HUSHED
IN DEATH

BY THE SAME AUTHOR
The Language of the Dead
The Wages of Desire

HUSHED
IN DEATH

AN INSPECTOR LAMB NOVEL

STEPHEN KELLY

PEGASUS CRIME
NEW YORK LONDON

HUSHED IN DEATH

Pegasus Books Ltd.
148 W 37th Street, 13th Floor
New York, NY 10018

Copyright © 2018 by Stephen Kelly

First Pegasus Books cloth edition November 2018

Interior design by Maria Fernandez

All rights reserved. No part of this book may be reproduced in whole or in part without written permission from the publisher, except by reviewers who may quote brief excerpts in connection with a review in a newspaper, magazine, or electronic publication; nor may any part of this book be reproduced, stored in a retrieval system, or transmitted in any form or by any means electronic, mechanical, photocopying, recording, or other, without written permission from the publisher.

ISBN: 978-1-68177-868-6

10 9 8 7 6 5 4 3 2 1

Printed in the United States of America
Distributed by W. W. Norton & Company, Inc.

For Bryan Denson, my lifelong friend.

Smile on, you newly dead, whose griefless masks
Are emptied of mortality of mind;
Safe is your secret from the world that asks
If death be dark—all lost and left behind.

—Siegfried Sassoon, from
"Words for the Wordless"

HUSHED
IN DEATH

ONE

—⚯—

JOSEPH LEE WAS DEAD. THE GARDENER OF ELTON HOUSE FLOATED facedown in the pond that lay along the path that led from the aging mansion to the village of Marbury.

A half-dozen members of the Hampshire Constabulary stood along the edge of the pond, among the tall, unruly grasses and reeds, as a slight breeze appeared from the south and stirred the waters of the pond and, with it, Lee's body, which began to float yet farther from their reach, like a toy boat gone astray.

Detective Chief Inspector Thomas Lamb stood about ten yards from the pond alongside police surgeon Anthony Winston-Sheed and Frederick Hornby, a psychiatrist who was the director of The Elton House Sanatorium, a medical retreat for military men who were suffering from the traumatic effects of combat. The pond lay within the sanatorium's grounds, which had once been the grounds

1

of the estate connected to Elton House; the house itself stood atop one side of an ancient, gently sloped valley, while Marbury, the village, nestled below.

Lamb looked at Detective Sergeant David Wallace, who was standing nearer to the pond, and thought about whether he should order Wallace to fetch Lee's body. Normally, Wallace would be exactly the man for the job. But Lamb worried that Wallace's fresh disability might cause him to fall into the cold water, which, besides embarrassing Wallace, would complicate matters unnecessarily.

Lamb looked also at Detective Inspector Harry Rivers, who stood next to Wallace; Rivers was twice Wallace's age and nowhere near as agile as the young sergeant, even given Wallace's wounded leg. But Rivers was indestructible and always had been. Even on the Somme, Rivers had never truly and fully broken down physically or psychologically, the only man—himself included—Lamb had known during the war about whom he could sincerely say that.

Lamb did not want to send out an obvious signal to his team that he harbored some doubt about Wallace's ability to do the job at hand. As a kind of compromise, then, he decided to send Wallace and Rivers into the pond as a team, expecting that Rivers, as the senior officer, naturally would take the lead.

He nodded at the waiting pair and said, "Fish him out, please, gentlemen."

In anticipation of the order, Rivers had already scoured up a longish fallen branch with a broken piece at the end that formed a kind of hook. He nodded his affirmation and began to move toward the pond's edge with the branch in hand, Wallace following and limping as he went. Lamb glanced at his daughter, Vera, and saw her wince slightly as she watched Wallace struggle to navigate the uneven, boggy bank. Wallace stumbled but caught his fall with his right hand, straightened himself, and went on. Vera looked away briefly.

In truth, Lamb thought, he should send Vera after the body. Not only was she more agile than either of the detectives, she was the best swimmer among them, including the other uniformed men her age.

She had been her secondary school's swimming champion and among its best cross country runners; in addition to which she was spirited, confident, and brave. But she was merely his driver, and merely a young woman, an auxiliary constable who owed her job to the coming of the war and the resulting shortage of men and her father's unfair intervention on her behalf, and to send her in Wallace's and Rivers's stead would publicly humiliate them, Wallace particularly.

As the detectives reached the pond, it became clear to everyone gathered along the bank that Lee had floated just out of the range of Rivers's branch, meaning that one of the men would have to wade partially into the pond after the body, whose feet pointed toward the men.

"I'll go," Wallace said. He immediately sat and began to pull off his shoes.

Rivers glanced at Lamb for instruction in the matter; Lamb nodded slightly, giving Rivers permission to stand aside.

Wallace removed his socks and began to roll up his expensive trousers. Rivers decided it best to remove his own shoes and socks and so sat next to Wallace and did so. Despite the relative seriousness of the proceedings, Rivers could not help but to goad Wallace a bit. He liked Wallace—and indeed had begun to see in Wallace a version of what he considered to have been his younger self—but found the sergeant's taste for stylish suits, neckties, and shoes an affectation.

"What about those lovely trousers, then?" Rivers asked as he pulled off his decidedly unstylish brown boots, which were blotted with mud stains even before they had reached the pond that morning. "A week's pay at least, right down the bog."

Wallace stood in his bare feet. "Sod the trousers."

Rivers suppressed a laugh. He removed his socks and also stood.

"All right, then," Rivers said. "It's your bank account." He then handed the hooked branch to Wallace and added, with a genuine smile, "But don't come crying to me for a bloody loan afterward."

Wallace took the stick and returned a slanted smile. "I'd drown first," he said.

This time Rivers could not entirely suppress a quiet chuckle. "Good luck, then," he said.

Holding the branch in his right hand, and Rivers's hand in his left, Wallace waded into the cold, murky pond nearly up to his knees, forcing Rivers to follow to his ankles. Vera watched intently but was careful not to utter a sound. She thought that Wallace's feet and legs must be freezing and worried that he would step on something that would cause his damaged leg to fail him. Lamb entertained an identical anxiety. The doctors—Hornby, the psychiatrist, and Winston-Sheed—also watched with anticipation, as did the other officer present, Sergeant Bill Cashen, a uniformed man whom Lamb relied on heavily, and the forensics man, Cyril Larkin. Rivers tightened his lips against the cold water and held firm to Wallace's hand.

"Careful now," he said, as Wallace moved the hook-end of the branch toward Lee's head.

But Wallace seemed blind to their concern. He extended his arm and the stick as far as it would go and was just able to snag the rear collar of Lee's jacket.

"Okay," he said to Rivers. "I've got him." With that, Wallace began to move methodically closer to the shore, pulling the floating body with him. Lee spun round like a leaf caught in a current, the top of his head coming round to face the bank.

Larkin moved to help Wallace and Rivers drag Lee's body from the pond and into the grass, where they laid it facedown. Lamb and Winston-Sheed knelt by the corpse and briefly examined it.

The back of Lee's head oozed with a fresh wound; someone appeared to have caved in the man's skull with "a blunt object of some kind," according to the doctor.

"I'd say that either the blow killed him outright or disabled him to the extent that, once he went into the water, he could not save himself from drowning," he told Lamb.

"Let's turn him over, then," Lamb said.

Rivers and Larkin turned the body faceup; Lee rolled stiffly, like a log. He was dressed in green corduroy trousers with muddy knees, a brown shirt of rough cotton, an olive tweed jacket that was becoming threadbare, and a pair of well-worn black leather boots. The area round his right eye was swollen and bruised.

Larkin straightened and pushed his wire-rimmed spectacles up the bridge of his nose. "Looks as if he also was hit in the face," he said.

"Yes," said Winston-Sheed, squatting again by the body to examine the wound as Rivers bent to the job of searching Lee's clothing and Larkin retrieved his boxy Rolleiflex camera and began to photograph Lee from a variety of angles and distances.

Lamb stood by silently, taking in the scene—the pond, the surrounding woodland, the worn muddy path to Marbury, and the gray, ivy-covered estate house on the hill, surrounded by long-neglected grounds. It had rained the previous morning, but not since. Still, the late April air remained moist and chilled. The spot reminded Lamb of the vaguely eerie rural places in which the Thomas Hardy novels he'd been required to read as a schoolboy had been set; places that always had seemed to him sodden with sorrow.

As Winston-Sheed tended to the job of moving Lee's body to a waiting van, Lamb moved thirty yards up the path, closer to the rear of Elton House, where he lit a cigarette and waited for Wallace to put on his shoes.

He spent a minute contemplating what the scene at the pond had told him about the killing of Joseph Lee. It appeared that someone had bludgeoned Lee and then dumped his body in the pond. He suspected the killing had occurred at the pond, though he couldn't yet be certain whether Lee was struck at some distance from the pond and then dragged there. But he had little doubt that the blow had incapacitated Lee. Lee's swollen eye suggested that Lee might have fought with his killer before the fatal blow was struck.

Given the proximity of the hospital, he had to consider the idea that one of the patients might have killed Lee for motives that were not yet apparent, or perhaps not even what one would normally consider logical, perhaps rooted in some form of illness to the mind. He took a drag from his cigarette and felt a stray drop of rain strike the rim of his fedora. He looked at the sky and saw that it had turned a slate gray.

The team had arrived in three cars—Lamb, Wallace, and Rivers in Lamb's aging Wolseley, with Vera at the wheel, with Larkin and nine uniformed men, including Sergeant Cashen, in the other vehicles.

Before climbing the hill for his smoke, Lamb had instructed Larkin to take two of the uniformed men and begin a search of the area surrounding the pond for any sign of a potential murder weapon and the possibility that the body might have been dragged or otherwise transported to the scene from elsewhere. He'd also assigned a pair of uniformed constables to Rivers and put the detective inspector to the job of searching Lee's lodgings, a small stone cottage near the pond. Lamb had obtained the key from Hornby.

Once all was settled by the pond, Lamb, Wallace, and Sergeant Cashen would return to the house, where the latter two would begin the job of taking statements from the staff and patients. He'd already sent Cashen and the remaining constables to the house to begin arranging for a room for the interviews. For his part, Lamb intended to interview in more detail Dr. Hornby and the two people who had reported finding Lee's body in the pond—a woman named Janet Lockhart, who Hornby said was a volunteer worker at the sanatorium, and a patient, Lieutenant James Travers—long enough to instruct all three not to speak to anyone about Lee until he'd had a chance to interview them properly. He'd also told Hornby that no one was to leave the grounds until he deemed it permissible.

From his vantage point up the trail, Lamb watched Wallace limp to where Vera stood, toting his shoes and lank woolen socks. He thought that Vera certainly yearned to comfort Wallace, but was resisting doing so in front of the others. Wallace eased himself into a sitting position and began to dry his wet feet and calves with a towel one of the uniformed men had fetched for him. Vera moved surreptitiously to his side and began to speak to him, though Lamb was too far up the path to hear what they said.

He watched Wallace tie his shoes and Vera help Wallace to his feet. During the team's last murder inquiry, ten months earlier, Wallace had taken a bullet in the leg during a tussle, sending him to hospital for two months, from which he'd emerged with a permanent limp. For three months Wallace had walked with a cane, but in recent weeks had taught himself to do without it.

Now, Vera took Wallace's arm and gently brushed off the back of his coat with her hand. The gesture was just shy of a caress, Lamb thought.

Another lone, heavy drop of rain struck his hat. He dropped the stub of his cigarette onto the path, ground it out with the toe of his shoe, then picked up the stub and put it into his coat pocket so it wouldn't be mistaken for evidence.

Wallace and Vera moved up the path to join Lamb and the three of them set off in the direction of the house. As they had done since Wallace had left the hospital, Lamb and Vera consciously slowed their pace so that Wallace, who was still learning to walk without the cane, could keep up.

Elton House loomed at the top of the hill, gray and silent. When they had arrived, Lamb and his team had found the estate's high wrought iron gates lying wide open; dead leaves, twigs, and other natural detritus had gathered near the base of the gates and their black paint had chipped away here and there, leaving small blots of rust. Lamb wondered if the gates hadn't stood open in just that way for years.

The paved drive that led to the house from the main road into Marbury was short, and the grounds on either side of it unkempt; a wood had begun to sprout up in what had once been a cultivated park-like setting. Several old large trees that had fallen across the drive over the years had been cut and cleared away at the point at which they met the road, leaving the bulk of the beasts lying where they had fallen, their long, barren branches, blackened with age, reaching up, Lamb thought, like giant crooked fingers from the grave.

The granite-and-stone three-story mansion—which had been cloaked in morning mist when they arrived—was compact and sturdy-looking rather than elegant, and possessed a patched-up quality, as if someone had endeavored to save it from the same neglect the estate's grounds had suffered. Its arched twelve-paned windows put Lamb in mind of a cathedral, though he noticed that a pair of them on the second floor had been bricked in.

As Lamb, Wallace, and Vera reached the front door of the house, Lamb ordered the detective sergeant to join the constables inside and begin the interviews. Wallace lingered for a couple of seconds. He seemed to move to touch Vera's arm, but refrained. Then he turned and went into the house.

The team's vehicles were parked along the edge of the semicircular driveway in front of the old mansion-cum-hospital, along with Winston-Sheed's Buick saloon and the van in which Lee's body would be driven to the morgue. Lamb walked Vera to his Wolseley and instructed her to wait for him there.

"If you get bored, you might have a look round the grounds," he said. He touched Vera's slender arm and said in a fatherly tone, "I'll fetch you when we're ready."

Vera looked at her father. Lamb believed that she wanted to say something to him; her expression contained almost a quality of beseeching, he thought. He waited several seconds for her to speak, but when Vera said nothing, he said, now in his chief inspector's voice, "All right, then. Carry on."

TWO

—◊◊◊—

DR. HORNBY HAD PRECEDED LAMB UP THE PATH TO THE HOUSE. During their initial conversation, he had told Lamb that the Elton House Sanatorium housed nine patients and employed fourteen staff, including himself, a cook, one kitchen assistant, a gardener—Lee, who also acted as a handyman—and ten nurses.

Now, as Lamb entered the hospital's foyer and removed his hat, he saw moving rapidly toward him down the main hall a middle-aged nurse neatly attired in a white hat and longish green cotton dress covered with a white apron. She introduced herself as Nurse Stevens and informed him that Doctor Hornby was waiting for Lamb in his office.

She led Lamb through double doors just off the foyer that opened onto an anteroom that contained a chair and desk and, along three of its four walls, floor-to-ceiling bookshelves that Lamb thought must have been a relic from the days in which Elton House served as a home to some titled family. Now the shelves were empty of books and anything else save several stacks of files and a few odds and ends—a hurricane lantern, and electric torch, and a potted aspidistra.

A door on the opposite wall led into Hornby's office. The doctor rose from behind a large cherry desk. "Come in, Chief Inspector," he said to Lamb, gesturing toward a pair of simple wooden chairs with worn green woolen cushions that faced his desk. "Please sit down. I was just going through some papers before we spoke."

Hornby was a tall, thin, balding man who possessed what Lamb considered to be an honest, somewhat haggard countenance, his tie slightly askew and jacket faintly rumpled.

"I'm afraid one doesn't really know exactly what to do in a situation like this," Hornby said, settling again in his chair. "I hope we have provided you with all that you need."

"Yes, thank you," Lamb said. "You've been helpful."

Hornby looked away from Lamb briefly and said, "Poor Mr. Lee. One almost can't believe it." He shook his head, as if not quite able to accept what had occurred.

"Yes, it is difficult," Lamb offered.

"Still, it does no good to lose one's head," Hornby said. He looked again at Lamb. "What else do you require of me, Chief Inspector?"

"Please tell me your version of this morning's events."

"I was at my desk when Nurse Stevens knocked and said that Mrs. Lockhart wished to speak to me."

"What time was this?"

"I suppose it was around nine, though honestly I didn't think to check. But I'm normally at my desk by seven and I had been working for two hours or so. At any rate, the pair of them entered—Mrs. Lockhart along with Lieutenant James Travers, one of our patients. Mrs. Lockhart said that she believed that there was a dead man floating in the pond—that she'd been on her way to the house from Marbury along the path and come upon the body. She seemed very shaken, on the verge of tears. You can imagine my shock. I asked her if she was quite sure and she said that, yes, she was certain."

"Did she say then that she believed the man to be Lee?"

"No."

"Did you ask her if she knew the man's identity?"

"I did and she said that she hadn't been able to see—that he appeared to be floating facedown and that she did not want to leave the path to look more closely. She said that, instead, she immediately came up the hill to inform me of what she'd found and on the way had run into Travers, who had just left the house for his morning walk and was coming down the path."

"What did you then do?"

"Well, I went to the pond to see the situation for myself, and found a scene that was exactly as Mrs. Lockhart described. When I saw the body, though, I felt pretty certain that it was Lee."

"What made you certain?"

"Process of elimination, really. Even facedown, it looked like Lee; you know how you become familiar with a person's size and shape. And I recognized the jacket on the body as Lee's."

"When did Lee begin working here?"

"Shortly after I bought the place and converted it into the facility it is today. No one had lived in the house—in the proper sense—since the last war, when the family that owned it moved away as the result of a tragedy. Since, it has either remained vacant for periods or been used for medical purposes. During most of the past two decades it served as a private sanatorium for consumption cases. I opened my small practice here in the summer of 1940—not the most auspicious time, obviously, but we've managed to survive and even thrive. We're really the only facility of our kind in all of England at the moment, though there should be more."

"Did Lee interact with the staff and patients?" Lamb asked the doctor.

"I spoke to him several times a week, but only briefly, to give him direction and to check on his work. Other than that, I left him to his job. He spoke to the staff and patients when he encountered them, I suppose. We encourage, and in some cases require, our patients to move about the grounds for certain minimum amounts of time each day. All of them are on the mend from the psychological and emotional shocks of war and the walks are part of their therapy. Exercise is very good for the mind as well as the body, and we encourage it."

"Do you know if Mr. Lee argued or fought with anyone in the past few days, either here at the hospital or in the village?"

"No."

"Had Lee complained to you about anything—or anyone—recently? Someone he might have had a disagreement with, perhaps? Or had you noticed that something might have been agitating him?"

"Nothing specific, though I doubt that he would have confided his troubles to me, in any case. Under the circumstances, though, I think it's fair to say that he could be difficult at times and therefore might have angered or irritated someone."

"How could he be difficult?"

"Well, he was a know-it-all, I suppose you'd call it. He kept an array of trivial facts about one thing or another at the ready and delighted in trotting them out when the opportunity arose; the dates of famous events and so on. He liked to steer the conversation toward topics in which he considered himself expert and took some pleasure in pointing out those items of which you were unaware or might be wrong. I'd be lying to you if I said I found him to be a pleasant man. I suppose that fancying himself expert on this or that trifling matter made him feel important. But he was a good worker and performed his duties."

"When is the last time you spoke with Mr. Lee?"

"Sunday. I asked him to get started on removing some of the weedy underbrush near the house and he said that he would. The grounds here still are rather a shambles, I'm afraid. They'll never be what they once were, of course, but Lee had done a fair job in the time he was here of straightening things."

Lamb removed a notebook and pencil from his pocket. "Please explain for me the work you do here, Doctor," he said.

"We're a private facility, as I said, for men who are suffering the psychological effects of combat. During the first war we erroneously called this collection of maladies shell shock, though I suppose that description is not necessarily wholly devoid of truth. There is a shock value to experiencing combat—being under lethal fire, having your life threatened, seeing others round you die."

"But you have no direct connection with the Royal Army Medical Corps, or any other branch of the military?"

"No, all of the men here have been discharged from service for reasons of emotional or psychological distress. All served between the outbreak of war and within as recently as the past six months. Each was referred to us through a private psychiatrist or doctor, or by a family member or close friend or associate. We evaluate them and accept them, as long as we have the room and they can pay the fee. Our work here is, if I may say, first class, and so involves some expense, obviously. Some have criticized us as being a place that only men of a certain means can afford, but we are working on correcting that. For example, we have a fundraising campaign ongoing that is designed to raise money to pay the fees of men who need the care but could not otherwise afford to reside here."

"Yes, I'm sure," Lamb said, moving the conversation back to the matter at hand. "What is your normal daily routine here, sir? And please be specific."

"We rise at six thirty. The men have a wash and then, at seven fifteen come to breakfast, which ends at quarter to eight. The men then have thirty minutes to straighten their rooms and make their beds and freshen up, if need be, or have a few minutes of time to themselves, for prayer or meditation. At eight fifteen we begin therapeutic group sessions, which go until lunch. The men have an hour to themselves after lunch. At two P.M. we begin individual therapeutic sessions, then have a break for tea at four. Then we have an exercise period. Dinner is promptly at seven. The men then have free time until lights out at ten."

"Why was Lieutenant Travers not in a group session this morning, sir?"

"Travers is farther along than most here; in fact, I would say that Travers is close to leaving us. A week ago I relieved him of the

responsibility of attending group therapy. I believe at this point he ben-
efits more from morning exercise. Indeed, I encourage him to go into
Marbury for a bit of normal interaction in the shops, or at the tea room."

"I see," Lamb said. "I take it that the doors are locked at night and
remain locked through the night."

"Yes, the doors are locked at ten."

"And during the day?"

"All of the doors save the front door are locked."

"Who has the keys?"

"Myself and Nurse Stevens."

"So Mrs. Lockhart has no key, then?"

"No."

"What is Mrs. Lockhart's role here, exactly?"

"She assists the nurses in some of their duties and socializes with
the men—plays cards with them and the like. To some of them she
even reads aloud for an hour or so from novels or volumes of poetry.
Some of the men find the sound of her voice soothing, to be frank.
It takes them back to a time before the war."

"Like a mother's voice, then?"

"You might say that, yes."

"Did her duties ever put in her contact with Joseph Lee?"

"Not that I'm aware—though I find her to be a kind woman and
not the type to have acted coldly toward someone such as Mr. Lee."

"Are any of the men whom you are treating at the moment capable
of doing violence to another?"

"Well, that's rather an open-ended question, Chief Inspector. You
could ask that of any man, even yourself, could you not? Is he capable
of violence?"

"I am speaking of violence that might be connected to, or result
from, their psychological distress," Lamb said patiently. "Put more
plainly, do you suspect that any of your patients might have either
fought with Mr. Lee or killed him?"

Hornby sat up straighter in his chair and his face reddened slightly.
"No—and I can say that categorically."

"I see," Lamb said.

Hornby sighed. "I apologize for my tone, Chief Inspector," he said. "I know that you must ask your questions. I can at times be a bit too protective of my patients, I'm afraid. As you might know, many people—even many psychiatrists—consider post-concussion syndrome nothing more than a synonym for cowardice."

"I'm sorry, sir. Post-concussion syndrome?"

"What we once called shell shock. We now know much more than we did during the last war about the effects of combat and trauma generally on the mind. The problem is not merely one of 'weak nerves,' but stems from a direct assault on the brain. That's what I am attempting to treat here." Hornby paused, then added, "But then you may know something of what I'm describing, Chief Inspector. You appear to be of the right age."

"I was on the Somme for a year."

Hornby nodded. "I was at Ypres, the first time round."

But Lamb was in no mood to speak of his personal experiences of war. "Where might I find Mrs. Lockhart, sir?" he asked.

"I had Nurse Stevens put her in the social room. She should be waiting for you there."

Lamb rose from his chair. "Thank you, sir," he said. "I think that's all I shall need for the moment."

Hornby also stood. "You're welcome, Chief Inspector. I'll have Nurse Stevens take you to Mrs. Lockhart."

When they reached the door, Hornby said, "I realize that this is a personal question, Chief Inspector, but I'll ask it anyway. Feel free, of course, to tell me to mind my own business, but I wonder how the war still affects you?"

The question so surprised Lamb that he did not speak for a full ten seconds. Still, he noticed that Hornby used the word "how" rather than "if."

"Obviously, it was wrong for me to have asked," Hornby said. "I hope you'll accept my apology. But it's my job, you see, to help men who have experienced what you have." He smiled. "I'm afraid I can't help myself."

"No need to apologize," Lamb said. Then the words escaped his mouth before he'd even had a chance to compose them: "Nightmares, mostly. Not as often as before, but they still come at times. And faces. I sometimes see faces and shapes. Faces and shapes of men who were lost."

Hornby placed his right hand on Lamb's left shoulder. "You're not alone, Chief Inspector. I also see the faces you speak of in my dreams. I hope you realize that it is never too late to seek help if you believe you need it."

Lamb smiled slightly. "Thank you, Doctor," he said. "But I decided long ago that I was beyond help."

THREE

—ɯ—

FEELING VAGUELY TROUBLED BY HIS BRIEF CONVERSATION AT THE door with Hornby, Lamb followed Nurse Stevens as she led him at a brisk pace down a secondary hall off the foyer to a room that had once been a study at Elton House, but which now served as the room to which the hospital's patients could retreat at the end of the day for conversation and quiet socializing.

Hornby's talk of combat trauma had forced Lamb back to 1917, and the Somme. Then, he'd known officers who'd been sent home to recover from cases of shell shock. Some had returned to the war, apparently cured. Lamb often had wondered, then and since, if *he* hadn't suffered from the affliction in some way. He had never fully been able to shake free of his memories of that time, and the dreams that still disturbed his sleep, and the misty, spirit shapes of the men he'd known who had died.

As he attempted to keep pace with Nurse Stevens, he mused on what he'd said to Hornby. *Was* he beyond help? He'd meant it as a joke, though he thought that Hornby had not taken it in that way. The psychiatric people he'd known mostly were like that: they tended to see hidden meaning in every word and gesture.

Nurse Stevens knocked upon the door to the common room—again, briskly; briskness seemed to be among the woman's signature traits, Lamb thought—before opening the door and striding in.

"Chief Inspector Lamb is here, Mrs. Lockhart," she said, as Lamb followed her into the room.

"Thank you, Nurse," said Mrs. Lockhart, who was sitting in a chair by a large window that looked out upon what once had been one of the estate's gardens, which, like the grounds surrounding the drive, had fallen into neglect and reverted to a wild state.

She was a well-turned-out woman of about fifty, Lamb thought, possessed of dark, intelligent-seeming eyes, shoulder-length graying auburn hair casually swept back, and a trim figure. She wore a yellow cotton blouse buttoned at the front, a black knee-length skirt, nylon stockings, and black high-heeled shoes. She sat in the chair with her legs crossed, and Lamb could not help but notice that her legs were slender and well proportioned. Indeed, he found Mrs. Lockhart attractive. She stood and held out her hand as Lamb approached and, as he took her hand to shake it, he caught the barest scent of her perfume, which he found pleasant.

"Sorry to make you wait, Mrs. Lockhart," Lamb said.

"Oh, no bother, Chief Inspector, really," she said.

She seemed, Lamb thought, rather well composed under the circumstances. If finding Lee's body in the pond had initially upset her, she seemed to have recovered from that.

Lamb turned to Nurse Stevens and thanked her for her assistance.

"I'll be on my way, then," the nurse said and departed.

Lamb sat in a chair facing Mrs. Lockhart, by the large window, and immediately got down to the business at hand. "Please tell me, in detail, the events of your finding Mr. Lee's body this morning," he said. "And please start from the beginning."

Mrs. Lockhart folded her hands and laid them in her lap.

"I left the house shortly before nine to come here," she said. "I volunteer with the patients, though it's not much, really. I help the nurses with their less dire duties. I also act as a kind of companion to the men. I suppose that's what one might call it. I play cards with them, mostly bridge—several of them are quite good players—and keep them company generally. We listen to the wireless or discuss whatever news has been in the papers. I also read to one or two of them, at night, you see, to calm them so that they can sleep. Some of them have a horrible time sleeping, Chief Inspector. Nightmares and the like. My late husband, Cyril, was in the last war and suffered from the same sort of nightmares. Reliving the war, you know. He'd awaken from a dream sodden from perspiration. So I know a bit about what some of the men here are enduring. It's the least I can do, really. So many other people are suffering such incredible hardships."

"Yes, I'm sure the work you do here is appreciated," Lamb said patiently. "Now, you were saying that you left the house a bit before nine."

"Yes, I left the house and came up the path from the village, as I usually do, but when I reached the pond my eye caught something out of the ordinary. At first I thought that it might be an animal that had somehow fallen into the water. But when I moved off the path for a closer look, I saw that it was a man and that he made no movement or sound at all. I even called out to him, but he simply floated there. I'm a bit ashamed to say that I did not get close enough to the pond to see if he was alive, in part because he was so still and silent. It sent a chill through me—the realization that he might be dead."

"Did you recognize the man as Mr. Lee?"

"No. He was facing down. But I could tell by the way that he was dressed that he was a working man."

"What did you do then?"

"I went to the house to report what I had seen to Dr. Hornby. As I went up the path I met Lieutenant Travers coming down it. He walks in the morning, you see. I must have appeared very agitated because he immediately asked me if anything was wrong, and I told him what I'd just found. He said that we should tell Dr. Hornby immediately."

"So Travers did not express any interest in going to see the body first?"

"No." She paused, then added, "At least not to my recollection."

"Go on."

"Well, Lieutenant Travers and I went to Dr. Hornby and the three of us then went to the pond, so that Dr. Hornby could see for himself what I was describing. He said that he believed the man was Mr. Lee; he recognized his clothing, I think. We returned here to the house and Dr. Hornby called the constabulary."

"Did the three of you have any other discussion regarding the body—about, perhaps, how Mr. Lee might have ended up in the pond, or why?"

"Lieutenant Travers remarked that perhaps Mr. Lee had become drunk and stumbled into the pond in the dark."

"So I take it then, madam, that you normally arrive here at about nine in the morning, is that correct?"

"Yes."

"And when do you normally leave?"

"I always stay through lunch, so I can help with that. On some days I might go home once lunch is finished, though I'll stay longer if needed. I normally return after the evening meal, to socialize with those men who desire it."

"Do you come here most days?"

Mrs. Lockhart uncrossed her attractive legs and then recrossed them in the opposite way. "Yes, though I have no set requirement," she said. "If I'm not going to come in I will call Dr. Hornby and let him know. But I'm normally here most days. Working here helps me to feel as if I'm connected to something and making a contribution. With the war on, I believe one is bound to make a contribution. And I suppose that I consider this mine."

She briefly touched the top button of her blouse, which was open at the neck, and raised her chin slightly. Lamb found himself briefly staring at the way in which her neck gracefully gave way to her slender shoulders.

"Would you then consider yourself well acquainted with the hospital staff and the patients and their daily routines?" he asked.

"Yes."

"Do you know if any of the staff or patients had relationships with Mr. Lee that went beyond casual acquaintance?"

"Not that I am aware."

"Did you see Mr. Lee about Marbury much?"

"Not really, though I suppose he must have come to the shops. And he came to the pub."

"Do you know this because you often saw him in the pub?"

"No. I don't go to the pub much. But, yes, I have seen him there on occasion."

"And how long have you lived in the village, madam?"

"Nearly thirty years. I moved here with my husband in 1915, just after we were married."

"And you mentioned that your husband was deceased?"

"Yes. He died in 1921."

"I'm sorry."

"Thank you."

Lamb was silent for a few seconds before steering the conversation back toward Joseph Lee. "I understand that Mr. Lee possessed a habit of trotting out his superior knowledge of this or that trivial matter."

"Yes," Mrs. Lockhart answered. "He seemed to have committed to memory the dates of famous events and tidbits of information about well-known people and historical figures."

"Did you find him irritating?"

"Not really. But then, I didn't encounter him often."

"Was he a violent man? Easy to anger, perhaps?"

"Not that I knew."

"Had you heard anything of Mr. Lee getting into a row or fight with anyone at the hospital or in the village recently?"

Mrs. Lockhart looked out the window and seemed to pause to consider the question. She sighed, then turned back to Lamb.

"I don't want to be a gossip, Chief Inspector," she said. "I detest gossip; it has no purpose but to wound others as far as I am concerned."

"All the same, madam; this is a murder inquiry and even the smallest bits of information can prove to be important," Lamb said. "I give you my promise that I will do my best to confirm the truth of anything you tell me. That is my job in the end."

She sighed again. "Well, I don't know all of the details, but James—Lieutenant Travers—told me that he'd seen Lee arguing with a local man on the High Street by the church on the night before last."

"What were they arguing about?"

She paused again before answering. "I'd feel better if you'd ask Lieutenant Travers about it, Chief Inspector. He was the one who saw it, you see. What I know of the incident is only secondhand."

But Lamb remained gently insistent. "It would be best if you tell me what you know and I will confirm that with the lieutenant," he said.

"He said he thought they were arguing about the daughter of the man who owns the pub in Marbury. It sounded to him as if Mr. Lee was perhaps jealous of the other man's attentions toward the girl."

"And did the lieutenant recognize this other man?"

"He didn't, but when he described him to me, I thought I knew who it was."

Lamb waited for Mrs. Lockhart to tell him the other man's name, but when she didn't, he asked, "And who did you believe it was?"

For a third time, Mrs. Lockhart turned away from Lamb to glance out the window and sigh before turning back to answer him. "It sounded very much to me like a man named Alan Fox. He lives just up the hill from me in Marbury, just off the High Street." Her face clouded with distress and she added, "But I can't really see a man such as Alan arguing in the street with a man such as Mr. Lee, Chief Inspector. I've known Alan practically since the day I arrived in Marbury; and I knew his parents well. His father was a solicitor and a prominent man locally."

"And is Mr. Fox also a solicitor?"

"No. He's an artist; a painter. I'm afraid he's rather lived off the money his father left him. But I believe him to be a decent man, all the same."

"What time did this argument occur?"

"I'm not sure. You'll have to ask Lieutenant Travers."

"And when did Lieutenant Travers tell you that he had witnessed this argument?"

"This morning, after he and I went to the pond with Dr. Hornby."

"And were the two of you speaking with Dr. Hornby at the time?"

"No. We were alone."

"I wonder if you might tell me the publican's name."

"Hitchens. Horace Hitchens."

"And his daughter?"

"Theresa Hitchens."

"Also, I wonder if you could tell me, specifically, where Alan Fox lives in Marbury, please madam?"

"On the eastern side of the village, just off the High Street and up the hill a bit from the village green. You will pass the church on your left and Alan's house is a bit beyond that, on the right. It's down a short lane, but his name is on the mailbox by the lane."

Lamb stood and offered Mrs. Lockhart his hand. "Thank you for being honest with me, Mrs. Lockhart," he said. "I think that we are finished for the moment."

Mrs. Lockhart stood and shook Lamb's hand. "You're welcome, Chief Inspector. It's such a terrible thing, what has happened to poor Mr. Lee."

"I'll have to request that you not leave Marbury at present," Lamb added. "I may want to speak with you again."

Janet Lockhart smiled. "Of course," she said.

FOUR

—⁂—

EARLIER THAT MORNING LAMB HAD BRIEFLY MET LIEUTENANT
James Travers, as he had Dr. Hornby and Mrs. Lockhart, before he'd
hiked down the path to the scene of Joseph Lee's murder. At that
time, Lamb had requested of Hornby that Travers remain in his room,
sequestered from the nurses and other patients until he, Lamb, had
interviewed him in detail. Hornby had assented to the request and
Travers had added that he didn't mind at all waiting in his room for
Lamb. Indeed, Travers had even explained to Lamb how to reach his
room when Lamb was ready to talk. Now Lamb tried to recall those
directions as he moved again into the main hall of the house.

Elton House had been built in 1725 by a man named Samuel Elton,
who made his fortune importing tea and other goods from China,
India, and parts of the Middle East. At the peak of its success in the
middle-to-late 17th century, the Samuel Elton Trading Company

had operated a fleet of more than twenty ships out of Southampton and Portsmouth, and Elton had built his mansion on a spot that was close enough to those port cities while, at the same time, removed from their hurly-burly. He married a young Hampshire woman named Bess, who bore him three children—three daughters and a son, whom he named after himself. The second Samuel Elton apparently had not possessed the same business acumen as had his father, preferring to live instead off the older man's wealth, and this, combined with the taxes levied on imported goods to pay for Britain's war with the French in the American colonies, meant that the family's traditional business had begun to decline during the final decades of the century. However, Samuel Elton Jr., who was not entirely without enterprise, turned to smuggling, mostly of Indian tea and American tobacco, but also rum and gin, streamlining his fleet and employing local men as go-betweens and confederates who depended upon his trade and, in some cases, became loyal to him. Indeed, the rumor had gone round the countryside surrounding Elton House that Samuel had dug a series of underground tunnels and storage areas—much like the priest holes of an earlier time—in which he stored the contraband until the time that he was able to sell it on a thriving black market centered in London. In this way, the younger Samuel had amassed a fortune of his own, which his heirs had lived upon through the end of the early years of the twentieth century, when the family had sold the house and the estate, not long after the outbreak of the Great War.

After the war, the house had successfully been converted into a working sanatorium for consumptives that, at its peak, treated up to seventy-five patients at once. Since buying the house for his much smaller operation, Hornby had closed off portions of the building. Even so, Lamb found himself slightly confused as he wended his way along a trio of halls and up a flight of stairs in search of Travers's room.

He was beginning to become frustrated when he again encountered Nurse Stevens, who recognized Lamb's predicament and asked if she could be of assistance. When Lamb told her what he was searching for, she led him directly to it and, as before, rapped briskly on the door.

"Lieutenant Travers, sir," she said. "Chief Inspector Lamb is here to speak with you."

Seconds later, Travers opened the door.

"Thank you, Nurse," Lamb said to Stevens, who nodded and went on her way.

James Travers was a tall, thin young man possessed of dark eyes and foppish brown hair cut in a sort of a Bohemian style. "Please come in, Chief Inspector," he said.

He ushered Lamb into what the Chief Inspector considered rather a large room, with a bed against the wall that lay to the left of the door, and a large window on the wall opposite the door that looked out upon the grounds behind the house, including the pond in which Joseph Lee had been found floating that morning. Against the right wall was a dressing table and armoire; between these and the bed lay a small round wooden table, well polished, with two chairs, which Travers led Lamb to and at which the two sat.

Travers pulled out a silver cigarette holder and opened it. "Do you smoke, Chief Inspector?" he asked.

"Yes, but I'll refrain for the moment, thank you."

"Do you mind if I smoke, then?"

"Not at all."

Lamb noticed that the cigarettes were an American brand, Lucky Strike, which had become scarce in England since the beginning of the war, as had cigarettes generally.

"American, then?" Lamb asked.

Travers smiled. "Yes. They seem to have an abundance of them about the place." He lit a cigarette, shook out the match, then tossed it into a glass ashtray that lay on the table. "And the comforts, generally," the lieutenant added. "I must say that Dr. Hornby provides you your money's worth. I'm sorry about Mr. Lee, by the way. I thought him a bit sad and lonely, but harmless in the end."

"At what time did you awaken this morning, sir?" Lamb asked.

"The nurses wake us at six thirty. Like clockwork."

"I notice that your window looks out onto the pond. Did you see or hear anything out of the ordinary from that area last night or early this morning?"

"No, nothing."

"After rising, did you follow your normal morning routine?"

"Yes."

"So you didn't leave the hospital at any time this morning?"

"Not until I went for my walk, which is part of my prescribed treatment. I walk for an hour in the morning and an hour in the afternoon. Weather permitting, of course."

Travers took a pull from his cigarette. "A few minutes after setting out on my walk, I met Mrs. Lockhart," he continued. "She was coming up the path from the village and seemed rather put out. She immediately told me that she'd just come upon what she thought was a dead body floating in the pond."

"Did she use that word—*dead*?"

"Yes. Otherwise, I would have thought it the right thing to do to check and see if the person was in distress. But I could tell from the way she looked and the way she spoke that she wasn't exaggerating."

"How did she look?"

"She was ashen, and trembling a bit."

"Then what happened?"

"She and I fetched Dr. Hornby and the three of us went to the pond."

"Did you have any notion, before you reached the pond, who the dead man might be?"

Travers sat back in his chair. "Well, I did, actually; I thought that the man might have been Lee."

"Why Lee?"

"Well, because the body was on the grounds, and in the pond specifically. Lee rather seemed to like the pond; he used to sit by it in the twilight. I saw him from my window many times. And he had full run of the estate. Also, he'd had an encounter with a man from the village, near the pub, a couple of nights ago. It had something to do with the publican's daughter, whom I gather Lee had his eye on. It seemed Lee was jealous of this other fellow and challenged him."

"And how is it that you know the details of this fight?"

"I saw it—or, that is, I heard it at first. I was walking along the path by the church in Marbury when I heard two men begin to argue rather loudly out on the High Street, so I went to have a look. I came to the end of the path, which intersects the street, and there, just up the street, I saw a man I recognized as Lee arguing with another man. They both sounded drunk and, as I said, seemed to be arguing about a woman—'Theresa' they called her. Lee accused the man of trying to 'steal' Theresa from him; that was the word he used. Stealing. The other man said he was crazy and told Lee to leave him be. When the other man tried to leave and head up the High Street, Lee grabbed him rather roughly, which turned out to be a mistake because the other fellow came round swinging and hit Lee squarely in the face, knocking him flat. He told Lee a final time to stay away from him and then walked off. I went to Lee and helped him to his feet; I offered to help him back to his cottage, but he shook me off and said he wanted to return to the pub."

"Did he appear to be seriously hurt?"

"Not that I could tell, though I supposed he must have ended up with a bruise of some sort on his face. He was drunk, as I said, but the blow didn't seem to have knocked him cold. In fact, he seemed to have a bit of fight in him still. He shook his fist at this other man and said something to the effect that he'd make him pay. That sort of thing."

"Do you recall his exact words?"

"Not really. As I said, it was along the lines of, 'You'll pay for this' or 'I'll see that you pay for this.'"

"And did the other man respond?"

"No. He continued up the street."

"Do you know if the other man saw you?"

"I don't think he did. I stayed out of sight until I went into the street to help Lee. There is a hedge along the path by the street and I stayed near to that, which would have put me out of their sight."

"Did you see anyone else in the High Street, or nearby?"

"No."

"Did Mr. Lee then return to the pub, as he said he would?"

"As far as I know. After I left him, I came back up here, up the footpath. I was on my way back here in fact when I heard the argument."

"What time was this, sir?"

"About nine thirty. Lights out here for patients is ten."

"And what were you doing in Marbury at that hour?"

"I was out for my evening walk. Dr. Hornby doesn't mind if I wander down into the village. Indeed, he encourages it. The patients here are on individual recovery plans, you see. After the evening meal, I am allowed to leave the house to walk the grounds and even to go into the village, as long as I return before the doors are locked. I usually walk just before dinner and then again afterward. Sometimes, though, I enjoy walking a bit later, especially with the days lengthening and becoming warmer."

"And yet, it rained two nights ago," Lamb said.

"A misting, yes, you're right," Travers agreed. "At least that's what it was doing during the time I was walking. It might have rained harder later on."

"Did you know the man with whom Lee argued?"

"Not until this morning, when I mentioned to Mrs. Lockhart that I had seen Lee arguing with a man by the church. When I described him to her, she said she thought she might know who it was—a man named Fox, she said. Rather an easy name to recall, though, that said, I'm not sure I remember what she said his first name was. Albert, perhaps, or Alan? I think it was Alan. Alan Fox."

"And do you know who Theresa is?"

"No—again not until I spoke to Mrs. Lockhart this morning, at any rate. She told me that the man who owns the pub has a daughter named Theresa. Apparently, she's known as a local beauty."

"So you have never met Theresa or her father?"

"No."

"Or Alan Fox?"

"No."

"Did you tell Dr. Hornby that you had witnessed this row involving Lee?"

"No, though I meant to do so. I suppose I should have told him earlier, but frankly I haven't seen him between then and this morning, when Mrs. Lockhart and I went to fetch him."

"Did you see Mr. Lee again between the time you saw him arguing with Alan Fox and this morning?"

"No."

"What was your relationship with Lee, Lieutenant? Beyond the incident you've just described?"

"I used to run into him now and then on my walks about the grounds and village. He liked to talk—enjoyed the sound of his own voice."

"Did you like him?"

"Not really. He was one of those people who seemed to have no inkling at all of how boring they are. And he possessed a sort of strange arrogance, as if he believed he was someone more important or impressive than he actually was. That said, I saw no reason to be rude toward him."

"And what is the nature of your relationship with Mrs. Lockhart?"

Travers shrugged. "She strikes me as a kind, helpful woman. And she misses her late husband terribly; she brings him up in conversation regularly."

"So you have no relationship with her apart from the one she shares with you and the other men, as a volunteer?"

"No. But in the interest of not wanting to be caught out lying to the police, I will say that she has been helping me a bit with my recovery here—though I fear that explaining how might come off as seeming a bit out of the ordinary."

"All the same, sir, it would be best if you told me. You are absolutely correct in your desire to avoid being caught out lying to the police."

Travers sat back in his chair, crossed his legs, and took a long drag from his cigarette before lightly placing it in the ashtray.

"Well, I suppose there is no good way to say it, but to say it without adornment—she has been helping me face my grief by helping me to make contact with those whom I am grieving."

"Meaning those who have died?"

"I know it sounds ridiculous on its face, Chief Inspector. But yes, that's essentially the goal. That said, I don't want you to conclude that this is some sort of fraudulent séance with the moving tables and the books falling off shelves and the candles suddenly going out for no reason. Instead, Mrs. Lockhart encourages me to remember those whom I grieve—how they looked, spoke, acted, even smelled; the clothes they wore; the books they liked; their favorite food and drink. Her theory is that we grieve best by remembering and not forgetting, and I have come to believe that's true."

"I see," Lamb said. "And whom have you contacted, if I might ask?"

"Some of the men I served with in France, for one. And both my parents are dead, Chief Inspector. And with Janet's—Mrs. Lockhart's—help, I have become reacquainted with them in a way, which, ironically enough, has aided me in allowing myself to let them go. She has done the same for herself as regards her late husband."

"Does Dr. Hornby know of this assistance that Mrs. Lockhart is rendering to you?" Lamb asked.

"Yes, and he approves. He believes in it, in fact. Hornby is not like the old-style psychiatrists, Chief Inspector. He is trying something new here and from what I can see he is succeeding. I certainly feel as if my time here has helped me to learn how to better face my past and some of my demons."

Travers glanced out the window, then back at Lamb. "I don't normally believe in that sort of thing, Chief Inspector; speaking to the dead and the rest of it. But I reasoned I had nothing to lose in trying it." He turned back to Lamb and smiled. "I suppose I was desperate enough at the time that I was willing to have tried anything. And yet, as strange as it all sounds, it has worked."

Travers again proffered his cigarettes to Lamb. "Are you sure you won't have one? As I said, we seem to have an endless supply of the things here." He looked at the ashtray, which was full of stubs. "Makes one rather profligate, I'm afraid. In France I smoked the bloody things down to the essence, until there was nothing left."

"No thank you, Lieutenant," Lamb said. He put his hands on the table and stood. Travers also stood.

"I take it we are finished, then, Chief Inspector?" he asked.

"For the moment, yes, though I might have further questions as the inquiry progresses."

"Well, I'm not going anywhere for the time being."

"Thank you for your time," Lamb said.

"Whatever I can do to help."

"I must request that for the time being you refrain from talking with anyone about the events of this morning. Your cooperation would be a great help to me."

"Of course."

"That includes Mrs. Lockhart as well, obviously," Lamb added.

Lamb searched Travers's eyes for a sign of surprise and thought he saw one flicker there. And then Travers smiled again.

"Obviously," he said.

FIVE

—ᴍ—

AS LAMB LEFT TRAVERS, HE FOUND HIMSELF SETTING OUT AGAIN on another search through the house. This time he was looking for the room in which Wallace and Sergeant Cashen were taking statements from the staff and patients. He realized suddenly that he had neglected to ask Hornby the location of this room and decided to retrace his steps to the foyer, where he might find someone he could ask. But before he reached the steps leading down to the main floor, Nurse Stevens suddenly appeared again—almost, Lamb thought, as if she had been keeping tabs on his movements.

"Lost again, Chief Inspector?" she asked.

"I'm afraid so. I'm looking for the room in which my men are collecting statements."

"I'll take you there. I've been assisting your sergeant in shuttling people in and out. I think, actually, that they are close to finishing up. As you might know, we run a relatively small operation here."

"Yes, thank you," Lamb said. "Lead on, please."

They followed the path along which they had gone to Travers's room, with the exception being that, once they reached the main foyer, they continued down a hall into the house's eastern portion, where Hornby had given Lamb's team a large room that the hospital rarely used.

"Here we are," Nurse Stevens said, opening the double doors to the room. "This once served as a kind of room for parties and dances, I think, though we have no use for it at present."

The room contained a large, polished wooden table at its center, with four or five matching chairs lined along either side. The wall opposite the door was dominated by a half-dozen high, wide windows, all of which were curtained. However, someone—Lamb guessed it was Nurse Stevens—had pulled back the curtains on the three middle windows to allow some natural light into the room. Cashen was seated at the table with his back to the windows, interviewing a young nurse who sat across the table from them. Wallace was leaning against the far end of the table sipping something from a blue-and-white china cup that Lamb at first guessed was tea. But as he entered the room he saw that the only other piece of furniture it contained was a rectangular table that was pushed against the wall to the right of the door and which had sitting on it a pot of coffee, a dozen more china cups like the one from which Wallace sipped arranged on a tea towel along with matching saucers, a bowl of sugar, and a container of milk. Lamb smelled the coffee, which put him in the mood for a cup and a cigarette. He had found that twice turning down Travers's offers of a Lucky Strike had tested his reserves of willpower, but he had not wanted to be taken off his guard while interviewing the lieutenant. Now, though, he felt as if he could at least briefly relax his diligence.

When Wallace saw Lamb, his eyes widened in surprise and he stood erect.

"Hello, sir; just taking a bit of a break," he said as Lamb approached him.

Lamb didn't begrudge Wallace his break and didn't want to seem to. "Do I smell coffee, then?" he asked.

"You do indeed; and quite good it is, too," Wallace said. "The nurse fetched it for us. Very kind of her, I thought."

Lamb poured a cup and added a spot of milk. He didn't like sugar in his coffee, but nonetheless lifted the lid on the sugar bowl to see if it actually contained the substance. The bowl was filled almost to brimming with sugar—another otherwise everyday commodity that, like cigarettes, had become dear and rationed since the coming of the war. The amount of sugar the bowl contained was more than Lamb had seen in any one place since the war began.

He took a quick sip of the coffee and found it to be hot, strong, and delicious, unlike the watered-down swill he'd grown used to drinking. He moved next to Wallace and lit a cigarette.

"How are we coming, David?" he asked.

"We're close to finishing; Cashen is interviewing the last nurse now, save the head nurse."

"Good," Lamb said. "I'd actually like to interview Nurse Stevens."

"Of course, sir."

"There's also a cook and a kitchen assistant, according to Hornby. Did you speak to them?"

"Yes, sir. Frankly, no one has had much of interest to say. No one saw or heard anything unusual last night and otherwise the general gist is that they knew Lee, or knew of him, but had little or no contact with him. Those who did say that they had spoken to him now and then described him as ill-mannered and boastful, and three of the nurses said outright that they avoided him because he had a habit of making lewd comments toward them. Nobody really admitted to liking him much. As for the kitchen people, both claimed never to have spoken to him at all; the cook said their paths simply never crossed Lee's."

The two stood together without speaking for a minute or so, as Lamb savored his cigarette and coffee. The brief silence discomfited Wallace, who found himself musing—as he often did now—how much Lamb knew of the extent of his relationship with Vera and whether he approved. Wallace always had considered Lamb a kind of sphinx, a man who rarely showed emotion and yet was tuned in to those of everyone round him. Wallace was glad, therefore, when he heard Sergeant Cashen, who was seated at the opposite end of the table, call the two of them over.

Lamb ground out his cigarette against the bottom of his shoe and placed the stub into the pocket of his raincoat.

Cashen still was seated across from the young nurse he'd been interviewing when Lamb had entered the room. He introduced the girl as Nurse Anderson and said she had an interesting story that he believed Lamb should hear.

"How do you do, Miss Anderson?" Lamb said. "I am Chief Inspector Thomas Lamb and this is Detective Sergeant David Wallace."

The nurse smiled at the men and said, "How do you do, sirs?" She had dark hair tied up and tucked beneath her nurse's cap, and a kind of flattish nose and round face. She wore a uniform that was exactly like the one Nurse Stevens wore, except that her bib and apron were brown, whereas Stevens's were green, which Lamb guessed signified the latter's superior rank.

He and Wallace sat next to Cashen, so that the three of them faced Nurse Anderson.

"Please tell the chief inspector what you were just telling me, miss," Cashen said.

Nurse Anderson straightened in her seat a bit.

"Well, I was saying, sir, that I had an experience with Joseph Lee that I found strange. Although I know he sometimes made unwelcome comments to some of the other nurses, he was friendly enough toward me during the few times we spoke, though always a bit strange-like too."

"How was he strange?" Lamb asked.

"He would say things that didn't necessarily have anything to do with anything else that you could put your finger on, really. I only ran into him a few times, in the cellar, when I had business in the kitchen. He used to come there to get his meals at odd hours of the day. A few months ago, I passed him in the hall down there and he lifted his hat to me, in a greeting-like, and rather than saying 'good day' or something of the kind, he blurted out that the following day would be thirty years exactly since the *Titanic* sank and that he'd known most of the people who had died on the ship that day. He seemed pleased by that, which I found morbid. And then, just two weeks ago, I happened upon him again in the hall by the kitchen. I tried to avoid him, but there was no getting around him. And that's when he told me that the cellar was haunted by the ghost of Lord Elton."

"And who is Lord Elton?"

"Well, I don't know for certain, sir, though Mr. Lee claimed that he was the former master of Elton House and that he'd been murdered here, during the first war, and that they'd found his body floating in the pond."

"I see," Lamb said. "And did he say anything else?"

"Well, he tried to convince me to come to a place in the cellar he knew and that he could prove to me there that the house was haunted. But I told him I had no intention of going to any haunted spot and went on my way as quickly as I could."

"Did he say where this haunted spot was?"

"Yes, sir. There's a door at the end of the hall in the cellar where the kitchen and the pantry are. It's locked and I've never had any cause to open it, nor has anybody else I know here. But Mr. Lee claimed it hid a secret passageway and that's where Lord Elton's ghost dwelled."

"And did you have any encounters with Mr. Lee after that, miss, especially during the last couple of days?"

"No, sir. That was the last time I spoke to him. And now I find out that he's been killed and found floating in the pond, and so when the sergeant started asking me questions, like, I thought I'd better tell him what Mr. Lee had said to me."

"You've done right to tell us, Nurse," Lamb said.

The door to the room opened and Nurse Stevens stepped in.

"We won't keep you any longer from your duties, miss," Lamb said to Nurse Anderson. "Thank you again for your assistance. You can go now."

Nurse Anderson stood and nodded at the three men. "Good morning, gentlemen," she said. She turned to find Nurse Stevens waiting by the door.

"Come now," Nurse Stevens said. "You're needed in the group activity."

"Yes, ma'am," the younger nurse said.

Once Anderson was gone, Nurse Stevens turned to the detectives. "Well, gentlemen, that's everyone. Is there anything else I can do to assist you?"

Lamb stood. "I understand that you have not been interviewed yet, Nurse," he said.

Surprise lit Stevens's eyes. "No, I haven't," she said. "I suppose I thought it wouldn't be necessary given that you've already spoken with Dr. Hornby."

"All the same," Lamb said. "We do like to interview everyone. I wonder if you have a moment now?"

Nurse Stevens stood rigid at the door for several seconds. Then she closed the door and said to Lamb, "Of course, Chief Inspector."

SIX

—⁓—

BEFORE SITTING DOWN WITH NURSE STEVENS, LAMB SENT CASHEN
and Wallace back to the pond to assist Larkin and Rivers in their
searches. Lamb took a minute to refresh his cup of coffee as Nurse
Stevens sat at the table and waited for him.

"Thank you for your assistance, today," Lamb said as he seated
himself across from her. "I don't think this will take long."

"As long as it takes, Chief Inspector," the nurse said.

"I wonder what you can tell me about Mr. Lee," Lamb began.
"My impression is that he was not well-liked about the place. I keep
hearing that he was a braggart and a bore."

Nurse Stevens folded her hands on the table and raised her chin
slightly. "He was those things, yes," she said. "Though I suppose it
depended on how one approached him. I did not have any trouble
with him, for example, though several of the nurses complained to
me about off-color comments he'd made to them."

"Did you speak to him about these comments?"

"No. That would be Dr. Hornby's job. I told him about the comments but don't know if he spoke to Mr. Lee about them. I assume that he did."

"So, do I take it then, that you spoke to Lee regularly?"

"When I encountered him, yes. As I said, he was not impolite to me and I was not to him."

"Did he ever speak to you about the publican's daughter, a young woman named Theresa Hitchens?"

"No."

"Do you know Theresa Hitchens, or her father, Horace Hitchens?"

"No. Then, too, I don't go into Marbury much. Only for the occasional walk. I don't have much of a respite from my duties here, nor do I need much of one. I believe in the work that Dr. Hornby is doing here for these men. I believe he truly cares about helping them to recover."

"How about a man named Alan Fox, a resident of Marbury? I'm told that Mr. Lee was heard arguing with him in the High Street two nights ago."

"I'm sorry. I don't recognize that name."

"So Mr. Lee did not mention to you, even in passing, that he had argued with someone in the village."

"Well, he wouldn't have, you see, because I hadn't spoken to Mr. Lee since the Saturday last, when Dr. Hornby asked me to order him to clear out some detritus—broken twigs and leaves and the like—that had collected in the rear courtyard over the winter. I gather that Lee was supposed to have done this weeks ago, but hadn't yet."

"Did you check to see if he had done it?"

"No—again, that would be Dr. Hornby's responsibility. I was merely acting as Dr. Hornby's intermediary when I asked Lee to do the job."

"How long have you worked here?"

"Slightly more than a year, since spring 1941. I was working as a private nurse in Portsmouth when I heard about the sanatorium that Dr. Hornby had opened here. Frankly, I had grown a bit tired of my previous posting and wanted something different. So I applied here and Dr. Hornby accepted me. He has since seen fit to promote me to head nurse, for which I am grateful."

"I take it you have quarters here?"

"Yes."

"And do they look out upon the rear of the house?"

"They do."

"Did you see or hear anything unusual coming from the area of the pond either last night or early this morning?"

"No. But then, I'm a sound sleeper. Even had there been something, I don't know that it would have awakened me."

"Do you know of anyone either here or in the village who disliked Joseph Lee enough to hurt him? Or anyone he'd rowed with?"

The nurse shook her head. During the interview she had not moved. Her hands remained folded together on the table and her chin erect. "No one," she said.

"And you had no conflicts with him?"

"None, sir. As I said, I didn't share the same aversion to him as others seemed to. I spoke to him when we met during our regular duties and when Dr. Hornby asked me to on his behalf. Apart from that we did not have a relationship."

"What is your relationship with Janet Lockhart?"

"Cordial enough. She is helpful, certainly."

"Are you responsible for assigning her duties?"

"No, as she is not an employee. Her arrangement here is with Dr. Hornby. She approached him and asked if she might volunteer her services and he agreed. She predates my coming here. As long as she does not get in the way of myself or the other nurses, I'm happy to have her assistance."

"And does she get in the way at times?"

"Not as such."

"Can you explain what you mean by that, please?"

"Well, she has no medical training but sometimes feels as if it is her place to offer medical opinions. But I let Dr. Hornby handle those situations."

"Are you speaking of her offering certain patients grief counseling?"

"If you must know, Chief Inspector, yes. I believe it to be a lot of nonsense and, in that way, potentially harmful. But Dr. Hornby approves of it and allows it."

"Are you aware that she is counseling Lieutenant Travers?"

"Yes."

"And is Dr. Hornby aware of this, do you know?"

"I believe that he is. But you would be best asking him that question if you want to make certain."

"Yes, of course," Lamb said. He paused to take a sip of his coffee. He sensed that Nurse Stevens was beginning to coil a bit tightly.

"This is delicious coffee, by the way," Lamb said, placing his cup again on its saucer. "Do you know where it comes from?"

"I think it's Brazilian. But I don't handle the food stores."

"Brazilian?" Lamb said. "I would think that hard to come by."

"Yes, well, one would think so. But Dr. Hornby does his utmost to provide his patients the best."

"I wonder if you heard that Joseph Lee told at least one of your nurses that the cellars here were haunted and asked to take her to a place in the house where he intended to prove this to her."

Nurse Stevens appeared surprised to hear this. "Haunted? No, I've heard nothing of that."

"Yes, he claimed that the cellar is haunted by the ghost of one of the former owners of the house, who apparently was murdered here sometime during the last war. Are you aware of that story? The story of the murder?"

"I've heard something about it, yes. I gather it's not spoken of much anymore, though."

"What have you heard?"

"Only that the master of the house was murdered. As you said. Nothing more."

"I understand, too, that there is a room in the cellar, along the same hall as the kitchen, that is never opened. This is the room that

Lee told the nurse was haunted. Do you know what this room was used for, or is it used for anything presently?"

"I have never been in it and I don't know that it is used for anything. Then, too, Chief Inspector, you must understand that this house contains several rooms that are not used or little used. Even the room in which we are now speaking is rarely opened."

"Yes," Lamb said.

As usual, he stood to signal that the interview was finished. The nurse also stood and Lamb bowed slightly in her direction.

"I want to thank you again for your assistance today," he said. "You've been most helpful. For the record, I would like to know your Christian name."

Nurse Stevens smiled slightly. "Matilda—though hardly anyone calls me that any longer."

"Thank you. Now, if you might do me one more favor," Lamb said. "I wonder if you can tell where I might find Mrs. Lockhart at this time of the day. I've a few more questions I'd like to ask her."

Nurse Stevens looked at the watch on her left wrist. "She would be on her break at the moment, I think. You might find her in the kitchen. She goes there sometimes to read and make herself a cup of tea."

"In the cellar, then?" Lamb said.

"Yes, Chief Inspector. If you'd like, I'd be happy to show you."

SEVEN

—⁂—

NURSE STEVENS LED LAMB BACK TO THE MAIN FOYER, FROM WHERE she directed him down the hall he'd traveled to reach the room in which he'd earlier met Mrs. Lockhart.

"If you go past the common room to the end of the hall you will find a door on your left that opens onto a set of stairs that lead directly to the cellar and the hall on which you will find the kitchen," she said. "I'm sorry that I can't accompany you, but I have some urgent work to attend to."

"Yes, of course," Lamb said. "I should be able to find my way."

"If you do not find Mrs. Lockhart down there, then please come back here to Dr. Hornby's office and I will do what I can to help you to find her."

Lamb moved down the hall to its end, where he found on his left a shallow and quite narrow alcove that contained a sturdy wooden door. He turned the tarnished brass knob; the ancient door creaked open, to reveal a narrow wooden stairway that led down to what looked to be a second door.

He looked for a light switch and found one just to the right of the door; he pushed it and the steps became illuminated by a single bare bulb in the ceiling of the narrow corridor. Lamb moved down the steps and into a hall much like the one he had just left, except that this one was darker; it, too, relied for light on a pair of bare bulbs in ceiling fixtures. He stood still for a moment, hoping to hear the sound of voices that might lead him in the direction of the kitchen, but heard nothing. He moved down the hall and soon came to an opening on the left; he peered inside and found a wide room with a blue tiled floor and a vast hearth along the far wall that he took to be the kitchen. He also found Janet Lockhart, who sat alone at a long, wide wooden table in the middle of the room. Behind her were two wide, deep, metal sinks with copper taps; set into a cut stone wall above these—at what Lamb understood to be the ground level at the back of the house, the stone wall being the uppermost section of the house's foundation—were two high windows hung with blackout curtains made of a heavy, green wool.

Mrs. Lockhart sat with her eyes looking down at the table and her hands cupped round a steaming cup of coffee. As Lamb entered, she looked up. "Oh!" she said, startled. "Chief Inspector!"

"I'm sorry to have startled you, madam. Nurse Stevens said I might find you here."

"Oh, yes. I was just taking a short break."

"Do you have a minute to talk? I have a few more questions."

"Of course. Can I get you a cup of coffee? I've just made a pot."

"No thank you. I've just had some as a matter of fact."

Before sitting at the table across from Mrs. Lockhart, Lamb glanced quickly round the kitchen in an effort to understand its layout. To the left of the sinks he saw a door with a hinged window in its top half that also was covered with the heavy green blackout material. Lamb reckoned that the door opened onto the rear of the house, from where, during its heyday, servants had taken delivery of the food and other items required to keep the household humming.

"Are you here alone, madam?" Lamb asked Mrs. Lockhart. "I would have thought there would be some staff around. Dr. Hornby said that he employs a cook."

"He does. But he and his assistant have gone into Marbury to buy supplies. Nurse Stevens released them to leave not fifteen minutes ago."

"She seems rather to run quite a tight ship here," Lamb said.

"Yes, indeed she does."

"I was just interviewing Lieutenant Travers and he told me about the support you are giving him—how you are helping him to face his grief."

Mrs. Lockhart smiled slightly. "I see," she said. "And you want me to assure you that it's all on the up and up, then."

"I would appreciate it if you would explain to me the nature of the assistance you render?"

Mrs. Lockhart sighed slightly. "All right, Chief Inspector; I've no secrets. The fact is, I knew that this was bound to come up eventually. Some of the people in Marbury seem to think I practice some sort of witchcraft, though I assure you I do nothing of the kind." She looked across the table directly at Lamb. "To put it plainly to you, I believe that I have a gift—a gift that allows me to sense the presence of, and even to communicate with, those who have passed to the other side. I discovered this after Cyril died and I found myself unable to disconnect my life from the one we shared together. More plainly speaking, I never really grieved his loss properly because I was not able to allow myself to accept the fact that he was truly gone. It was only after a time that I began to realize that the only times in which I felt his presence—the presence of his spirit, I mean—was when I wasn't trying to. I realize that might not make sense to you, but there it is. Some people describe the kind of person I believe myself to be as a medium. But I prefer the term *empath*. I am empathetic with the dead, if you will, and this allows me to truly hear and sense their presence."

"I see," Lamb said. He tried not to sound skeptical.

"You think I'm batty, of course," Mrs. Lockhart said. "Many people do and I suppose I can't blame them. Before my husband died I might have said the same thing about someone who claimed to have a connection with the spirits of those who have passed on."

She looked down at her coffee for a few seconds before returning her gaze to Lamb. "My husband committed suicide, you see, Chief Inspector. In that way he was a casualty of the war, like the young men here, a victim of something larger than himself that he was never able to adequately reckon with."

"Yes, I understand," Lamb said. "And I'm sorry for your loss."

"Please don't apologize. I believe that one must learn to accept death, of course, but also that the spirit can live on, can transcend the flesh. I often feel as if Cyril is near me during those moments when I need him to be. Some people have accused me of running séances, but I do nothing of the kind. Instead, I encourage the people who come to me to do what I eventually learned to do with my husband—to let the dead go, so that one may reconnect with what they have become, as opposed to what they were in life, which we fervently, but fruitlessly, long for them to continue to be."

"Does Dr. Hornby know of your work?"

"Yes, and I wouldn't have it any other way. In fact, he approves of what I do and believes it can be beneficial. But Dr. Hornby is a very forward-thinking man. I don't suppose I'd be as welcome in other, similar places as I am here."

"And Travers? How are you helping him?"

"He has suffered a great deal of loss in his life for a man so young. His father died of heart problems when James was young, and his mother died very tragically soon after. And of course he lost comrades in the war, as my husband did. But I believe that you might know something of that yourself, Chief Inspector."

"Yes," Lamb said. "I understand the power of grief."

"But I fear you find me a charlatan all the same."

Lamb shrugged. "I believe one can feel the presence of the dead," he said. "But I don't believe in being able to speak with them."

"But if you can feel their presence then what's to stop you from taking the next step and endeavoring to discover if they can sense, or feel, yours?"

"Perhaps 'presence' is the wrong word, then," Lamb said. "I believe that we maintain memories of the dead—at times very vivid memories—and that through these we maintain lasting impressions of those who have died. We remember how their voices sounded, how they walked, or some quirk they possessed. And in these impressions they can remain 'alive' for us, I suppose you might say. But this is a kind of remembering, rather than experiencing anything new."

"Perhaps you will change your mind one day."

"Perhaps."

"Marbury, and this house, is filled with spirits, after all."

"So I understand," Lamb said. "One of the nurses implied that a murder had occurred here during the last war."

"That is true, yes."

"You know about it, then?"

"I was living in the village with Cyril at the time. We had only just moved to Marbury a few months earlier."

"Can you tell me what happened?"

"The victim was the man who owned and ran Elton House at the time. His name was Henry Elton—or Lord Elton, as I knew him. His wife, Catherine, killed him; she poisoned him and then put his body in the pond to make it appear as if he'd drowned by accident, but the police saw through it. Lady Elton was brought to the bar on a charge of murder, but her lawyer successfully argued that she had killed her husband as an act of self-defense—that Lord Elton had abused and humiliated her in the most terrible manner during their marriage, thereby forcing her to act in order to protect herself. Several members of the Eltons' staff testified that they had either heard or witnessed some of these instances of abuse, and, in the end, a jury acquitted her. This was in 1915. After that, she shut down Elton House and left Marbury and has never returned. The house lay unoccupied for a time until it was brought by a group of medical people who converted it into a sanatorium that treated consumptives. They packed up and left a couple of years ago and the house sat vacant again until Dr. Hornby bought it. The rumor is he got the place for a song, though it was showing its age by then."

"In what way had Lord Elton mistreated his wife?" Lamb asked.

"Well, it was all rather strange and scandalous; one might even describe it as depraved. In short, Lord Elton was said to have had a kind of a perverted sexual obsession with the figure of Ondine, a mythical water nymph who rises from the depths searching for a human man as a husband so that she also can then become human. Do you know the story?"

"I'm afraid I don't."

"I don't really, either, though it has apparently inspired several artists, and Lord Elton fancied himself an artistic type. He was a painter and sculptor both, but not a very good one if the truth be told. In any case, he eroticized the character in his mind and this led him to ask of his wife sexual favors that she refused to grant, as she considered them deviant and humiliating. But Lord Elton insisted and, according to what came out at her trial, forced her to play the role of his Ondine, his eroticized water nymph. I followed the trial at the time because I had been friendly with Lady Elton; she and her husband had invited my husband and me to the house several times for parties. I couldn't say, of course, what it all meant; one would need a psychiatrist for that, I suppose. But it is ironic, given what has happened to Mr. Lee—the way they both involve the dark water beneath the surface of which we cannot see and which holds close its secrets. It's rather like that line between life and death that we were just discussing."

Mrs. Lockhart smiled again. "Now I *do* fear that you find me off my rocker, Chief Inspector," she said in a joshing tone.

"Not at all," Lamb said. He found the story of the Eltons rather fantastic, but had no reason to doubt that it was true. Nearly two years in the trenches and twenty as a detective had convinced him that the depths of human depravity knew no limits. He doubted the case had any connection to Lee's killing other than their common setting.

Still, to be certain, he would have to check to see what else he could discover about the previous murder at Elton House.

"Anyhow, there is a rather nice young man in Marbury named Arthur Brandt who has written about the case," Mrs. Lockhart continued. "He fancies himself a playwright. He could tell you more about the case if you really want to know. His cottage also is in the High Street by the church."

Lamb jotted the name in his notebook. "Thank you, Mrs. Lockhart," he said. "I hope I shall not have to take up too much of your time, but I must ask again that you remain in Marbury for the time being."

"I've enjoyed speaking with you, Chief Inspector. I sense that you will find some justice for Mr. Lee. In fact, I hope I am not being too forward in saying that I sense that you feel responsible for the losses of other people you have known in your life and that this might be the reason you became a policeman—to seek justice for those who have had their lives unjustly ended."

Lamb did not at first know quite what to say in response. She was, in a way, correct, he thought. "That is very interesting, madam, and I can't say it's entirely wrong," he said.

"I don't mean to be presumptuous, Chief Inspector. And I certainly don't mean to be morbid. But it's just that none of us, really, can fully hide from our grief, nor should we."

EIGHT

—ɯ—

WHILE LAMB WENT ABOUT HIS BUSINESS IN ELTON HOUSE, VERA had taken his advice and decided to have a look round the estate's grounds. She headed first toward the right side of the house, which faced away from the path, the pond, and Marbury. Here, the grass was moist and her shoes became a bit wet, but she didn't mind. She could see that the grounds must have been impressive at one time—trimmed and neat and park-like, with well-spaced trees and rows of hedges and shrubs marking former terraces and other spots—but had since fallen into a neglected and shabby state.

Inevitably, her thoughts turned to David. Indeed, since her father had dropped her at the car and bade her wait, she had thought of little else. For nearly ten months she had been serving as her father's driver in what everyone round them understood to be a clear-cut case of nepotism her father had cooked up to keep her from being called up into a more dangerous war-related job. Vera had never liked the idea of her father using his influence on her behalf in that way, but she had swallowed her distaste for that because her job kept her close to David, who, in recent months, had become her lover.

She could not chase away a sense of concern about David's need to prove that his wound had not crippled him. That was the word David himself used. *crippled.* He hated the idea that someone might consider him crippled. She understood why he felt this way and sympathized with him. She even sometimes felt that she shared his sense of embarrassment—and sometimes even his physical pain—as she watched his attempts to negotiate the world as if his wound didn't exist. And yet his insistence on going into the pond that morning had struck her as too desperate an attempt on David's part to prove that he remained the same man he'd always been. He could have easily allowed Rivers to go, she thought.

David was essentially courageous—selfless in his desire to protect others from harm and reckless in defense of himself. These traits had attracted her to him, along with his smile and wit and easy charm and something else besides those surface allures—a kind of emotional vulnerability that he normally did not display but had shown to her. And so she had fallen in love with him—a love that, she believed, had not diminished since his wounding.

She and David had become lovers during the initial three months of his recovery, when his doctor had forbidden him to work. During that time she had stolen whatever time was available to her in which she could visit him in his flat in Winchester. She had always been anxious to see and touch him and to hear his voice. Occasionally they had made love, mostly in the late afternoons and usually too quickly.

But since David's return to duty they had found it harder to find time to be together alone, in part because David had thrown himself back into the job with the zeal of a man with something to prove. While on duty, the two of them had done their best to hide the fact of their relationship from the others, though they understood that her father knew that they were in love and probably had guessed that they had become lovers. Or had he? Vera was unsure on that point and believed that their shared silence on the matter acted as a wedge between herself and her father. She had discovered—just as Wallace had discovered before her—that her father could be maddeningly intractable while on the job. Before becoming his driver, Vera had never seen this side of her father's personality and she hadn't fully decided yet what to make of it. Was his inscrutability a way of politely avoiding addressing the subject of what he might know about her and David? Or was he holding his cards close to his vest with the goal of laying them on the table at some point in a winning flourish?

David's wound meant that he would not be called up for war duty, and this, along with their lovemaking and the subterfuge they were forced to practice while on duty, had caused David to begin speaking of marriage. He wanted to end the sneaking round, he said, and make their love an open fact around which they could build a life together. All of this made sense to Vera—and when she and David had become lovers she had thought then that she would marry him.

But although she believed she loved him, she had found his sudden enthusiasm for marriage a bit frightening. And indeed, though David had not yet proposed marriage, she had begun to realize that she might be dreading the notion that he soon might.

Enough, she thought and tried to direct her thoughts elsewhere.

She continued to walk along the side of the house to its rear where, she reckoned, she would find herself heading back toward the trail that led to the pond. That way she could make an entire circle of the house, which seemed to her very old and caused her to wonder about its origins and history. She knew nothing of its current use except that it was a hospital for men suffering from psychological illnesses related to the war and she thought this as good a use as any for the place.

She came to a kind of courtyard at the rear of the house that was laid in gravel and was muddy in spots. From here, the grounds of Elton House sloped downhill toward Marbury. The slope also was untended, covered in high grass, and spotted with patches of low brush and young trees, and not too far down the hill, a full-fledged wood. To the left of this lay the path to Marbury, which passed the pond.

She went into the level courtyard, which contained a pair of old wooden buildings that Vera took to once have been the house's stables and carriage house. To reach them, she descended a flight of stone steps that were part of a retaining wall that was built into the slope and faced the house from across the courtyard. With the sun having disappeared once more, the setting in the muddy, neglected spot, with the three-story high rear wall of the old, stone mansion looming to her left, struck Vera as rather spooky.

She moved first to examine the stables, which she found shuttered and padlocked, its windows boarded up. The rear of the stables abutted the retaining wall, giving the place a bunker-like aspect. She lifted one of the heavy iron padlocks, which also seemed a relic of a much older time, conjuring in her mind's eye an image of a stable boy in his flat cap, black boots, and mud-stained trousers moving among the skittish horses in the midst of a summer thunderstorm at twilight, holding a hurricane lantern above his head and whispering to the animals to hush as the wind rattled the wooden doors and indifferent mice scurried along the rafters—an image she knew came from books and films and her own imagination, which tended to visualize the past in a sentimental, amber light. Even so, the thought of a thing so seemingly elemental and romantic having passed away left her feeling fleetingly sad, and she realized that she had not thought of David for some minutes.

She moved next to the carriage house, the high double doors of which—something like barn doors—faced the courtyard at a ninety-degree angle to those of the stables. These too she found secured with iron padlocks. Taken together, the two buildings gave off a feeling, like the grounds, of neglect, locked up tightly not only against trespassers but time itself.

She decided to head back to the car—but a flash of color at her feet caught her eye. She looked down and saw what appeared to be a stick of gum. She bent to pick it up and found that it indeed was a stick of

Wrigley's Spearmint Gum, wrapped in a plain brown, waxy paper with green lettering. She had not seen a stick of Wrigley's Spearmint Gum in nearly three years; since the war began such American luxuries had all but disappeared in Britain. The wrapper was damp and a bit dirty from having lain in the mud. Vera considered opening it to see the condition of the gum, but decided instead to save it and show her father. Who knew, after all, if it might not be a clue?

He had suggested she have a look round to see if she found something interesting and now, she thought, she had.

NINE

—◊—

ON HIS WAY TO THE POND TO ASSIST LARKIN AND RIVERS, WALLACE
had stopped by the front door of Elton House to smoke a cigarette.
Sergeant Cashen, who did not smoke, had gone on ahead of him with
a reminder not to take too long.

Wallace had hoped to find Vera alone, tending Lamb's Wolseley,
and was disappointed to see that she was not there and wondered
where she might have gone. He decided to wait a bit to see if she
showed.

He knew that he'd been stupid to rush into the pond in the way
he had. But he'd also sensed that Lamb had paused to think about
whether to send in Rivers rather than himself after Lee's body. Before
his wounding, he knew, Lamb would have entertained no such second
thoughts about his abilities. In the meantime, Lamb maintained a
belief in Rivers as unbreakable, despite Rivers's age. It all went back

to the time they'd spent in the trenches on the Somme. Lamb therefore refused to allow that Rivers also possessed weaknesses. He had therefore gone ahead and jumped into the pond ahead of Rivers and reckoned he might do something similar again until he convinced Lamb that he was not crippled.

Although the morning had been chilly, he hadn't bothered with an overcoat. Now he turned up the collar of his jacket and hunched his shoulders against the damp. He didn't relish becoming bogged down in a murder inquiry; the damned things required all of your time and he wanted to spend more time with Vera. The last one he'd handled had occurred nearly a year ago, when he'd been shot in a scuffle involving a man who had been at the end of his rope and was holding Lamb at gunpoint. The whole mess had been partly his fault because he'd failed to properly follow Lamb's directions before storming in on the two of them. And so he'd come out of it with a permanent limp and a pass on the call-up. He didn't mind the limp so much, especially when so many men were being maimed in much worse ways, or killed outright.

But his pass from combat duty had left him feeling guilty, and the fact that the army now looked upon him as too defective to even consider for such duty vexed him; he did not feel weak and hated the idea that he might be seen as such. More than anything he despised pity, though he'd found that other people enjoyed dispensing it, mostly because it made them feel well disposed toward themselves.

He stepped out into the drive to see if he could spy Vera somewhere in the vicinity, but did not see her. He was anxious to speak with her; he wanted to tell her again that he loved her, which he tried to do as often as possible in those rare moments on the job when they found themselves alone and out of earshot of the rest of the team. But he also wanted to check her mood, given that she'd seemed to him in recent days somewhat distant and even irritated with him, and he thought he knew why—three days earlier, he had brought up the subject of their possible marriage and she had surprised him in her reluctance to discuss it in depth. The day was a balmy, sunny Saturday, the sort of day he normally looked forward to in June. Vera had taken the bus from her parents' house and met him at his apartment in Winchester; most of their meetings and all of their sexual trysts had occurred in the daytime, and on weekends, in his apartment.

They had not gone out; rather, he had lit candles in the room and prepared them lunch. Afterward, when they were finishing off what was left of the bread and strawberry jam, he had told her that he loved her. She had smiled and taken his hand and said that she also loved him. And then he had spoken the words he now regretted. He was not even certain what had possessed him to utter the words when and in the manner he had, but he now believed that he'd gone about the thing the wrong way and bollixed it.

"I want to make it official," he'd said, and she had looked him, confused, and said, "Make what official?"

"Us," he said. "Our being together."

When she hadn't answered right away, he'd added, "I'm tired of the sneaking around and having to watch the clock whenever we're together."

"So am I," she had said, then added: "But we mustn't move too fast."

These last words had pierced him, and when he had asked her why they must wait, she had looked away from and said, "I don't know."

Then she had looked him in the eye and said, "I do love you, David, but it's too much for me to think about. I'm sorry. I'm confused."

She had taken his hand again and said, "I realize I'm not giving you the answer you want, and I'm not sure if I'm even giving you the answer you deserve. But I need some time to think about it."

He had then said that he was sorry and that he hadn't meant to upset her and was willing to give her as long as she needed, all the while thinking that *he* needed no time to make up his mind. He was certain. Shorty afterward, she had left to go home.

They had not had another chance to speak before that morning, when she stood by him as he put his shoes and socks back on and they were out of earshot of the others. She had quietly asked him how he was feeling and he'd answered "never better," hoping that his bravado would erase some of the unease left over from their last meeting.

She had gently scolded him for going into the pond, saying, "You shouldn't take those sorts of risks with your leg the way it is," and, annoyed, he had answered, "But here I am, none the worse for wear," not bothering to camouflage the pique in his voice.

Now he longed to find her to apologize for his impatience and to gauge whether she was angry with him. Once again he scanned the area in front of the house but saw no sign of Vera and, as he did, a thought occurred to him: Lamb might be coddling him—protecting him—not for *his* sake or safety but for Vera's.

He believed the arrangement that the three of them seemed to have quietly agreed upon could not last. That arrangement, which none of them had spoken of, had simply fallen into place, as his and Vera's relationship ripened. It consisted mostly of Lamb acknowledging, in his own silent way, that he knew of their growing romance but had chosen not to intervene in it in exchange for their remaining discreet about it while on the job. But Wallace still was not certain that Lamb's recognition meant that he had come to accept the fact of his and Vera's relationship. Perhaps he had merely resigned himself to it temporarily—again for Vera's sake, so as not to upset her. Indeed, Lamb seemed blind to the idea that his daughter was anything but an innocent, a person without adult wants, needs, desires, and ambitions.

Frustrated, but for the moment resigned, he flicked his cigarette butt to the ground, then turned and walked down the path to Joseph Lee's cottage.

TEN

—m—

LAMB WAS ANXIOUS TO GO INTO MARBURY TO SPEAK WITH ALAN FOX. But he first went to check to see if Larkin and Rivers had recovered anything worthwhile in their searches of the area round the pond and of Lee's nearby lodgings.

The iron clouds that had earlier dropped rain on him had cleared off to the south and given way to scudding, flat, gray-white apparitions that allowed the sun to peek through here and there.

Larkin, who had been searching the area round the pond, saw Lamb approaching down the path and went to him, carrying the one bit of possible evidence he'd found in the grasses along the pond edge, not far from where they had pulled out Lee's body—a stub of a thin white candle that had been burned nearly to its end.

Larkin showed Lamb the candle and explained where he'd found it. "It's still clean, as you can see," the forensics man said. "It can't have been there long."

Lamb examined the candle, turning it over. He had not seen any similar candles in Elton House.

"We also found a boat—a row boat—lying in the reeds not far from the wood on the far side of the bank there," Larkin said, pointing to a place where a short, narrow, rickety-looking pier entered the pond. "It shows no sign of having been used recently, though; its hull is dry and there is no water in its bottom, so I'm inclined to think that Lee's killer made no use of it. I've also found no indication that Lee's body was dragged to the pond either unconscious or dead. I think he was struck near the pond but I've found no spillage of blood in the grass and reeds and am concerned that the rain might have washed it away."

"Any sign of a possible weapon?" Lamb asked.

"None, sir. But we haven't quite gotten fully round the pond yet."

The news was hardly encouraging. "All right, Mr. Larkin," Lamb said, as he handed the candle back to the forensics man. "Thank you."

—⁂—

The chief inspector continued down the path a short way until he came to an intersecting path that led a bit into the wood on his right, at the end of which lay the cottage in which Joseph Lee had lived, a small stone structure covered in ivy that once had served as the gamekeeper's residence at Elton House. About twenty yards away lay what was left of an ice house, through which, two centuries earlier, a stream that fed the pond had run. But the stream had been rerouted more than a century earlier and the little house had been allowed to fall into disrepair.

Lamb found the weathered wooden door of the main cottage standing open, its hinges and latch rusted nearly to the point of futility. He peered inside and saw the dark figures of Rivers and two constables within. The only light came from a rectangular window that took up most of the left side of the cottage's front wall and an oil-fired hurricane lamp that Rivers had found, lit, and hung from a rusting iron hook hammered into one of the wooden ceiling beams.

The room contained a narrow wooden cot along one wall; its rough straw-in-gingham mattress was askew and lay at the foot of the cot. A small wooden table with a single chair stood at the center of the room, while the corner of the far wall held an iron wood-burning stove and, next to it, a water pump and metal wash basin. Along the opposite wall was a shelf that appeared to have held books, cooking utensils, and other sundry household and personal items, most of which seemed to have been knocked to the wooden floor just below it. Indeed, the place clearly had been ransacked, Lamb thought as he entered.

Several stacks of what appeared in the dim light to be notebooks lay on the table next to a bundle of cash. Dust drifted in the shaft of light that came from the window and the ceiling was so low that Lamb found himself ducking a bit to avoid colliding with the lamp as he entered. He nodded at the two uniformed men who were assisting Rivers in the search.

Rivers greeted him with, "Kind of you to stop by, sir."

"Well, I thought I'd come down and check to make sure you weren't slacking on the job, Harry."

"The place has been tossed recently, as you can see."

"Yes." Lamb nodded at the cash on the table. "I see that you found some money."

"Yes, and more than you might expect a man like Lee to have. Eighty quid so far, all in cash, mostly ones and fives. We found it in the usual place, tucked beneath the mattress. If someone ransacked the place looking for money then they appear not to have been too savvy about where to look for it. We've also found more than a dozen notebooks of various sizes filled with what appear to be lists of things Lee fancied or was interested in—his favorite foods and the names of cities he's visited and the like. He appears to have written dozens of these lists."

Lamb noticed two thin white candles, each of which stood within a tin holder; one sat in the middle of the table, while the other had been placed atop the shelf. He picked up each and examined them. Each had been burned down very close to their nubs.

"Larkin found a candle stub very similar to these by the pond," he told Rivers. "Make sure we include them in whatever we pack up and take away from here."

"Right," Rivers said.

Lamb glanced round the room hoping that something might jump out at him. He went to the stove and examined it. He found a small shovel used to remove ash but no tool with which to poke the fire in the stove's belly.

"The poker seems to be missing," he said.

Rivers looked up. "I hadn't noticed. I'll have a look round for it."

Having seen all he thought worthwhile for the moment, Lamb moved to the door and ducked out of the cottage, followed by Rivers. A brief ray of sun lit the clearing, warming it. Lamb stopped to light a cigarette, but did not offer one to Rivers, who did not smoke. He took a drag and then said, gesturing toward the ice house, "What about that little building there?"

"It looks like it might have been an ice house at one time," Rivers said. "I had a peek inside but we haven't searched it yet. There appears to be nothing in there save cobwebs."

"Given the amount of cash he had stashed away, we've got to consider whether he was blackmailing someone," Lamb said, returning to the subject of what the search of the cottage had yielded.

Rivers nodded. "I agree."

Though he reminded himself that he must not get ahead of the game, Lamb could not help but to weigh the possible targets of blackmail whom he'd so far met. Hornby struck him as the most obvious; if the doctor was up to something untoward, then Lee, who moved about the place freely, might very well have discovered it.

He briefly updated Rivers on what the interviews at Elton House had yielded, including that Travers had claimed to have seen and heard Lee arguing with a local man named Alan Fox.

"How well do you trust this Travers bloke?"

Lamb dropped his butt on the ground, extinguished it with the toe end of his shoe, retrieved it, and deposited it in his pocket.

"I'd like to trust him; he seems right enough on the surface," he said. "But he apparently came out of the campaign in France a bit shattered, so it's hard to say. I'll tell you once I've spoken to the fellow Alan Fox. I'm about to go into Marbury now to see if I can't hunt him down."

Rivers smiled just a little and said, "Tally ho."

—m—

Lamb returned to the house to tell Hornby that he could now allow his patients and staff to come and go from the house. He was met in the hall by Nurse Stevens, who said that Hornby was not available—he was in a session with a patient—and that she would relay the message to him and let the staff know.

Lamb then went out to his car, where he found Vera waiting for him, leaning against the bonnet.

"Have you been terribly bored?" he asked her.

"Not really. I took a stroll round the place, as you suggested. It must have been quite a nice place in its day, but it's just kind of ragged now. It's sad, really."

She dug into her pocket and withdrew from it the stick of gum. "And I found this: American gum; Wrigley's Spearmint. It was lying on the ground behind the house. It looks as if it might have been lying there for a while, though it's clearly never been opened."

Lamb took the gum and briefly examined it. He thought of the American Lucky Strike cigarettes that Travers had offered him, and the lieutenant's comment that the sanatorium "seemed to have an endless supply of the things."

Lamb thought he knew the origin of the gum and the cigarettes. For two years, through the "lend-lease" program, American ships laden with food, war matériel, vehicles, and other essential supplies had called at British ports, including Southampton and Portsmouth, from which the supplies were distributed both to the military and civilians. The goods shipped into the southern ports moved through

Hampshire on their way to London and the rest of England. Many of these goods were rationed, including some foods, and, as always, a black market had arisen to barter goods stolen from the ships that had become either scarce or hard to obtain because of rationing. Some people were willing to pay exorbitant prices for certain commodities, mostly petrol, food, liquor, and cigarettes. This did not necessarily mean that the food and cigarettes he'd seen in Elton House had been obtained illegally. But all of it taken together—the coffee, the milk, the "endless" cigarettes, and now the gum—made him suspicious.

"What's behind the house?" he asked.

"Some old stables and a carriage house. But they are shuttered and boarded up."

"Do you mind if I keep this?" Lamb said, pulling a handkerchief from his jacket pocket and placing the gum within it before folding and replacing it.

Vera smiled at her father. "Only if you promise not to chew it—finders-keepers after all—though I'd be happy to split it with you."

Lamb returned the smile. "I promise."

ELEVEN

—⁌—

VERA PUSHED THE WOLSELEY'S START BUTTON, BUT THE CAR MERELY sputtered.

"Wonderful," she said under her breath. Her father's aging car, she knew, had a habit of developing a case of the fits and starts, though they had experienced no problems with it since she had become his driver.

"Try again," Lamb said patiently. "It can be obstinate."

Vera pushed the button again—and again the car only coughed.

"Give it a few seconds and then try a third time," Lamb said, trying to sound optimistic.

Vera did as her father advised; when she pushed the button a third time the car rumbled to life.

"You know what they say about the third time," Lamb said.

Vera knew, but said instead, "That it's too many?"

"Then you do know," Lamb said, kidding her.

Vera headed the Wolseley down the driveway to the road, where she made a left and moved down the hill into Marbury. As they drove, Lamb stole a glance at his daughter. He was certain that Vera had wanted to say something to him when he had dropped her at the car earlier, but had held back from doing so. He thought that Wallace's actions at the pond might have distressed her. But he decided for the moment not to broach the subject.

The slope flattened as they entered the outskirts of Marbury, which lay in a valley formed by an insistent, tea-colored brook called the Bottle. They began to pass stone cottages with slate roofs and well-tended front gardens.

As they reached the center of the village, the High Street split and snaked its way round both sides of an oval-shaped green that was roughly seventy-five yards long and perhaps thirty wide. On the opposite end of this oval the split lanes converged again and headed uphill to the village's eastern end.

Vera maneuvered down the lane on the left side of the green, which was lined with small shops, including a tea shop called London House. Near the place where the lanes converged sat a pub called the Watchman, and just east of it, a small gravel-and-dirt lot that lay hard by a stone arch bridge that conveyed the High Street over the Bottle.

Vera parked in this lot and shut off the car, which wearily sputtered into silence. "It doesn't sound right," she said of the motor.

"No, it doesn't," Lamb agreed. But he had no time to worry about the car. And he was concerned that Vera had eaten no lunch. He put his hand to his brow and squinted across the green. At its center was a vertical marble obelisk that he guessed contained the names of the men from Marbury who had given their lives for England in various wars.

"The tea shop looks friendly," he said to Vera. "Why don't you take a bit of a break and see if they've any sort of worthwhile lunch. I'm going to hike up the hill and see if I can't locate this man who argued with Lee."

Vera was hungry and the idea of getting lunch appealed to her. "All right," she said. "But what about you; have you eaten?"

"I had some very delicious coffee at Elton House."

"Yes, but coffee isn't lunch, dad."

"I'll survive. Go ahead now and I'll see you back here in a bit."

—⁂—

Climbing the High Street from the village center, Lamb soon reached the Church of All Saints. He paused to gaze at the 17th-century building and saw the path leading round to the rear of the church along which Travers claimed he'd been walking when he'd heard Lee and Fox begin to argue. According to Travers, this path led round to the back of the church, where it connected to the path that led to Elton House and that passed the pond.

He continued up the road for about fifty yards, until he spied, on his right, a wooden mailbox with the name FOX painted on it in white letters. Next to the name was a small cartoonish drawing of a fox's face, made with two dots on either side of a cross, all of which was contained inside a *V*. A narrow lane led off the High Street to a cottage about thirty yards distant. As Lamb made for the front door, he heard the faint sound of orchestral music. He knocked upon the red door and waited a full minute before trying again; but neither try resulted in anyone answering.

He stood by the door and listened more closely and soon determined that the music was coming from the rear of the house. He moved round to the left side of the house, where he found a low whitewashed wooden gate and stone path leading round back to a small stone terrace that had at its center a single round table made of metal, painted bright red, with four matching metal chairs circling it. The table held a half-dozen empty ale bottles and a yellow ceramic bowl filled nearly to its brim with cigarette butts. And it was here that Lamb found the source of the music—a large wood-slat garden shed. The shed's door was open and the sound of an orchestra cascaded from it. Through a smudged window to the left of the door Lamb could just make out the figure of a man who appeared to be standing before a painter's easel.

As he moved to the door, the first thing Lamb saw inside was a Victrola, perched upon a rickety wooden table, from which the music emanated. Next to the table, a collection of phonograph records lay in what had once been a case for wine bottles. Lamb now saw the man, who had his back to the door. He was indeed standing before a large easel that he was filling with blotches of green and blue oil paint. The rest of the room was filled with canvases—some finished and some blank—leaning against the walls and a potting table beneath the window that was covered in scattered painter's supplies: brushes, tubes of paint, glass jars full of oils and thinners. Most appeared to Lamb to be portraits of people done in what he thought must be the modern fashion, people rendered as multicolored geometric shapes.

Unaware of Lamb's presence, the painter stepped back from his work, as if appraising it, a half-smoked cigarette hanging on for dear life from his lips. He wore paint-stained green corduroy trousers held up by a leather belt inlaid with red, yellow, and blue beads and a rough brown cotton shirt. Fingers of his hair stuck up slightly, as if he'd recently run his hands through it.

"Mr. Fox?" Lamb said. He nearly had to shout the name to be heard over the music. "Alan Fox?"

Startled, Alan Fox turned round quickly, causing the lengthy ash clinging to his cigarette to fall away onto the well-trodden wooden floor.

"Who are you?" Fox said, squinting at Lamb. He seemed poised to defend himself with the sable-haired brush, filled with blue paint, that he held in his left hand.

Lamb pulled his warrant card from the pocket of his jacket and showed it to Fox.

"Detective Chief Inspector Thomas Lamb," he said. He nodded at the Victrola. "Might you turn that off for a moment, so that we can speak properly?"

Fox stood still. "I'm busy," he said. "Come back later. I'll speak to you then." He began to turn away from Lamb.

"Joseph Lee was murdered last night, and I intend to speak to you about that now, Mr. Fox," Lamb said, deciding he had no time to waste with Fox. "We can do it here or in a cramped little room in Winchester, with no windows. The choice is yours."

Fox turned back round to face Lamb; he sullenly walked to the Victrola and switched it off with an angry flourish. He took the cigarette from his lips, dropped it on the floor, and ground it out with the toe of his boot.

"Did you say that Lee is dead?" he asked Lamb.

"Yes. He was found this morning on the grounds of Elton House with his head battered in."

Fox sighed, then nodded toward the table in the middle of the terrace. "All right," he said. "We can talk out there."

Fox moved toward the door and Lamb stepped back to let him pass, then followed him to the metal table, where they sat across from each other with the empty beer bottles and the ash tray between them. Fox immediately took a packet of cigarettes from his shirt pocket and lit one. Lamb noticed that the brand was not American, but French.

"You don't seem too surprised to hear that Joseph Lee is dead," Lamb said.

"Well, I'm not—then again, if you told me he'd just gone off and married Greer Garson, I wouldn't be surprised, either," Fox said nonchalantly. "I know nothing about the man, really, and care even less."

"And yet you struck him in the face two nights ago during an argument over a woman," Lamb said without emotion.

Fox sat back in his chair and struck a contemplative pose, with his arm across his chest and the fingers of his right hand pressed against his mouth. He did not speak for about ten seconds before he took his hand from his mouth and said, "I hit him once and knocked him down in self-defense. He was badgering me and had been for at least two hours in the pub. Then he tried to follow me home and accosted me on the way. The stupid sod had it in his head that the publican's

70

daughter was in love with him and that I was trying to steal her heart away. The whole thing would have been laughable if it wasn't so bloody pathetic. I knocked him down and I went on my way and I haven't seen him since."

Fox took a drag from his cigarette and added, "He struck me as a repugnant little man who lived in a fantasy world of his own construction."

"Do you have any connections to Elton House?"

"None."

"Have you ever been in Joseph Lee's cottage?"

"Never."

"So I shan't find your fingerprints about the place, then?"

Fox smiled. He exhaled smoke, then looked directly at Lamb and said, "No."

"Was Joseph Lee blackmailing you, Mr. Fox?"

"Blackmailing me? Absolutely not."

Lamb did not answer.

Fox then smiled—a cracked, leering grin. "You're just guessing, Lamb; yes, I see it. You've nothing, no evidence, and yet you've still got a murder you must clear up, else your boss won't be pleased. Am I right? Perhaps you've bollixed a whole string of cases recently and this one could be your last chance."

"Where were you last night?" Lamb asked.

"Here, from tea time on."

"Can anyone else confirm that?"

"Not that I'm aware of."

"What is your relationship with Theresa Hitchens?"

"Ah—so you know her name. You have been on the job, then. But to answer your question, nothing. I have no relationship with her beyond her serving me a drink now and again."

"Why did Joseph Lee single you out, then, as his competition?"

"As I just said, there was no competition, except for the one that sprang from Lee's pathetic fantasy world. I suggest you ask Theresa if she had even the slightest interest in Lee. He was a sad nonentity who drank too much and who had created a dream world in which he was a man of consequence. It's not an uncommon occurrence after all."

"Neither is murder."

Fox stood. "You're fishing, Chief Inspector, and I've grown tired of it. I've answered your questions truthfully, but you seem uninterested in the truth. And so I'm going to have to insist that you leave now."

Lamb also stood. "Very well, Mr. Fox. I advise you not to leave Marbury."

Fox took a drag from his cigarette and nodded toward the gate, encouraging Lamb on his way.

"I wish I could say it was a pleasure meeting you, but I'd be lying if I did," he said.

TWELVE

—m—

LAMB HEADED BACK TOWARD THE CENTER OF MARBURY, THE
landscape leveling as he reached the stone bridge beneath which
flowed the Bottle.

He stopped on the bridge to smoke a cigarette. He had found Fox
arrogant but also genuinely confident. He smoked the cigarette to a
nub then dropped the butt into the Bottle; the thing hit the water
with a fizzle and final pant that put Lamb in mind of a man's dying
sigh, and he watched it sail away beneath the bridge, on the stream's
swift current. Beneath the brook's surface, rushes clung to the stones
just below the surface, looking very much, he thought, like a woman's
long hair flowing behind her, putting him in mind of mermaids—and,
he thought, the tale of the water nymph, Ondine. He wondered if
the flowing rushes were the source of such myths—of the stories of
beautiful half-human female beings who lived beneath the water but

yearned for men, and to enter into the light and air of human experience. He could not think of a tale or myth that told the opposite story, of feminine beauty pulling a man down to a depth from which he could not return, and in which he must inevitably drown. But this, he thought, was the more common occurrence.

He reached the lot by the pub in which they'd parked the car, but did not find Vera there. He looked across the green and hoped that she had taken him up on his suggestion to get lunch at the tea house, and then set off in that direction to find her.

—⁂—

Vera reckoned that news traveled quickly in a small, rural place such as Marbury and that, by now, some word of the discovery of Joseph Lee's body had managed to trickle down the hill and into the village.

For that reason, she was reluctant at first to cross the green and enter the tea shop. Given her uniform, she was sure to draw questions. Not that she would mind answering them; she'd happily do so if she knew anything—anything at all, really—about what had happened at Elton House. All she really knew was that the gardener's body had been found floating in the pond; beyond that, she was as ignorant as any passerby whom she might encounter.

She found herself becoming irritated by her father's standing suggestion that she "have a look round" whenever he left her to mind the car. She believed it was meant to mollify her—to help her ward off the boredom of having to stand by while he and the others went to perform the actual police work.

She was beginning the believe that perhaps the time had come to cut herself free from her parents' anxieties for her—to declare her independence from their desire to protect her and take her chances with the call-up, or even to enlist in one of the military organizations for women. The army had begun to allow women they considered fit for the duty to join coastal antiaircraft batteries and she reckoned she could handle that. And yet, she must also consider David, who, she worried, probably would be as opposed as was her father to her taking on any sort of dangerous war duty.

Her pangs of hunger urging her on, she put aside her concerns about fielding questions from villagers and headed toward the tea shop—though she found its door locked and a handwritten sign affixed to it that read, "Back in twenty minutes."

Frustrated, she decided there was nothing for it but to have a "look round" and so began walking up the High Street. She passed several people but none stopped to ask her questions, though they did indeed notice her uniform and nodded greetings to her as they passed, which she returned. Perhaps the uniform intimidated them, she thought; if the presence of a stranger dressed in police garb assuredly meant bad news, then perhaps the locals didn't want to hear it. Except for these few people, though, she found the High Street strangely deserted, as if most of Marbury had gone into hiding.

She walked for what she reckoned was ten minutes, then turned round to head back toward the green. But as she turned, she found herself suddenly colliding with someone—a man. He had been approaching her from the left and she had walked directly into him as they crossed paths. Or he had walked into her. She wasn't entirely sure. She looked to her left and saw there a narrow side street leading up the hill from the High Street—and she became aware that the man's glasses had fallen from his head and that he had dropped something else besides. She took a step back and watched the man bend to pick up his glasses.

"Oh, my," she said. "I'm very sorry."

The man found his glasses and put them on. He straightened and looked at Vera through them, squinting a bit. "Oh, no, no," he said. "No, please. My fault—my fault entirely. I hope you aren't hurt."

"I'm fine," Vera said.

The man smiled. "I wasn't looking where I was going; I had my nose in a book, I'm afraid."

He looked at the ground. "Speaking of which, where is the culprit?" He saw the book lying in the road on its spine. "Ah, here we are," he said and picked it up. As he bent over, his glasses slid down his nose and, when he straightened again, he pushed them back onto the bridge with his left index finger.

Vera saw that the book was Voltaire's *Candide*, which she'd read in school and liked. The man was a few inches taller than she and rather thin. He had longish sandy hair and, Vera thought, a nice face—both handsome and friendly—marked out by large, expressive brown eyes, a smallish, almost feminine, nose, and an unaffected, genuine-seeming smile.

"I'm afraid I wasn't looking where I was going, either," she said.

"No harm done, in any case." He paused a couple of seconds before saying, "You're with the police, then?"

"Yes. I'm an auxiliary constable."

"I see," he said. "Are you here about the mess up at the hospital; the man in the pond?"

"Yes—or, I'm here with the chief inspector. I'm his driver. He's off interviewing someone at the moment, so I was just having a look round."

The man shook his head. "Terrible thing, murder," he said. "We don't get it round here, much—though it is rather eerie how much this one resembles the last one."

"The last what?"

"Oh, I'm sorry. Perhaps you don't know. The last time we had a murder in Marbury, the body also was discovered floating in the pond at Elton House; the lady of the house poisoned her husband, you see. At her trial, she claimed self-defense and it worked. She disappeared after that."

"Oh, my," Vera said. "It all sounds so Agatha Christie."

"Indeed. I sometimes forget how moldy the whole affair has become."

"Did you know the man?" Vera asked. "The dead man, I mean?"

"The husband? No, I'm afraid that all occurred before my time."

Vera smiled. "I'm sorry," she said. "I meant the dead man found this morning."

"Oh, yes, I see. No—no, I didn't know him. I gather that he was the gardener up there, though."

"Yes, that's right."

A few seconds of silence passed between them, before the man said, "I'm sorry, but I didn't catch your name. Mine is Arthur Brandt."

Brandt extended his hand and Vera shook it lightly.

"I'm Vera Lamb," she said. "Constable Lamb."

Brandt bowed slightly. "I'm pleased to meet you, Constable Lamb."

"Well, in truth, it's really Auxiliary Constable."

"All the same; if you wear the uniform, you assume the responsibility."

"Yes," Vera said, pleased by Brandt's answer. She raised her chin and fixed her eyes on a figure moving toward them up the High Street from the direction of the green.

"Here comes the chief inspector now," she said. "He'll want me to drive him somewhere, I should imagine."

Brandt turned to see Lamb approaching them. Vera hoped that her father would understand not to address her in a familiar or unofficial manner. She didn't want Arthur Brandt to know she was the head man's daughter.

"Hello, Chief Inspector," she said as Lamb reached them.

To Vera's relief, her father nodded and said, "Constable." Better yet, he added, "Anything to report?"

"Nothing as of yet," Vera said. She turned toward Brandt. "This is the Chief Inspector," she said, purposely leaving the surname unsaid.

"This is Mr. Arthur Brandt," she said to her father.

"Pleased to meet you, sir," Brandt said, offering Lamb his hand.

"The pleasure's mine," Lamb said. He recognized the name as the one that Mrs. Lockhart had mentioned, the journalist who'd chronicled the murder of Lord Elton.

"We were just discussing the fact that there was a previous murder at Elton House some years back," Vera told her father.

"Yes, Janet Lockhart mentioned to me that you had done some research on the matter," Lamb said, speaking to Brandt.

"Ah, so you've spoken to Janet, then."

"Yes, she found Mr. Lee's body in the pond this morning."

Brandt's brow clouded with concern. "Oh my," he said. "Poor Janet. I hope she hasn't had a shock."

"She seemed fine," Lamb said.

"Yes, well, that is Janet. She's nothing if not stoic. And she told you of the case of the Eltons, then?"

"Briefly, yes. She said you had written about it for the newspapers."

"Yes, I wrote a piece that appeared in the Sunday *Times*—looking back on a scandalous, though mostly forgotten case of murder twenty-five years after the fact. That sort of thing. Sells newspapers, you see. Something about twenty-five years having passed lends a thing a unique importance, apparently, though I've never understood why. Same with ten, or fifty, or seventy-five. At any rate, having grown up here in Marbury, I felt it was a natural story for me to write."

"You're a journalist, then, Mr. Brandt?" Vera said.

"Oh, no. No. Hardly a journalist. I'm a playwright—so to speak. I guess you'd call me one of the starving variety."

He turned again to Lamb.

"Not that it makes much difference to your current problems, Chief Inspector, but I'd be happy to give a copy of the piece if you'd think it worthwhile."

"Thank you for the offer, Mr. Brandt," Lamb said. "I might take you up on it if, as you say, it comes to matter. In the meantime, I wonder if you knew Joseph Lee?"

"The gardener? I'm afraid I didn't, no. I was just telling Constable Lamb that it seems such a sad affair."

"Had you heard anything about him getting into a row with another man by the church two nights ago?"

"No, and I live quite near to the church."

"Do you know Alan Fox?"

"Of course. Everyone in Marbury knows Alan." He looked quizzically at Lamb. "I hope you don't think that Alan had anything to do with this man's murder, Chief Inspector. That is, if I'm not out of line in asking."

"No, you are not out of line," Lamb said simply. "How well do you know Mr. Fox?"

"Well enough, though I would hesitate to call us bosom companions. Alan also is a native of Marbury, so I have known him most of my life—though, of course, he's quite a bit older than I. When I was a young boy he was already a man."

Lamb touched the brim of his fedora. "Well, thank you for your time, Mr. Brandt."

"Glad to be of help."

Lamb turned to Vera. "I have at least one more stop I'd like to make in the village this morning and I'll need your assistance, Constable," he said.

"Right away," Vera said, trying her best to sound like an eager-to-please underling. She turned to Brandt and said, "Thank you for the information, Mr. Brandt." She found herself reluctant to say goodbye to Arthur Brandt with such an air of finality.

Brandt blinked. "Of course. It was my pleasure."

He turned to Lamb. "Let me know if you'd like the story on Lady Elton," he said. "It's no problem, really."

Lamb nodded, then turned back toward the center of the village. Vera followed, nearly turning round to take a final look at Arthur Brandt, who stood by the lane and watched them leave.

THIRTEEN

—⁓—

AS THEY HEADED BACK DOWN THE HIGH STREET, VERA THANKED her father for not giving her away to Arthur Brandt.

"I'm still a bit touchy about the nepotism," she said.

"Is that what has been bothering you, then?"

"It's not that I don't appreciate what you're trying to do for me, dad. But it's so obviously unfair."

"It is indeed," Lamb agreed.

Vera looked at her father. She wanted to tell him that she was ready to break free, but found she could not quite speak the words. The time and the setting were wrong, she decided. Even so, given that they had broached the subject, she didn't want to let it pass without saying something that might move them toward a resolution of the problem in the future.

"I feel guilty," she said. "Not only am I protected, but I'm doing so little to earn my keep. I'd feel better if I could at least contribute something."

By then, they had reached the car.

"I understand why you feel as you do," Lamb said. "In fact, I'm glad to hear that it bothers you; if it didn't, I'd be more concerned." He placed his hand on Vera's arm. "I'm sorry that I've put you in this predicament, Vera. It wasn't my intention, but I'm afraid I didn't see all of the consequences as clearly as I should have when I came up with the bright idea of making you my driver. Perhaps I didn't want to see them. At any rate, it is probably time for you and I and your mother to sit down again and discuss your future. I realize, as your mother does, that you can't spend the rest of your life shuttling me here and there."

"I would like to talk about it," Vera said. "It is time."

Lamb cocked his head in the direction of the pub, which lay to their right about fifteen yards down the High Street. "I'm afraid, though, that for the moment, I'm going to leave you with the car yet another time, while I interview the landlord of the pub and his daughter. By the way, did you ever get anything to eat?"

"No, the tea shop was closed. The proprietor was out."

Lamb glanced across the green in the direction of the shop. "Now might be the time," he said. "Once I finish here at the pub I'll want to go back to Elton House."

He simply cannot stop acting like my father, Vera thought. Still, she *was* hungry now. Very hungry.

"All right," she said. "I'll make it quick."

"I hope I won't be too long, either," Lamb said.

They stood facing each other in silence for a couple of seconds.

"Thank you, dad," Vera said finally.

"You're welcome, Vera."

He watched her head off across the green, then turned for the pub.

—⁂—

The Watchman had yet to open for its evening hours. Lamb peered through the leaded glass of the front door but could see nothing inside. He knocked and waited but no one answered. He knocked again, louder this time. A few seconds later, the door opened and Lamb found himself facing a tall, stout, imposing-looking man he took to be the owner, Horace Hitchens.

"Mr. Hitchens?"

"Yes."

Lamb produced his warrant card and introduced himself. "I'd like a word with you and your daughter, Theresa, please."

"This about Lee, then?"

"Yes."

"I had nothing to do with that, nor did Theresa."

"All the same. I'd like to speak to you and your daughter. I know that Lee argued with Alan Fox in your pub two nights ago."

"We had nothing to do with that, either. That were between Fox and Lee." Hitchens did not move from where he stood. He was at least six inches taller, close to three stone heavier, and five or six years younger than Lamb.

"Nevertheless, I'd appreciate your cooperation in the matter, and so I will ask again: May I come in?"

"You can't just barge into a man's house. I know my rights, after all."

"Quite so," Lamb said. "But I also have rights, Mr. Hitchens. I could, for example, arrest you for obstructing a murder inquiry and we could have this conversation at the nick in Winchester, where we tend to conduct our business in small, cramped windowless rooms."

Hitchens's eyes widened in surprise briefly, then narrowed in anger. Even so, he stood back from the door.

"Thank you, sir," Lamb said as he crossed the threshold into the pub's main room, which featured a bar along the wall opposite to the door, a trio of booths along the front window, and four square wooden tables in the center of the room. Just to the right of the bar a short hall ended at a closed door painted a bright red.

Hitchens went to one of the tables in the middle of the room and silently sat down, glaring at Lamb, who sat across from him at the table.

Lamb found Hitchens's petulance annoying and suspicious. He wondered if father and daughter, having heard of Lee's death, had discussed how to respond to questions about the altercation between the dead man and Fox. Indeed, he wondered if Theresa Hitchens wasn't at that moment standing on the other side of the red door with her ear pressed against it, hoping to hear what her father said so that she could parrot it.

"Will you fetch your daughter, please?" Lamb asked Hitchens. "I'd like to speak to her first."

He expected Hitchens to claim that his daughter was not at home. However, the publican pushed his chair back with more force than Lamb believed necessary and walked to the red door, which he opened.

"Come out here, Theresa," he said.

Theresa Hitchens appeared in the room behind her father. She was of average height, plump and curvaceous, with shoulder-length blond hair and small black eyes. Lamb reckoned that she was about Vera's age, perhaps a year older. Her father led her to the table. She said nothing as she sat and seemed uneasy. Lamb wondered about the source of her anxiety. Was it his presence or her father's that worried her?

"This man is from the police," Horace Hitchens said to his daughter. "He wants to ask you about Joseph Lee."

Rather than sit again, Hitchens stood behind his daughter with his arms crossed.

"I'm Detective Chief Inspector Lamb, Miss Hitchens," Lamb said. "I'd like you to tell me what happened in the pub two nights ago involving Joseph Lee and Alan Fox."

Theresa turned to her right a bit, as if to look back at her father, then seemed to think better of doing so and turned back toward Lamb.

"Mr. Lee started in harassing Alan—Mr. Fox," she said. "Mr. Fox mostly minded his own business, but Mr. Lee was persistent."

"And what was Mr. Lee harassing Mr. Fox about?"

This time Theresa did turn fully round to glance at her father before answering. Horace Hitchens nodded.

"He said Mr. Fox was sweet on me," Theresa said. "He said Mr. Fox was trying to steal me from him. But he was wrong, sir—Mr. Lee, I mean. I never had any interest in him, though he used to pay a lot of attention to me, flirt with me, like. But nothing ever happened between us. He said he had a letter—a love letter—from Mr. Fox to me. But Mr. Fox never sent me any love letters, sir."

"Did you see this letter?"

"He was holding it up, waving it in the air, like, but I couldn't see what was written on it."

"Did you notice what he did with this letter once he finished waving it round?"

"No, sir."

"Did he say how he came to possess this letter?"

"No. I wondered about that too. As I said, I never had no love letters from Mr. Fox, or anybody. I wondered if Mr. Lee wrote it and only said that Mr. Fox had written it."

"How did Mr. Fox react to Mr. Lee's accusations?" Lamb asked.

"He ignored him at first. Then after a time, he told Mr. Lee to shut up."

"Did he yell at Mr. Lee or threaten him?"

"No, sir. He just sat at the bar, quiet, like, as he always does. Then he paid up and left. But Mr. Lee followed him out."

"Did anyone else follow Lee out?"

"No, sir. At least not that I saw."

"Did you follow them?"

Theresa sat back in her chair as if Lamb had taken a swing at her. "No, sir," she said emphatically. "I thought their leaving would be the end of it."

"Did Mr. Lee interact with anyone else at the pub that night?"

"Not that I saw."

"Do you know if anyone was outside of the pub when the two of them left? Someone they might have encountered there?"

"No."

Lamb looked at Horace Hitchens. "And you, Mr. Hitchens? Did you see anyone follow Fox and Lee out of the pub? Or do you know if anyone was outside the pub when they left?"

"I saw no one."

"Did either of them return to the pub at any time that night?"

"Lee did," Horace said. "His nose was bloody. He asked for a towel and I gave him one."

"Did you ask him how he'd managed to get a bloody nose?"

"I figured that Fox must have punched him. Were I Fox, I'd have punched him, the way he was going on."

"Did he say, specifically, that Alan Fox had punched him?"

"No, and I didn't ask. I got him the towel and he sat in the corner booth there for a bit nursing himself and then he left."

"Did anyone else offer Lee assistance?"

"No. I don't think anyone wanted to go near him, the way he was acting. He was not well-liked to start with. He were a braggart and a liar."

Lamb turned back to Theresa. "Did you offer Mr. Lee any assistance, Miss Hitchens?"

"I just said no, we hadn't done," Horace Hitchens said, the blood rising in his face.

"I'm asking your daughter, sir."

"No," Theresa said, as her father made a noise of displeasure. "It was like my father said; I didn't want to get tangled up in it. I don't know where he got the idea that I was his girl, sir. I never led him on or said anything to him. I swear it. He just sort of seemed to have made it up in his mind, like."

"He was a queer man," Horace added. "Not right in the head."

Horace put his large right hand on his daughter's shoulder.

"This is partly down to me," he said to Lamb. "Theresa had nothing to do with any of this. I should have said something to Lee about his bothering her."

"Have either of you spoken to Mr. Lee or Alan Fox since the previous night?"

"No," Hitchens said. "Neither of us have."

Lamb wondered if that was true but knew that Theresa would not contradict her father in Horace's presence.

With that, he stood, thanked the Hitchenses for their time, and left the pub convinced that at least one of the three people to whom he had spoken to in Marbury that morning had lied to him.

FOURTEEN

—◊—

LAMB RETURNED TO THE WOLSELEY TO FIND THAT VERA WAS NOT there. He walked across the green and found her just finishing a plate of toast, jam, and cheese and a cup of tea. He waited for her to finish and pay and then the two of them headed back to the car. As they reached it, Arthur Brandt appeared, moving down the High Street at a jog. He held up in his right hand what appeared to be a newspaper.

"Chief Inspector," he yelled, "might I have a word?"

He reached them, panting slightly.

"So sorry to hold you up," he said somewhat breathlessly. He bent over slightly and put his hands on his knees. "Whew! My fitness level is appallingly low." He straightened again, took a deep breath. "All that time sitting at a desk staring at a typewriter has ruined me, I'm afraid."

"How can I help you, Mr. Brandt?" Lamb asked.

87

Brandt held up the thing he'd been toting. It was indeed a newspaper—a portion of the *London Times* from a Sunday edition published in the spring of 1940.

"I wanted to give you this; it's the piece I wrote on the first murder at Elton House," he said. "I know you said that you'd take it if you needed it but I thought it might prove useful and I wasn't sure if I'd run into you or Constable Lamb again. I imagine you should be quite busy doing other more important things."

Lamb took the newspaper from Brandt and thanked him.

"My pleasure, Chief Inspector," Brandt said. He drew in another deep breath, which he released with a kind of happy shrug.

—⁓—

Like Sisyphus rolling his rock up the hill yet another time, Lamb returned to Elton House. He wanted to check a final time on the progress Larkin, Rivers, and the others had made and wrap up for the day. On the following day, he would send Rivers into Marbury to conduct a house-to-house canvass of the village. He wanted to know who else in Marbury had witnessed the set-to between Lee and Fox in the Watchman and if anyone besides Travers had seen the men arguing by the church.

Before heading to the pond, though, he asked Vera to show him the place where she had found the gum wrapper. She took him round the back to the horse sheds and pointed out the spot by the stables. Lamb squatted down to look at the spot, then glanced round the courtyard. He tried to open the double doors to the stables but found them locked, just as Vera had. The same was true of the doors to the carriage house.

He looked at Vera and said, "Are you interested in doing a bit of snooping?"

"Of course."

"All right, then. Let's have a closer look round these buildings and along the back of the house. I'll take the stables and you take the carriage house."

Lamb spent fifteen minutes patiently searching the area round the stables, but found nothing. Neither did he find anything along the base of the back wall of the house, though he recognized the doors he found there as those he'd seen in the kitchen that opened onto the courtyard.

He did, however, notice tire tracks left in the mud by vehicles that had moved through the yard. It made sense that the clinic would take deliveries of food and other supplies round the back of the house and that some of this would be delivered by lorry. He wondered, though, if a secret cargo might also have found its way to the house by lorry. He made a rough measurement of one of the tracks and estimated its width at six inches and that it had made an impression in the hard packed mud that was perhaps a half-inch deep.

Vera had more luck in her search round the carriage house. A mix of dried leaves and other natural detritus, blown there by the autumn and winter winds, had gathered in the one of the corners where the rear of the side of the house met the stone wall abutment, built into the slope that faced the house. Among this brown-gray pile of litter Vera spotted what appeared to be the yellowing edges of a slip of white paper. She stooped to pluck it from the pile and found that it was indeed a piece of paper, moist and partially balled. She was careful as she unfolded and flattened it. She saw that a portion of it seemed to have been torn away, leaving a jagged edge. She flipped it over and found written on its opposite side, in faded black letters: U.S. ARMY FIELD RATION D and just beneath that: 2 OUNCES NET WEIGHT. A horizontal fold line ran just below the writing and beneath that Vera found these words, stacked in three horizontal lines:

MANUFACTURED BY
HERSHEY CHOCOLATE CORPORATION
HERSHEY, PA.

She brought the paper up to her nose and sniffed it and found that it smelled as the dead leaves smelled. She moved the toe of her shoe through the detritus but found nothing else there. Believing she had struck gold, she went to her father and showed him the wrapper.

"Look at this," she said, gently handing the paper to her father. "Careful, it's damp."

Lamb took the paper by its edge and laid it in the palm of his left hand. He took a second to read what was written on the paper.

"Is it important?" Vera asked.

"I think it might be."

Lamb handed the wrapper back to Vera and asked her to hold it while he removed from his pocket the handkerchief in which he'd placed the stick of gum. He opened the handkerchief and laid it on the ground between them and moved the gum to the corner. Vera then laid the chocolate wrapper in the middle of the handkerchief and Lamb carefully folded it and returned it to his pocket.

"What is it?" Vera said.

"I think it's from a field ration—the sort of thing combat soldiers eat when they are in the line. The food comes in packets of this and that, wrapped in paper or foil. When I was on the Somme they gave us tinned meat and condensed milk, and crackers and biscuits in little packets like the one you just found."

"Yes, but do soldiers get gum and chocolate?"

"We got hard little sweets sometimes," Lamb said. "I imagine that the Americans have moved well beyond that by now. Gum and chocolate, certainly. And cigarettes. And who knows what else."

"Is this lend-lease, then?"

"It's got to be lend-lease. But I believe it's meant for military rather than civilian use. This wrapper and the one round the gum you found are plain; but normal Hershey's chocolate and Wrigley's gum don't come in plain wrappers. The ones you've found are from field rations meant to be issued to soldiers on the line. I'm nearly certain of it."

"Maybe Elton House is allowed some because it serves shell shocked men."

"That could be. That's a question I intend to ask Dr. Hornby. The place also has a healthy supply of American cigarettes."

Lamb nodded toward the stables.

"Perhaps it's time we found out what's behind those locked doors."

—m—

They went round to the front of the house and entered the foyer and found the door to the anteroom of Dr. Hornby's office closed. Lamb tried the knob but it was locked. He knocked on the door but received no response.

He looked round for someone who could help him but saw no one. With Vera at his heels, he moved down the main hall to the room in which Wallace and Cashen had interviewed the patients and staff, but found it empty. Frustrated, he went back to the foyer, where he again knocked on the door to the anteroom—and again received no answer.

He turned back to the hall with the intention of checking the kitchen, when he saw Nurse Stevens heading toward him, apparently having just come from the cellar.

"Chief Inspector," she said, surprised to see Lamb again. "How can I help you?"

"I'd like to speak with Dr. Hornby."

"Oh, I'm sorry," she said. "He's gone to Southampton on business."

"Can you reach him there by telephone?"

"I'm sorry, I can't. You see, I'm not exactly sure where he's gone."

"Did he not tell you where he was going?"

"No. He seemed to be in a bit of a hurry. He left a note on my desk in the anteroom. It said that he was going to Southampton and that he would return tomorrow morning. He didn't say where he was going. He sometimes does that—leaves in a bit of a hurry. He has so many responsibilities."

"Did he leave you in charge?"

"Yes."

"Then I'd like to request your permission to open the stables and the carriage house at the back of the house. Both are locked."

"But why would you need to look in the stables, Chief Inspector? I doubt they've been used since the last war."

"I wouldn't ask if I didn't believe it important," Lamb said.

"It would be irregular for me to do so without first speaking to Dr. Hornby," she said. "In any case I haven't the key."

"Is there only a single key to those locks?"

"Yes, I'm afraid so. We simply don't use them, you see, so there is no need, really, for duplicate keys. I'm surprised Dr. Hornby hasn't had the sheds removed, to be honest. I should think they would be nothing more than vermin nests."

"Who has this single key?" Lamb asked, believing he knew the answer.

"Dr. Hornby, of course."

Lamb found Dr. Hornby's sudden trip to Southampton suspicious.

"Very well, Nurse," he said, then turned on his heel and strode out of Elton House with Vera at his elbow.

FIFTEEN

—⚏—

ON THE FOLLOWING MORNING, THE TEAM MET AT THE NICK WITH Superintendent Harding to go over the day's plan.

Lamb began by running down all they had learned on the previous day, including the fact of the large sums of cash they'd found in Lee's lodgings, and his and Rivers's suspicion that Lee might have obtained it through blackmail. He also mentioned that they had found no fireplace poker in Lee's cottage.

Harding liked the notion that Alan Fox might have been a victim of blackmail. "That and the fact that the two fought; it's our best connection of anyone with Lee," he said. "Now we've got to figure out what Lee had over Fox."

"If anything," Lamb added, aware that Harding enjoyed making giant leaps toward a quick result, even if those leaps were not always in the proper direction.

Larkin said he'd spent some time examining the cash and discovered something odd on a five pound note.

"It appears to be a doodle of a fox," Larkin said. He held up the note and pointed out the drawing, which was just beneath the government's rendering of Saint George slaying his dragon. Lamb recognized the doodle as the same one he'd seen on Fox's mailbox and mentioned this.

"It does resemble a fox," Wallace said.

"Indeed it does," Harding agreed. "There you go, then, Tom. Another connection."

"Yes, but we have no idea whether Fox drew it, of course," Larkin gently reminded the superintendent.

"Isn't just a bit too obvious, though, sir?" Wallace said to Harding. "What if someone is trying to frame Fox?"

"How did it get in among Lee's cash, then?" Harding parried.

"Maybe someone planted it there. Lee's room was tossed."

Harding looked at Lamb. "Tom?"

"I don't know," Lamb said. "Fox is an artist—a painter. He might well doodle on his bank notes. But I think Sergeant Wallace is right. I wouldn't jump to any conclusions for the moment."

Lamb then briefed the team on the chocolate and gum wrappers that Vera had found by the horse sheds and the seeming prevalence of American cigarettes at Elton House, all of which had led Lamb to wonder if Hornby was not obtaining black market lend-lease goods. He pointed out that one of Larkin's duties that day would be to see if a facility such as the Elton House Sanatorium was eligible to receive lend-lease goods that normally would go to frontline soldiers. Lamb added that he had tried to discuss the matter with Hornby on the previous day, and to gain permission to open the horse sheds, but been frustrated by Hornby's sudden disappearance to Southampton. He hoped to speak to Hornby later that morning, he said.

"You don't think he's done a runner then?" Wallace asked.

"No. He has too much invested in the sanatorium and his experiment. But it's possible he's worried that we might find something if we continue poking round the estate."

The team's main goal that day was to complete a house-to-house canvass of Marbury, Lamb said. "It's not a particularly big place so I hope that we can wrap it up before dark."

Rivers would lead the operation, seconded by Wallace, Cashen, and nine uniformed men.

Larkin would remain in Winchester, where, in addition to checking on whether the sanatorium legally received lend-lease goods, he was to check the land records to see if a blueprint or some other document showing the layout of Elton House existed. Lamb also wanted the forensics man to sort through the notebooks and other papers they'd retrieved from Lee's cottage, and to check on the criminal backgrounds—if any existed—of Joseph Lee, Alan Fox, Dr. Hornby, Janet Lockhart, James Travers, and the nurse, Matilda Stevens.

Finally, he brought up Lord Elton's murder at the house nearly three decades earlier and briefly described what had happened, as best he knew the details, including the fact Lord Elton's body also had been dumped in the pond. He also said that he and Vera had met a local man named Arthur Brandt in Marbury who had given him a newspaper article he'd written that looked back on the case, and that he intended to read it when he got a chance, but only for the purposes of edification.

"I tell you this because the subject is likely to come up as you interview the residents, and particularly the older ones who were living there at the time. That said, there is no reason to believe that it has anything to do with Lee's murder—and please inform your teams that they should not speculate on whether or not it does with anyone in the village. If the people whom we interview don't mention it, then we shouldn't either."

Before the team left for Marbury, Vera and Wallace found a moment to talk alone. But their conversation devolved into an argument about marriage when Wallace had asked her why she was reluctant to discuss the matter.

Did she not love him? he asked.

"That's not fair, and you know it," Vera said, believing he had deployed the word—and indeed the very concept of *love*—as a kind of conversational weapon. Whenever he wanted to attack he brought up the word, she thought. *Love.* Did she not *love* him? Did she not believe that he *loved* her? It was almost as if he wanted her to swear an oath to him: *I hereby love you.* It was as if having given herself to him—in mind and body—hadn't been enough proof of her love.

Later, when the pair got into Lamb's car along with Cashen, Lamb found the tension between them palpable, leaving him to wonder if the relationship between his daughter and his detective sergeant was coming to a head.

SIXTEEN

—⚹—

LAMB BURIED HIMSELF IN READING ARTHUR BRANDT'S NEWSPAPER account of Lord Elton's murder as Vera, icily quiet, drove to Marbury. Wallace, who also made nary a sound, sat in the back with Cashen.

The chief inspector found intriguing the story of Lady Elton's botched attempt to make her husband's killing appear to be an accidental drowning, and her being acquitted of the crime on the grounds of self-defense. Brandt, however, did not paint a portrait of Lady Elton as an innocent, frightened, and unalloyed victim-turned-killer; his story quoted several people who had lived in Marbury at the time describing Lady Elton as essentially cruel; they spread the rumor that she might gave had a lover who helped her to murder Lord Elton—a rumor for which no evidence ever had come to light.

As they entered Marbury, Lamb noticed that the village had come to life since the previous day. More people were moving along the

High Street near the green and the Watchman had opened. Vera parked in the same lot by the pub and the four of them exited the car to meet with Rivers and the uniformed men, who had come in two other cars. Lamb stuck around as Rivers deployed the men in three teams, each led by an officer—himself, Wallace, and Sergeant Cashen. Wallace would take his men into the east side of the village, while Cashen would take the west and Rivers and his men the shops and central Marbury.

That done, Lamb and Vera returned to the Wolseley; Lamb was anxious to get back up the hill to Elton House and to speak with Dr. Hornby. But as he slid into the passenger seat, he glanced at Vera and saw the disquiet in her expression. She pushed the starter button with what he considered a bit too much force, though the car did not turn over.

"Damn this thing," Vera said under her breath. "Has it ever worked properly?"

Lamb touched her arm and said, "Do you want to tell me what's wrong?"

Vera slumped behind the wheel. "No," she said without looking at her father. Then she sighed heavily and said, "I don't know."

"You argued with David this morning?"

"Yes."

She looked at her father. "He wants to marry me."

"Do you want to marry him?"

"I don't *know*," she said, looking away again. She felt as if she might cry, but did her best to stop the tears. "It's not that I don't love him." She shook her head. She looked at her father again. "It's just that I feel as if I haven't had a chance to live my own life yet. Everyone seems to want to create a life for me."

"I think I know what you mean," Lamb said.

"No—I don't think you do, dad." Tears welled in her eyes. "I know you only want the best for me, but I feel as if I don't even know what I'm capable of. And yet I also feel as if I'm capable of so much. But I haven't had a chance to find out what those capabilities are. And now David wants to marry me and I can't help but feel as if I'd be agreeing to let myself be sewn up in a bag."

She began to cry, though softly, and wiped a tear away from her right cheek.

"Would it help if I told you that what you're feeling is perfectly natural?" Lamb said.

Vera shook her head. "I don't know. I don't think so."

"I hope you know that you haven't displeased me, or your mother," he said. "And that takes in whatever you've done—or haven't done—with David. Your mother and I could not be more pleased with the woman you've become."

Vera looked at her father. "Yes, but I'm not quite there yet, am I?" she said. "I feel as if I'll only be there when I can make my own decisions about my life. I used to be frightened of that. But I don't think I am anymore."

She wiped another renegade tear from her cheek. "Even this stupid bloody war doesn't frighten me anymore. It only makes me wonder sometimes if I'm losing my mind."

"You're not losing your mind. Nothing is the way it should be at a time like this."

"Not even love?"

"No—not even that."

Vera turned away. "It makes you wonder what good any of it is, then," she said.

She pushed the Wolseley's starter and its motor sputtered to life—then, almost as quickly, sputtered out. She pushed the starter again, but the result was the same.

"Once more, please," Lamb said patiently.

But the car only coughed a second time then died.

"Wonderful," Vera said.

"It would be easy enough to walk to Elton House from here; in fact, I'd like to have a look at the trail that leads from here to the estate," Lamb said, already thinking ahead. "But we'll have to see if someone here can fix the car in the meantime."

"I don't remember seeing a garage," Vera said.

"Nor do I."

They exited the car and Lamb lifted the bonnet. In truth, he had only the most rudimentary idea of how cars worked. As he scanned the oily engine he could see nothing that appeared to him to be obviously amiss. He closed the bonnet then looked round; none of his men were in sight and he did not want to interrupt their work in any case.

"Why don't we ask Mr. Brandt if someone in the village knows how to fix a car?" Vera suggested.

Although Lamb was reluctant to involve Brandt in their problem, neither did he want to waste time poking round Marbury in the hope of finding a mechanic who might not even exist.

The pair headed past the church and up the hill where on the previous day Brandt had said his house was located. Sure enough, they came to a house with a front garden shielded by a line of poplars and a waist-high cut-stone fence that paralleled the High Street and appeared to be less-than-adequately maintained.

"I wonder if this might be it," Lamb said.

He and Vera went to the door; if the house wasn't Brandt's then whoever came to the door would be able to point them in the right direction.

But Lamb's guess had been correct; Brandt answered Lamb's knock, smiling. He wore the same green corduroy trousers as he had the previous day and a rust-colored woolen tie that was slightly askew. His brown hair was slightly mussed, as if he'd been running his fingers through it in deep concentration, and his glasses sat near the bridge of his nose at an awkward angle.

"Chief Inspector," he said, clearly surprised to see Lamb standing at the threshold. "And Constable Lamb; this is a pleasant surprise indeed."

He pushed open the oaken door and bade them to enter. A cat with extravagant orange fur appeared in the foyer and, purring loudly, began to move through Brandt's legs.

"Hello, Walter," Brandt said to it, touching his glasses to set them aright. He plucked the cat from the floor and cradled it. "We have visitors, as you can see, so I haven't time for you at the moment."

The cat squinted at Lamb, its eyes like small black slits in a profuse, feathery ball of burnt orange yarn.

Brandt put the cat on the floor, massaged its sides briefly with his fingertips, then touched the top of its tail, which was sticking straight up, like a ship's mast. "Off with you now," he said. "We've work to do." But the cat merely sat in the middle of the foyer and began to lick its paws.

Brandt shrugged. "He rarely listens, I'm afraid. I sometimes wonder if he even understands English."

"We're sorry to bother you, Mr. Brandt," Lamb said. "But we're wondering if you can point us toward someone who repairs motorcars. Mine has broken down."

"Oh my," Brandt said. "We did have someone at one time. Old Mr. Donatelli—Italian chap; came here before the turn of the last century as a laborer. Taught himself all about cars and opened a shop and made himself indispensable. My father used him, whenever his car went on the fritz. But I'm afraid he died a couple of years back and no one else has taken up the mantle. It really hasn't been worth it since the war began, given that no one has any petrol anymore."

A look of disappointment crossed Lamb's face, which Brandt noticed. "I say, you've a Wolseley, am I right?" he said. "I saw it yesterday."

"That's right. A Wasp 6."

"Well, I've a 1935 Wasp 6 mothballed in the garage. I haven't even tried to start the thing since the war began. But I know a bit about how they work. Perhaps I could have a look at your car."

"That would be very kind of you," Vera said.

Brandt smiled warmly at Vera. "All right, then," he said to her. "If you'll allow me just a minute, though, please. I really should feed my snake before we go. He's been acting rather famished all morning."

"You've a snake?" Vera asked. "An actual snake, I mean?"

"Indeed I do. A python; a West African breed. If you'd like, you're welcome to watch me feed him. It will only take a minute."

Lamb had not counted on being delayed by Brandt feeding a snake; but beggars could not be choosers.

"Right this way, then," Brandt said and he led them into a room that looked as if a gang of thieves had just finished rifling it. Nearly every surface, whether table or chair, was piled with books, newspapers, typescripts, magazines, and photographs, not to mention cups, saucers, plates, and potted plants. Two of the four walls were lined with shelves also brimming with books and papers. A third contained a large window, beneath which various boxes and other odds and ends were stacked, and the fourth a hearth.

"This is my study," Brandt said. "I apologize for the mess. I realize it seems chaotic to most people, but I find it comfortable."

Vera noticed a helmet hanging on a nail just to the right of the door. She recognized it as that issued to some of the Home Guard. Nearly every village in Hampshire had some form of civil defense committee, a vestige of the bad summer of 1940, two years earlier, when the Germans had bombed southern England. Vera had served for a time that summer as an air raid warden in a village called Quimby.

"You're in the Home Guard, then, Mr. Brandt," Vera remarked.

"Yes. I've been the air raid warden here since the beginning. The army passed me over, I'm afraid. The RAF, as well. They claim I've an irregular heartbeat, though I've never felt it. So the Home Guard it is."

He took them to the wall just inside the door, where a large glass terrarium sat upon a side table. Within the terrarium sat a small bowl of water surrounded by twigs and fresh leaves. To one side sat a large wooden cigar box turned upside down. Brandt removed the top from the glass enclosure and put it aside. Then he lifted the wooden cigar box, revealing beneath it a rather large and fat bronze-colored python with a mustard-yellow stripe, curled into a tight ball.

"Hence, their name—*ball* python," Brandt said. "They rather like to curl up in a ball and hide beneath something. Now, if you'll just excuse me for a minute, I'll fetch his dinner."

Brandt disappeared from the room for about thirty seconds, during which Lamb and Vera at first were silent.

"Well, it's different, at any rate," Vera said finally.

"Yes, it is."

"And interesting, too, don't you think?"

"Of course."

Brandt returned with a large gray mouse hanging limp from a pair of long bamboo tweezers.

"Freshly caught," Brandt said. "I trap them in the rear garden with spring traps. It breaks their necks you see and kills them instantly. He's quite dead now, so you needn't worry. He won't suffer."

The snake now uncurled from its ball and began to move across the terrarium floor, flicking its elastic tongue and raising its head into the air.

"Hello, there, my good man," Brandt said to it. "Ready for a bit of lunch, I hope?"

"Is it dangerous?" Vera said.

"He's quite harmless, actually. His name is Terry, after pterodactyl." He smiled. "I've always enjoyed that word—pterodactyl; something about that silent *p*. Ball pythons are among the most sweet-natured animals on the face of the earth, actually. Unless, of course, you're a rodent. Then they're rather deadly."

"Wherever did you find him?" Vera asked.

"A dealer in London." Brandt glanced at Lamb and smiled. "All quite legal, Chief Inspector, I promise."

Brandt now dangled the mouse, head first, into the terrarium. Terry moved very quickly toward it then stopped, almost as if confused. It flicked its tongue another time. Then it struck the mouse in a blur and wrapped its body round it. The killing movement was so sudden and quick that Vera found herself taking a step back from the terrarium and uttering, "Oh!"

Lamb was growing impatient to return to the Wolseley. Even so, he found himself impressed by the display. "He's quite fast," he said. "Blindingly so."

"Oh, indeed," Brandt said.

He put the tweezers aside and replaced the top on the terrarium. He turned to Lamb and said. "Terry will take it from here. I'm ready to go and have a look at your car whenever you are, Chief Inspector."

SEVENTEEN

—— m ——

AS THE TRIO DESCENDED THE HILL TO LAMB'S MOTORCAR, THE chief inspector took the opportunity to ask Brandt a few questions he hoped would tap into Brandt's knowledge of Marbury, and perhaps some of its secrets.

"How well do you know Janet Lockhart?" Lamb asked.

"Rather well. She and her late husband were friends of my parents. I've known Janet all of my life in one way or another."

"Are you aware of the work she does at the sanatorium?"

"Yes—though are you speaking of the spiritualism aspect as well?"

"Yes. She has spoken to you about that, then."

"Oh, yes. She has several times offered to help me commune with my parents. But I'm afraid I don't believe in that sort of thing."

"Do you think that her belief is genuine?"

"Janet is a lovely woman who wouldn't dream of hurting anyone or anything," Brandt said. "But she has never quite gotten over the loss of her husband. You know how it is, Chief Inspector—we men tend to die off sooner than the women do, leaving many more widows than widowers. And when you throw in two major wars in a quarter century . . . well, you see what I mean. I know that what Janet does would strike many people as fraudulent but I have no doubt that she believes that she is doing the people who seek her out some good."

Lamb mentioned that he'd read the account of Lord Elton's murder that Brandt had written for the *Times*. "You portrayed Lady Elton as not quite the victim that she seemed to convince everyone at the time she was," he said.

"Yes, well, some of the people whom I interviewed, particularly a few who had been on the staff of Elton House, painted a picture of her as someone who could be cruel and vindictive. The problem was, none of those people were called on to testify at her trial, though my guess is that if they had been they would have been reluctant to speak ill of her, for fear that it would ruin their chances of being hired elsewhere. Lord Elton also apparently possessed a hair-trigger temper. But the people to whom I spoke said they preferred him to Lady Elton. And they contradicted the story Lady Elton told at trial of her suffering abuse at the hands of her husband."

"The Ondine defense?"

"Precisely. One of the women I spoke to, who had been a maid at Elton House, claimed that it was not Lord Elton but Lady Elton who seemed unusually fond of the story of Ondine. Indeed, she said Lady Elton kept a small statue depicting Ondine rising from the depths in their bedroom and that she rather treasured the thing, even though it was a cheap knockoff of a statue done by some nineteenth-century French sculptor or another."

"Did you attempt to track down Lady Elton for your story?"

"Of course, but I had no luck. The general consensus since her release is that she went abroad and either changed her name or remarried and took her husband's name. I did manage to track down the solicitors who acted on her behalf when she sold Elton House just after the war. But they refused to speak with me. The same maid who claimed that Lady Elton had an interest in the story of Ondine also claimed that she had been orphaned as a child and that she had a younger sister. Indeed, Lord Elton at some point had apparently been interested in the sister first, but once he got a gander at the future Lady Elton he changed his mind."

"You did not include that fact in your story."

"I was not able to entirely confirm the truth of it nor was I able to find out the younger sister's name."

"Do you believe that she exists?"

"I'm not really sure. But had I been writing a novel rather than a piece of journalism I certainly would have included her."

He smiled at Lamb. "I daresay you have access to sources that I did not as a mere hack writer looking to make a pound or two digging up the story of a salacious murder."

They were crossing the stone bridge and nearly to the car.

"I also noticed that you made reference to a rumor at the time that Lady Elton had a lover who might have acted as her accomplice in the murder, but that no evidence of such a person ever came out," Lamb said.

"Yes."

"Have you a guess about who this mystery lover might have been?"

Brandt sighed.

"One hates to be a gossip—unless, of course, one is a gossip," he said. "However, a lot of people speculated at the time that Lady Elton was having an affair with Alan Fox, though it's possible, of course, that his name came up merely because he's always had a reputation as an outsider in Marbury and a Lothario besides. I think people also are jealous of his wealth and the advantages it has given him. Alan has never had to work in the proper sense, you see. He's always been an artist kept afloat by a private income that he himself did not earn, and most people don't find that at all fair, I'm afraid."

"So he had a reputation as a ladies' man, then?"

"He did, yes."

"Does he still?"

"I think that would depend upon who you ask."

"What's your opinion?"

"I don't know, really. Alan has retreated from life in the village over the years, and it's common knowledge that he drinks a bit too much; the only place anyone might find him with any regularity in Marbury is the Watchman. He's become rather craggy and ill-kempt besides. Then again, some women—and particularly the younger ones—seem to find that sort of thing romantic. The struggling artist and the rest of it. Except that he's not actually struggling and I suppose the jury is still out on whether he's an artist. Alan tends to paint his life; if something happens to him, affects him in some way deeply, he tends to paint it. Not an exact reproduction of the event, of course. He is very allegorical and all the rest of it. But in the end, it's Alan's life as he has experienced it."

Vera had been listening with interest to her father's interview of Brandt, and had not interrupted it. Now she spoke. "But wouldn't you also describe yourself as kind of a struggling artist, Mr. Brandt?"

"Oh indeed so," Brandt said. "Though I'm not so sure about the artist part in my case, either." He looked at Vera and smiled. "My main problem, you see, is that I'm not nearly as handsome or as rich as Alan Fox."

EIGHTEEN

—◠◡—

WHEN THEY REACHED THE CAR, BRANDT OPENED THE WOLSELEY'S bonnet and began to poke round the motor, lifting this and that fitting or cap and tugging at the odd wire. When he was finished with this brief initial examination, he pulled a red handkerchief from his pants pocket, and began to wipe motor oil from his hands.

"I think I see the problem," he said. "It appears your distributor has bit the dust."

"Is that bad?" Vera asked.

"It's hardly ideal. But I can replace it with the one from my Wasp. I think it should work."

"I certainly wouldn't expect you to cannibalize your own motorcar on my account," Lamb said. "Though I appreciate the offer, certainly."

"Oh, please don't worry about that, Chief Inspector," Brandt said. "As I said, I haven't driven the bloody thing in years anyhow and won't be able to any time soon. Better that we get this one running."

Lamb decided that he had little choice but to take Brandt up on his offer. "I shall see that we get you a new distributor from our motor pool in Winchester as soon as possible," he promised Brandt.

"Not to worry, Chief Inspector, really. I'm glad to help."

"Thank you, Mr. Brandt," Vera added. "You're very kind."

"Oh, it's nothing, really, Constable. It's actually nice to have an excuse to leave my desk. I'm afraid I sometimes forget how interesting the outside world can be."

—⁓—

Lamb left Vera with the car along with instructions to drive it to Elton House once Brandt had repaired it—if indeed he repaired it. If not, she was to wait for him to return. In the meantime, she should seek out Harry Rivers, Cashen, or Wallace to inform them of the problem and that it was being addressed.

Lamb decided he would ascend the trail to Elton House in the meantime, giving him an opportunity to explore the route Janet Lockhart had taken the previous morning. He believed he still had much to learn but a narrowing window of time in which to learn it. Soon someone might begin to feel pinched and try to make a decisive move, either to clear evidence they'd neglected to hide, silence a witness, or make a run for it.

Although Lamb knew that the path to the village began somewhere behind the church, he did not know where exactly and so asked Brandt to step away from the car for a moment to show him the spot. Hence, he and Brandt retraced their steps up the hill to the church, where Brandt led them off the High Street and onto the flagstone path that led round to the rear of the church. To their left, the path was bordered by a high hedge.

"Just on the other side of the hedge is Janet's Lockhart's cottage," Brandt informed Lamb. "As you will see when we get round back, she can walk directly through her back garden to the place where the path begins to climb the hill to Elton House."

The path led round the back of the church and past the church cemetery, which was surrounded by a waist-high wrought iron fence and gate. Twenty yards beyond that the cleared land gave way to wood and began to noticeably slope upward. Brandt pointed to a break in the hedge on their left that he said led to Janet Lockhart's rear garden.

The cemetery caught Lamb's eye—and particularly a small granite mausoleum at its center, where someone had laid a half-dozen paper lilies and lit some candles, which had burnt out.

"Who is buried in the mausoleum?" he asked Brandt—though he thought he knew.

"Lord Elton," Brandt said, confirming Lamb's guess. "As you might have noticed from my story, today is the anniversary of his death—June twenty-second. I'd actually forgotten it until just now."

Lamb opened the cemetery gate. "I wonder if we might make a little detour, Mr. Brandt," he said.

"By all means."

Lamb went to the mausoleum and squatted down to inspect the flowers and the candle stubs. The latter appeared to be identical to the stubs they'd found by the pond and in Lee's cottage. He took one and slid it into his jacket pocket. He fingered the petals of the paper lilies and found them to be well made, of a high-grade stock.

"Is there anyone in Marbury who felt particularly close to Lord Elton, or the family?" he asked Brandt.

"Not that I'm aware of, though of course one never knows."

Brandt led Lamb from the cemetery to a place just inside the wood, where the flagstone path ended and the footpath to Elton House began. Lamb thanked Brandt, told him that he would return soon, and began the climb, as Brandt returned to the car.

Although hemmed in on either side by the wood, the path was well-worn and wide enough to accommodate two people walking side by side. After roughly a quarter-mile the steepness of the rise began to soften and the wood began to fall away. Here Lamb came upon a sign that was staked into the ground to the right of the trail: YOU ARE NOW ENTERING THE PROPERTY OF ELTON HOUSE SANATORIUM.

Fifty yards later, the portion of the wood to his right ended and gave way to the open area behind Elton House, which included the pond. On his left, the wood continued for a short distance farther, taking in the former gamekeeper's cottage in which Joseph Lee had lived.

Lamb spied a lone figure standing along the edge of the pond who he recognized as Nurse Stevens. She stood only a foot or two from the water and seemed to be staring into it; indeed she was so engrossed in what she was doing that she did not notice Lamb's approach. Lamb looked at the surface of the pond but could see nothing that might have caught the nurse's attention.

Not wanting to startle her, he spoke quietly as he approached: "Hello, Nurse Stevens."

She abruptly turned to face Lamb with a look of frank surprise.

"I'm sorry, I didn't mean to startle you," Lamb said.

She looked intently at Lamb. "I thought you had finished here, Chief Inspector."

"Not quite. I still want to speak with Dr. Hornby, as I said yesterday."

"He hasn't returned yet from Southampton."

"That is disappointing," Lamb said. "You said yesterday that you expected him to return this morning."

"Yes. Well it seems he's been delayed."

"Do you still expect him to return today?"

"I hope so. Is there anything else I can do for you?"

Lamb removed the candle stub he'd taken from Lord Elton's grave and showed it to the nurse. "Do you recognize this?" he asked. "I found it on a grave in the church cemetery in Marbury. It's identical to several we found yesterday while searching Mr. Lee's cottage. I wonder if it might have come from Elton House?"

Nurse Stevens looked at the candle briefly. "No, I don't recognize it," she said.

Lamb then showed Nurse Stevens the paper lily he'd taken from the grave, which, she said, she also did not recognize.

She stepped back from the pond. "Now, if you'll excuse me, I must get back to work," she said.

"Please tell Dr. Hornby that I will return later to speak to him," Lamb said.

Nurse Stevens's face clouded for an instant—almost as if, Lamb thought, she'd suddenly remembered something she instantly wished she hadn't forgotten.

She looked at Lamb. "Of course," she said. Then she turned and made her way up the path.

NINETEEN

—◊◊—

RELUCTANTLY—AND FEELING VERY SUSPICIOUS OF FREDERICK Hornby—Lamb turned round and headed back down the path. He hoped that Brandt would not take long repairing the Wolseley. In the meantime, he could check with Rivers and the others on the progress of the canvass of the village.

As he descended the path he noticed a familiar figure climbing the hill in his direction. It was Janet Lockhart.

"Hello, Chief Inspector," she said as the two converged. Despite the fact of her climbing an unpaved footpath, she wore high-heeled shoes and a simple yellow dress. Once again, Lamb caught the scent of her perfume and found himself thinking that she was an attractive—and even a seductive—woman.

"Hello, Mrs. Lockhart," he said. "I assumed that you were already at the sanatorium by now."

"Well, I took a bit of time this morning; I suppose I'm still getting over the events of yesterday. I don't mind admitting that I found them overwhelming."

"Yes, I can certainly see why," Lamb said. "I hope you are feeling more like yourself."

"I am. Still, it's very troubling to think about what happened to Mr. Lee. Murder is so disturbing."

Lamb recalled Brandt's assessment of Mrs. Lockhart—that she had, in effect, dedicated herself to denying the finality of death.

"Indeed it is."

"And yet you must encounter it regularly, Chief Inspector. I wonder if you've found a way to inure yourself from its disturbing aspects."

"I suppose that I must have, at least to a degree. But, of course, I still find it disturbing."

"I hope you don't think I'm criticizing you, Chief Inspector. On the contrary, I sense you are a truly honorable man—and perhaps even a bit heroic in your pursuit of those who kill."

"I wouldn't say that. I'm no different in that regard from any other policeman."

"Still," Mrs. Lockhart said. She paused for a couple of seconds in which Lamb felt her appraising him. "Do you mind if I ask you a personal question, Chief Inspector?"

"I suppose that depends on the question," Lamb said, though in a cordial tone.

"I want to ask you if you were in the war. I sense that you were."

"I was on the Somme in 1916 and '17."

"It must have been terrible, having to live with that knowledge—that each day you awakened might very well be your last."

"It was terrible, yes."

"And yet, as terrible as it is, there comes a point at which you accept it. Is that right?"

Lamb nearly said, *It depends on the man*, but thought of Mrs. Lockhart's husband and brought himself up short.

"Yes, after a time you come to accept it. Or maybe it is more accurate to say that you lose an idea of yourself as somehow different from all the rest, which is a feeling that nearly every man who goes into combat for the first time carries with him. A feeling of, *Yes, others will die, but I will not.* You come to realize that those who die and those who live is all down to chance. No one is especially protected in any way, by God or fate. Then again, neither is anyone naturally inclined toward being among those who won't live to see the end of the day, even those who are the worst sinners or whose hearts are brimming with evil. It all comes down to a series of events that no one could possibly have predicted or had even an inkling of ahead of time."

Lamb could not recall the last time he had spoken at such length about what the war had left him believing. But something in Janet Lockhart's eyes—a kind of pleading—loosened something within him he normally kept reined in.

"Well, I want to thank you for answering my question, Chief Inspector. I realize that such sentiments are enormously personal."

"I hope that it was of some help to you."

"Yes—yes, it has been."

Lamb pulled the candle stub and the paper lily from his pocket and showed them to Mrs. Lockhart. "Before you go on your way, I wonder if I might ask you if you recognize these?" he asked.

"Well, the candle does resemble some that we keep round the sanatorium. But then, I suppose one candle looks much like another. As for the lilies I have noticed that someone has been putting something similar on Lord Elton's grave, especially recently, but otherwise I don't recognize them. They are not something I've ever seen for sale in Marbury."

"I found this on the grave of Lord Elton. Do you know of anyone in Marbury who might have had a close connection to him and therefore might feel compelled to mark the anniversary of his death, which I understand is today?"

"I don't really—at least among those people in the village who are still living or haven't moved away. I suppose I would have to say that, among those who still live in Marbury, I would be the most likely choice. My late husband and I were among their closest acquaintances from the village."

"Did you remember that today was the anniversary of his death?"

"Yes. I don't think I shall ever forget that date. His death and the events that followed it shocked everyone in Marbury at the time. It greatly upset me. I don't know what sort of man he really was, but I couldn't understand then—and still can't—how his wife could kill him."

"Has anyone in Marbury ever sought you out to assist them in communicating with Lord Elton?"

"No."

"How about from the sanatorium?"

"No, and I'm quite certain that if Nurse Stevens found out that I was dredging up the old sins of Elton House with one of the patients, she'd have a fit. She has in the past complained about me to Dr. Hornby—accused me of being a negative influence on the men. I know because Dr. Hornby himself has told me. But he has ignored her, thankfully."

"So she disapproves of your interactions with patients such as James Travers?"

"Yes. And James has mentioned to me that she has tried to dissuade him from seeing me. But James feels as if I have helped him, as I told you yesterday, and so he also has ignored her."

"What is Nurse Stevens's relationship to Dr. Hornby? He seems to rely quite heavily on her."

"He does, though I'm not sure why. Frederick Hornby is a brilliant man, Chief Inspector—a man who is devoted to his work and his patients, for whom he has a great understanding and a great deal of empathy. And yet he seems blind to some of Nurse Stevens's more obvious shortcomings. I hope you'll excuse me if this sounds catty and small-minded, but she is not as crucial to the smooth running of the sanatorium as Dr. Hornby seems to believe she is. At least she isn't in my opinion."

"She strikes me as very efficient."

"She can be indispensable when it comes to the small duties—the fetching of the correct file or a cup of coffee or the prompt answering of the phone and the noting down of the caller's message. She would make an excellent secretary, I shouldn't wonder. But she's not much of a nurse; she seems to know next to nothing about medical matters and has little patience with the men, nor any sympathy for them. Her duties seem to consist mostly of bossing them and the other nurses about, ensuring that they are never late for this or that appointment or duty, especially if it involves Dr. Hornby, or would be something he would notice."

Mrs. Lockhart drew in a deep breath. "Well, I've gossiped enough, Chief Inspector. And here only yesterday I told you that I detest gossip. You must find me a terrible hypocrite."

"Not at all."

"You're very kind." She smiled. "I should be on my way. I'm sure Nurse Stevens is wondering where I've gotten to."

TWENTY

—◊—

ARTHUR BRANDT HAD EXTRACTED A PART FROM THE MOTOR OF Lamb's Wolseley, which he'd laid on the ground atop the same red handkerchief on which he'd cleaned his hands.

"What is that?" Vera asked.

"A distributor. It fires the car's spark plugs."

"Have you fixed it?"

"Oh, heavens no. It's shot and needs replacing." He wiped his brow with his right wrist, which left a smudge of grease on his forehead.

"What happens next, then?"

"Well, as I told the Chief Inspector, I can probably fit the one from mine into this one. I'm off to fetch the part. Would you like to come and have a cup of tea, or does duty keep you glued here?"

Vera glanced behind her, up the High Street, hoping that Harry Rivers or David or Sergeant Cashen didn't suddenly appear. She believed she could risk leaving the car long enough to have a cup of tea with Arthur Brandt.

"I'd love a cup of tea," she said. "But it will have to be quick."

"Splendid. We'll have a break and then get back at it. I expect the whole job shouldn't take more than an hour or so."

They walked together to Brandt's cottage. He cleared a space on the sofa in his cluttered study for them to sit on, then went to the kitchen and put the kettle on. He then went to unlock the shed behind the house in which he'd mothballed his Wolseley. He pulled away the sheet of green canvas with which he'd covered the car and opened its bonnet. He had a look at the distributor and knew that it would fit. As he exited the shed, he heard the kettle come to the boil in the kitchen and jogged back inside, where he made a pot.

While he was gone, Vera had a snoop round the study, feeling relieved that she had spoken to her father about David and her future. She was uncertain if her father also had spoken to David in the same way, but doubted it. His relationship with David was too dependent on chain of command for the two of them to speak as equals. She had not foreseen such problems as she had fallen in love with David and was certain that David had not either. But love *was* blind, especially in the beginning. She believed that the next conversation she must have with her parents was one in which she told them that she was leaving the constabulary to take her chances with the call-up. That was coming soon, she was certain now.

She found herself perusing Brandt's bookshelves, where she found a mix of some of the more popular novels, along with an eclectic mix of English, German, and French literature, histories and biographies, and a fair amount of poetry, including the Great War poems of Wilfred Owen, which she had studied in school and remembered mostly because of the opening lines of his "Greater Love," which she considered both beautiful and disturbing:

> *Red lips are not so red,*
> *As the stained stones kissed by the English dead.*

She took the volume down from the shelf and read the poem anew, which made her think of her father. She knew that her father had served with Rivers on the Somme, but not much else. He did not speak of his war experiences, nor did Rivers.

Brandt entered carrying a tray that had on it a pot of tea and a container of milk. "Here we go," he said, putting it on the table in front of the sofa. "Sorry there's so little room, by the way," he said, clearing a few more magazines and papers from the space by tossing them on the floor.

Vera returned the book to the shelf and joined him.

"The distributor will fit by the way; I'm sure of it."

"Good news," Vera said.

They sat in silence for a bit sipping the tea as people did when they were in a hurry. Vera rose, though, and went to Terry's terrarium. She had been intrigued by the snake and wanted to see if he had indeed eaten his mouse. But she did not see him.

"Has he gone back into his box?" she asked.

"Probably," Brandt said, rising and joining her by the cage. "They spend most of their time hiding away."

Brandt put down his tea and removed the top of the cage.

"Really, it's not necessary," Vera said, realizing what he was doing. "I'm happy to leave him be."

"He doesn't mind," Brandt said. "I'd like to say hello to him myself."

Brandt lifted the cigar box, revealing the curled python, which he lifted gingerly.

"There we are, my friend," he said, as he removed the snake from the enclosure. Terry hardly seemed to notice. Indeed, he laid tightly curled in the cupped palms of Brandt's hands, looking very much, Vera thought, like an oversized pastry. After several seconds, though, he began to slowly uncoil, raise his head, and flick his tongue.

"Why do they flick their tongues so?" Vera asked.

"It's how they smell; they actually 'taste' odor."

"May I touch him?"

"By all means."

She reached out to stroke the area just behind Terry's head. "Hello, sir," she said. "You are quite a handsome and dignified fellow, aren't you?"

The snake seemed to look right back into her eyes, she thought.

"There are tribes in West Africa that believe the ball python to be a spiritual creature and consider it taboo to kill them. Some African kings kept them as pets and wore them round their necks as ornaments. Most people misunderstand snakes; they believe them to be evil, when they are nothing of the sort. It all goes back to the story of the Garden of Eden and the temptation of Eve, I suppose. The snakes ended up with rather a bad break in that story, I'm afraid."

"Yes, but it's not like having a dog or cat, is it?" Vera said. "They can't curl up beside you on the sofa."

"Oh, you'd be surprised. I often walk round my study with Terry draped round my neck. He quite enjoys it. In fact, I take him for walks twice a day round the village; once in the morning and once in the evening. The fresh air is good for him. He rests on my shoulders and off we go."

"But don't you worry that he might choke you?" Vera asked. "Isn't that how they kill their food, wrap themselves round it and squeeze?"

"Not at all. They only constrict their prey, which in Terry's case are rodents. They seem to understand instinctually that if they took on something our size, they'd come out the worse for it. Their docility is actually a kind of defense and it tends to work quite well."

Vera touched Terry's head again. "I have to admit that I do find him surprisingly charming."

"He charms most people who take the time to really notice him. That's because he *is* charming, of course. But I believe it also has something to do with the positive feeling one gets from facing and overcoming one's fears. Most people naturally fear snakes; and then they meet Terry and realize they've nothing to fear."

Brandt lifted the snake. "All right, then, son," he said to it. "Time to go back into hiding."

He gently placed Terry back into the terrarium, whence the snake immediately headed for the cigar box. He and Vera watched the snake slowly slip through the hole and out of sight. Brandt put the top back on the cage and turned to Vera.

"Well, now," he said. "I suppose we should get a move on and drink our tea so that we can get back to the matter at hand."

—◊—

Lamb made his way back to the Wolseley only to find Vera and Brandt gone. He told himself that there must be a good reason for their absence—that Brandt might have gone to home to check his own car for whatever parts he needed to make the repair. But he was somewhat put out that Vera seemed to have left her post to go with Brandt. Resolving to check back on the pair later, he went in search of Rivers, in part to bring the inspector up to speed on the subject of the disabled car, but also to check and see if the canvass had turned up any useful information yet.

After fifteen minutes of searching, Lamb found Rivers emerging from a cottage on the western edge of the village green.

"I didn't expect to see you back here so early," Rivers said.

"My car broke down. We found a local man who can repair it—the same one who wrote the newspaper article on Lord Elton's murder."

"A jack of all trades, then?" Rivers said.

"We'll see."

Lamb said that Hornby had not yet returned from Southampton.

"Sounds as if we might have to put a ball and chain on the good doctor before it's all over," Rivers said.

"What we need is probable bloody cause for a warrant to search the place. I'm hoping that we will find something today."

Rivers brought Lamb up to date on what the canvass had so far uncovered. The people whom he and the three constables under his command had interviewed so far had mostly denied knowing Joseph Lee personally, though a couple had admitted they would have recognized him if they saw him on the street. The gist of their statements was that Lee came into the pub regularly and normally left drunk, but that before the incident with Fox nobody had seen him act belligerently. Everyone knew Alan Fox and a couple of them had seen Lee harassing Fox in the pub on the night in question and waving around what he claimed was a love letter that Fox had sent Theresa.

Although several people had seen Lee follow Fox out of the pub, none had witnessed the fight near the church. Two people had confirmed Horace Hitchens's story that Lee had returned to the pub with a bloody nose not long after he'd left it. None had seen Fox return to the pub that night.

Rivers halted briefly to retrieve his notebook from his pocket and flip it open. He glanced at it, checking his notes.

"One of the women I spoke to said that when Lee returned to the pub bloodied, she heard him tell Horace Hitchens that he intended to 'ruin' Alan Fox and that Fox could do nothing about it," Rivers said.

"Did she know what Lee meant by 'ruin'?"

"No. She thought it just another case of Lee mouthing off, as he often did in the pub when he was in his cups."

"Has anyone else mentioned hearing Lee tell Hitchens this?"

"Not so far."

"All right, then, Harry, nice work," Lamb said. "Sounds as if I'll have to pay another visit to the pleasant Mr. Hitchens."

—⁂—

Vera waited as Brandt set to the job of replacing the Wolseley's distributor, humming the tune to Cole Porter's "Begin the Beguine" as he worked. Occasionally she came round to the front of the car to check his progress and to ask how he was doing, to which he three times answered, "Nearly there."

Having briefed Rivers, Lamb now arrived back at the car, glad to see that Vera and Brandt had returned. Brandt had slid beneath the front of the car and was fiddling with something.

"How is she coming, Mr. Brandt?" he asked.

The sound of Brandt's voice floated up from beneath the car. "Chief Inspector—ah, you've returned. Nearly there. Just a few minutes more, I hope."

Lamb debated whether he should say something to Vera about having left the car unattended, but decided he hadn't the stomach for it, and that it was unnecessary besides. In the end, she and Brandt had achieved their mission.

Five minutes later, Brandt reappeared from beneath the car, smiling and wringing the red handkerchief with his oily hands.

"Well, she's done, I should say." He added for Lamb's edification, "It was the distributor. Shot, I'm afraid. But the one from my Wasp fit perfectly."

"Thank you again for your efforts, Mr. Brandt," Lamb said. "As I said earlier, we will see to it that you are made whole."

"Well, don't thank me until she starts, Chief Inspector. Hopefully I haven't crossed any wires."

Vera sat in the driver's seat and pushed the starter. The car coughed, and then the motor caught and turned over. Vera turned to her father and Brandt and smiled.

"Success!" she said.

Lamb smiled.

Brandt emitted a sigh of relief. "Will miracles never cease?" he said.

TWENTY-ONE

—◁◁—

LAMB AND VERA WASTED NO TIME IN HEADING BACK UP THE HILL to Elton House. Lamb knocked upon the door and was surprised to see Frederick Hornby open it.

"Good morning, Chief Inspector," the doctor said. "I understand you've been anxious to speak with me. I'm sorry; I've been away on business in Southampton that took longer than I had reckoned. Nurse Stevens was saying that you were interested in opening up the horse sheds for some reason."

"Can we speak privately for a moment first, sir?" Lamb asked.

"Of course, of course. Let's go to my office."

Although Hornby sat behind his desk, Lamb did not take the chair opposite it and instead remained standing. "What sort of business kept you in Southampton?" he asked.

STEPHEN KELLY

"I was speaking with a couple who might send their son here. They are making up their mind. It's a question of cost, truth be told."

"Can you give me the name of the couple to whom you spoke?"

Hornby's brow furrowed. "Well, I'd rather not, obviously, for reasons of confidentiality. Why would you need that information in any case?"

"To check your story."

"Meaning that you believe that I might be lying to you, Chief Inspector?"

"You might be, sir."

"But why would I want to lie to you?" He smiled briefly, almost as if he was testing whether Lamb was putting him on.

"For the same reason that anyone lies," Lamb said, keeping his tone just this side of conversational. "To conceal something."

Lamb expected Hornby to become defensive and even to lose his composure—and in so doing perhaps give away some tidbit of information that he might otherwise have kept hidden. But the doctor remained composed. Lamb thought that Hornby likely had practiced reining in emotion during conversation; doing so was part of his profession.

"It seems as if you've got it in your head that I'm hiding something from you, Chief Inspector," he said. "But I assure you that I am not. Perhaps if you'd tell me straight out what your suspicions are I can clear them up."

"I've evidence that you are in possession of American lend-lease goods, including gum and cigarettes, which, as you know, are rather hard to come by these days. These goods seem to have come from field rations meant for soldiers. As I'm sure you're aware, quite a lot of lend-lease shipments come through Southampton and Portsmouth, so I would expect a bit of it to end up in the local economy. But the goods of which I'm speaking would have to have been stolen and traded on the black market to have ended up in civilian hands."

"I see," Hornby said. "You suspect, then, that I'm supplying the hospital with ill-obtained goods?"

"One of your patients was smoking American cigarettes—again a very scarce commodity. And yet he described the supply of cigarettes here as bottomless. You also seem to be unusually well supplied with certain hard-to-obtain foods."

Hornby stood. "Yes, I see," he said. "I'm not going to claim that I have personally inventoried every morsel of food that has come through here, Chief Inspector. We might very well have a few things round here that are out of the normal bounds. It's possible that some of the patients brought them in, or even some of my employees. Especially the cigarettes. But I promise you that we are not know-ingly taking in stolen lend-lease goods here. We do have approval for amounts of coffee, tea, sugar, milk, eggs, and the like that probably exceed the normal rations for those commodities in part because we are considered a medical facility. I can have Nurse Stevens show you the paperwork on that if you'd like. As for the gum, I don't know about that, unless it, too, has come from the patients or staff."

Lamb believed that Hornby was attempting to outflank him—suddenly getting to his feet; rapidly taking control of the conversation; making assurances that all was well, while at the same time shifting the blame for anything that might be amiss onto the patients or staff.

"I'd like to see the inside of the horse sheds in back," Lamb said. "The stables and the carriage house."

"That can be done, Chief Inspector. Of course. I have the key on my chain."

With that, Hornby led the way round to the rear of the house, where he first opened the stables. Stepping into them, Lamb was nearly overcome by the twin scents of mildew and rotted hay. The interior was dark and musty, full of nearly indistinguishable gray shapes.

"There's no light, I'm afraid," Hornby said. "The last time this building was used with any regularity they lit the place with paraffin lanterns. I've a torch, though."

Hornby pulled a battery-powered torch from his pocket and handed it to Lamb. The pair of them moved about the interior of the shed, with Hornby always keeping a step behind Lamb, who played the light on every corner of the room and along its walls and ceilings. But other than weathered wood, rotted hay, and this or that rusted metal implement related to equine care, he found nothing.

They searched the carriage house in the same manner and the result was the same, with the exception that the building contained a lightweight delivery van with a roofed bed, which Hornby claimed had not been used since the previous year due to the lack of petrol. Lamb made silent note of the fact that the van's tires possessed a diamond-shaped tread and that the front tire had what appeared to be still-damp mud stuck among some of the grooves. He reckoned the tires were roughly six inches wide—the same width as the tracks he'd found imprinted in the courtyard on the previous day. Strangely, though, the rear tires appeared to be clean.

"All right, Doctor, I think I'm finished," Lamb said to Hornby, who stood between the door and Lamb. As Hornby turned to lead the way out, Lamb scraped some of the mud from the van's front right tire onto his finger. It was still damp, though barely. As he followed Hornby back into the sun, he wiped the mud from his finger onto the inside lining of his trousers pocket.

"Well, Chief Inspector, I hope that puts your mind at ease about the way we operate here," Hornby said as the two stood in the courtyard.

Lamb ignored the remark. His mind was not at ease. "I'd like to see one other room, if you please," he said.

The doctor's patience finally began to wear a bit. "Really, Chief Inspector, I don't see why you should want to. I've told you we've nothing to hide, but you clearly don't believe me."

"I don't believe—or disbelieve—anything anyone *tells* me, Doctor. I prefer to gather evidence that I can see and hold."

"Yes, but I can't help but feel as if you are overstepping your mandate. You came here to investigate a murder and Mr. Lee was not murdered in the house."

"Frankly, I have no idea yet *where* Mr. Lee was murdered, nor, I think, should you. Unless you know something you haven't told me."

For a second time, Hornby reined in his rising emotion.

"Very well," he said. "What would like to see?"

"The room in the basement at the end of the hall off which the kitchen is located."

"But why that? I don't think anyone here has ever opened that door or had any cause to."

"One of your nurses told me that Joseph Lee had attempted to lure her into the room with a story that it was haunted by the ghost of the former owner, Lord Elton. Are you aware of the history of this house?"

"If you are speaking of the murder of Lord Elton, yes, I know about it. But what has that to do with Mr. Lee's murder?"

"Perhaps nothing. But it's clear that Mr. Lee knew about the room and might even have used it for something other than attempting to impress young women."

"All right," Hornby said. He led Lamb through the door at the rear of the house and down a flight of wooden steps into the kitchen, through which they passed as they moved into the hall and thence down the hall to the door.

"I have no idea where this door leads to," Hornby said as he found the key that fit its lock. "This will be the first time I have opened it."

"Has anyone on your staff opened it?"

"Not to my knowledge. The only other person with a key would be Nurse Stevens."

The door swung open on creaking hinges; Lamb caught sight of a set of wooden steps leading up to a spot that appeared to end at what he guessed would be the level of the courtyard at the rear of the house. The steps seemed to mirror those they'd descended into the kitchen.

"May I have your torch, please?" he asked Hornby. He shined the light on the stairs and followed them with the beam of light to the top, where they ended abruptly at a solid stone wall.

"That's very curious," Hornby said.

"Yes."

Lamb carefully ascended the steps, which creaked beneath his weight. At the top he examined the wall where they ended and saw there what appeared to be the outline of a former door. The stone within this outline was a lighter shade of brownish-gray than that of the blackish-gray stone that surrounded it.

Seeing nothing more, he and Hornby retreated through the kitchen and back into the rear courtyard, where Hornby locked the horse sheds.

"I hope I've convinced you that nothing untoward is going on here," Hornby said.

Again, Lamb ignored the question and countered with one of his own.

"Are you aware that Janet Lockhart sometimes meets with your patients to help them commune with dead people whom they knew in life?"

"Yes, I am."

"And you approve?"

"I do. I look on what Mrs. Lockhart does as a therapeutic exercise for people who are grieving."

"Did you know that she was working with James Travers?"

"Yes. They both informed me and I endorsed it."

"Thank you for your time, sir," Lamb said. "I can see my own way back to my motorcar."

Hornby began to turn to leave, but stopped and addressed Lamb.

"I feel terrible about your suspicions, Chief Inspector. But perhaps you'd understand us better if you had a chance to really see how the staff and patients work together here toward success. What we do here is important and I would hate to see it disparaged."

"As would I."

With that, Hornby seemed finally to surrender to Lamb's refusal to allay his anxieties, bid Lamb good day, and disappeared round the corner of the house.

When the doctor was fully out of sight, Lamb squatted and dredged up some of the moist soil of the courtyard and compared it to the mud he'd scraped from the tire of the small van in the carriage house. The two samples looked and felt similar—gray, rather thickish and hard-packed, almost like clay and flecked with small bits of a lighter-colored gravel. He also found faint, diamond-shaped tire tracks near the door of the carriage house that looked to be identical to the tread on tires he'd seen on the delivery van. He thought that if Hornby was dealing in stolen lend-lease goods—perhaps as a way to finance the operation of his sanatorium—then Lee's murder might be connected to that. And yet he had still had no real evidence of either of those suppositions.

He looked up at the gray walls of Elton House and felt as if the old mansion itself was intent on defying him.

TWENTY-TWO

—ɯɯ—

THERE WAS NOTHING LEFT THEN BUT TO KEEP DIGGING. FEELING very much like a boomerang, he returned again to Marbury with Vera and parked in the lot by the Watchman. His teams still were out canvassing residents, but this time he did not seek them out for a debriefing.

Instead, he left Vera to watch the car and went to the door of the Watchman. Because the time had gone past three, the pub was closed for the afternoon and would not open again until half-past six. Lamb rapped on the door soundly and added in a loud, clear voice, "It's Chief Inspector Lamb, Mr. Hitchens. Open the door, please."

He waited patiently for nearly a minute and was about to thump on the door a second time when it swung open. Horace Hitchens stood in the doorway, looking sleepy and disheveled, as if he might have been napping.

"What is it?" he said. "I told you all I know yesterday."

"I have some new information."

"What new information?"

"I'd rather discuss it inside."

Hitchens retreated a step. "All right, but Theresa's not here."

Lamb doubted the truth of that. But he did not dispute it with Hitchens as he had no need this time to speak with Theresa. He stepped through the door and went into the darkened main room of the pub. Hitchens did not bother to turn on a light, nor did he offer Lamb a seat. "What's your new information, then?" he asked.

"A witness overheard Joseph Lee speaking to you when Lee returned to the pub after Alan Fox punched him. This person said that Lee told you that he intended to 'ruin' Alan Fox and that Fox had no way to stop him from doing so. Did Lee tell you this?"

After a couple of seconds, Hitchens said, "Yeah, he said that."

"Do you know what he meant by it—*how* he intended to ruin Fox and why Fox couldn't stop him?"

"No, and I didn't ask. Lee was the type who liked to mouth off. He had a bigger mouth than he had a brain. I didn't put much stock in much of anything he said, as I told you yesterday."

"Perhaps Lee had some information about Alan Fox's relationship with your daughter." Lamb was fishing. But it seemed that Hitchens took the bait.

"Here now, what are you getting at? I've already told you that my daughter has nothing to do with Fox and had nothing to do with Lee."

"Was Joseph Lee blackmailing you, Mr. Hitchens?"

"Absolutely not! You're off the bloody beam."

Hitchens pointed to the door and shouted, "Now get out. You've no call to come here and disparage myself and my daughter."

"Very well," Lamb said. "But I assure you, Mr. Hitchens, that the truth will come to the surface. It always does."

—⁂—

When he stepped outside, Lamb found Sergeant Cashen standing by the car chatting with Vera. The uniformed men Cashen had overseen that day were gathered near the war memorial in the center of the green, smoking cigarettes.

"All finished, then, Sergeant?" Lamb asked.

"Yes, sir. Constable Lamb was just telling me about the car troubles you had today."

"Yes, but we've managed to get it squared away, luckily enough. What did you find, then?"

Vera listened in as Cashen delivered to Lamb a rundown of what he and his team had learned. All of it was in line with what Rivers had reported earlier. For the most part, people denied having known Joseph Lee. A few people said they had briefly engaged him in conversation and found him unappealing—a bore and a braggart. Although two people, both men, had seen Lee follow Fox out of the pub on the night in question, neither had followed them nor had they seen Lee and Fox fight near the church. Several people said they also had seen Lee in the pub on the night following his set-to with Fox, but had not seen Fox as well. None had noticed when Lee had left the pub on the night he was killed.

Lamb thanked Cashen for his work and asked him to wait for Wallace and Rivers to return with their teams.

"In the meantime, I'm going to stroll up the High Street and see if I can't have another talk with Alan Fox," he said.

As he turned to go, he saw Vera moving across the green to join the uniformed men smoking by the memorial and considered this to be a positive development.

—⁂—

As he ascended the hill, Lamb mused on how he did not yet have a good enough bead on Alan Fox. If Lee had possessed some sort of compromising information about Fox and had been using it to blackmail Fox, the latter, who appeared to have a rather generous private income, might have decided that he was better off paying up rather than attempting to silence Lee. Indeed, given the amount of cash they'd found in Lee's cottage, it appeared that Lee had not been bleeding Fox too harshly. But all that might have changed if Lee, believing that Fox was about to "steal" Theresa Hitchens from him, had threatened to reveal Fox's secret as he drunkenly confronted Fox by the church. Fox, who also apparently had been drunk, had slugged Lee. Lamb believed that Fox was too smart a man to have killed Lee in such a public place as the High Street, even while intoxicated. Fox therefore might have waited until the following night to creep up the hill to kill Lee.

But was Fox capable of such violence? Janet Lockhart believed not and Brandt seemed unsure.

As Lamb neared Fox's cottage, he heard the sound of someone playing a piano coming from the rear garden. He went through the gate and into the garden where he found a scene identical to the one he'd found on the previous day—the red metal table dotted with empty ale bottles and the ceramic bowl brimming with cigarette butts; the garden shed with its door wide open, and, just within, the Victrola perched upon the small wooden table, a recording—the source of the music Lamb had heard—spinning upon it. He stood and listened to the music for a couple of seconds and found it enchanting enough, full of glissandos and rises and falls in pitch, volume, and tone that brought to mind the sound and movement of flowing water.

As the music continued, he peeked into the shed, but saw no sign of Fox. From the door, he could see the canvas upon which Fox was working. Fox seemed to have done quite a bit of work on it since the previous day, having turned the greenish and blue blotches into what appeared to be a painting of the sea.

He stepped into the shed and went to the easel. The painting, which he saw now was only partially finished, depicted in the foreground a single human hand—presumably from a drowning person—protruding from a dark green sea. What appeared to be a strand of sea grass clung to the outstretched fingers; near the hand, an ornate wide-brimmed woman's hat, adorned with yellow ribbons and blue feathers, floated on the surface. The background was dominated by a twilight sky unobstructed by land forms and suffused with what appeared to be an almost infinite array of colors. Separating this sea and sky was a blurred horizon upon which the dark figure of a distant ship—a large ship; a liner, perhaps—appeared to be steaming away from the drowning woman, trailing a lazy plume of gray smoke that mingled with the colors of the sunset.

As he moved to exit the shed, he stole a glance at the recording and found that it was Maurice Ravel's *Gaspard de la Nuit*. Although rudimentary, his French was good enough for him to translate it as "Gaspard of the Night." He had no idea who Gaspard was and did not care to know, but as he looked at the recording he noticed in reading its label that *Gaspard de la Nuit* had three movements, each with a name. The second and third were called, respectively, *Le Gibet* (which Lamb translated as "the Gallows") and *Scarbo*, the meaning of which he did not know. But it was the title of the first movement—the movement to which he'd been listening—that truly caught his attention: *Ondine*.

Lamb left the shed and went to the double doors that led into Fox's cottage and peered through them but saw no one inside. He banged on the doors and announced himself. But Fox did not answer, leaving Lamb to wonder if Fox had passed out from drink or was purposely avoiding him, as he suspected Hornby was.

He went round to the front door of the cottage and banged on it, but had no better luck there.

Feeling uneasy, he retreated again down the hill.

TWENTY-THREE

—∿—

BY THE TIME LAMB RETURNED AGAIN TO THE CAR, WALLACE AND Rivers and their teams had finished their canvasses and gathered by the green. After a quick debriefing—no one had discovered anything appreciably different from that which River and Cashen already had reported—the group decamped to Winchester.

Back at the nick, Lamb received a briefing from Larkin, who had spent the day immersed in the papers and notebook they had removed from Lee's cottage and checking on the backgrounds of Lee, Fox, Hornby, and the others.

Only one of the people had a criminal record, Larkin reported. Joseph Lee.

"In 1927 he was convicted of stealing nearly seventy-five quid worth of cash and jewelry from a passenger on an ocean liner he'd served on as a steward. He served a year in jail in Liverpool and was dismissed from the line—the Blue Star Line. At the time he was a first class cabin steward on a ship called the *Algiers*. It seems he spent some time working as a steward on liners."

Lamb immediately thought of the painting he'd seen in Fox's studio an hour earlier. "Blue Star—that's a bit of a tramp outfit isn't it?" he said.

"Well, it's not Cunard, sir, no, but it might be a stretch to call it a tramp line. It does a fair amount of work out of Southampton, mostly to the Mediterranean—or at least it did until just before the war, when it apparently had to cut back a bit due to a decrease in demand. I've called the company offices to see what else I can find out about Lee's tenure with them. I spoke with a clerk who promised to have someone of a higher rank get back to me. But they've not done so yet."

"When you speak with this ranking person ask him if they have any record of Lee serving on a ship in which someone went overboard during a voyage."

"Right."

"What did you say the name of the ship was—the one Lee was serving on when he was caught stealing?"

"*Algiers*."

Lamb tried to recall if, in Fox's painting, the departing liner had its name on its stern, but could not. He described the painting to Larkin.

"Lee also pasted into one of his scrapbooks a few things from his days as a steward; after I spoke to the Blue Line man I checked the books to see if Lee had kept anything from that time and, sure enough, there it was," Larkin said.

He retrieved the scrapbook and opened it, so that Lamb could see of what he was speaking.

"There's a few dinner menus from first class and a couple of photographs of what I assume to be Lee, given what I saw of his face yesterday, posing with other uniformed people whom I assume were also employees of the shipping line," Larkin said.

Lamb studied the photos, several of which showed Lee wearing a light colored uniform that looked like that which a steward on a liner would wear. Other than Lee, he recognized no one in the snaps.

"The menus come from three ships—*Acadia*, *Winnipeg*, and *Algiers*; two ships named after places in Canada and one after a Mediterranean port," Larkin said. "The Blue Star man told me that until the war they sailed regularly to Nova Scotia, Boston, and Portland, Maine, along with their Mediterranean service, which called at Gibraltar and Malta, among other ports."

"And then there is this, sir," Larkin said, flipping the pages until he reached a place where one was missing.

"The book's intact except for this page, which, as you can see, obviously has been torn out, and recently," he said. "The pages have begun to yellow with age but the paper at the place where the page was torn is much lighter and newer looking."

Lamb ran his finger along the jagged, ripped edge of the page. "Have you anything else for me?" he asked.

Larkin adjusted his glasses and opened a notebook on his desk.

"I've also done some checking on Elton House," he said. "It was owned for a time by a medical consortium based in Southampton that from 1919 through 1938 operated a sanatorium for people suffering from consumption. Just as with the shipping line, I called the company headquarters and spoke to a representative there who was helpful once I told him I was calling from the police. He said the company bought the house from the estate of Lady Catherine Elton in March 1919. Apparently the place had sat vacant from the time of her acquittal in 1915 until then. The transaction was handled by her solicitors in London, as she had left the country several years earlier. They sold the place to Frederick Hornby in June 1939. I asked him if Hornby had financial backers and he said that he probably did but that he did not know who they might be."

"They have no floor plan of the house, then?"

"Unfortunately, no."

"There is one other detail, though. The solicitor I spoke to—he sounded quite an old gent—said that by the time she sold the estate, Lady Elton had remarried in Malta—a man named Berkshire—and therefore sold the property under her new name of Mrs. Catherine Berkshire."

"Did you ask him if she was still married to this Mr. Berkshire?"

"I did and he claimed not to know. He said that once she sold the estate she dropped their firm in favor of her husband's, which was based in Malta. After that, they lost track of her. He didn't know the name of her husband's firm."

Larkin pushed the notebook aside and withdrew a cardboard folder from a small pile of papers on his desk. He took a handkerchief from his shirt pocket and used it to pluck a typewritten document from the folder.

"I also found this among Lee's things," he said, laying the document before Lamb. "It's a love letter to a woman named 'Theresa'—who I assume is Theresa Hitchens—from 'Alan,' who I have to believe is Alan Fox."

Lamb read the brief letter.

> *My darling Theresa,*
>
> *I just wanted to let you know how much I enjoyed our tryst of last evening. You are the sweetest, most beautiful woman I have ever known and I can't wait until we can be together again, my love. I shall come to the pub tonight, where I hope that we can talk and meet afterward. I am sorry that the horrible little gardener from Elton House has been harassing you and intend to do something about that.*
>
> *Until then, I remain your devoted lover,*
> *Alan*

Lamb found the note odd. For one, its language struck him as clichéd and insincere, as if "Alan" knew nothing about how to write a proper love letter and had copied what he thought was correct from what he'd read in melodramatic novels. Although he did not know Alan Fox, really, he nonetheless doubted that Fox would have written such drivel. Indeed, Fox struck him as the kind of man who would take seducing a young woman such as Theresa Hitchens for granted. What need would he have for love letters and flowers and the rest of it? He also wondered why Fox—or anyone—would type a love letter rather than write it in their own hand.

"Have you checked it for fingerprints?" he asked Larkin.

"Not yet."

"All right, then," Lamb said. "Keep at it and I'll check in again with you tomorrow morning."

—m—

While Lamb spoke to Larkin, Wallace took the opportunity to approach Vera, as she moved down the hall from the bathroom.

"I'm sorry about this morning," he whispered as he sidled up to her.

"So am I," Vera said.

"We must find some time to be together without anyone around."

"We will. I promise."

She glanced behind them to see if anyone was following. But they had the hall to themselves. They stopped and looked into each other's eyes. Vera could almost feel David's desire to speak—to say something he had been wanting to say since that morning. And yet he was communicating all the same, telegraphing a sense of anxiety and vulnerability that made her feel as if she were keeping a secret from him.

Wallace burned to ask her again if she loved him. But he also understood that even if Vera gave him the answer he sought it might not be wholly genuine.

Vera broke the tension between them by violating her own rule about how they should act toward each other while on duty. She put her hands on his chest and reached up and kissed him on the lips, quickly.

Before Wallace could speak, she said, "Please don't worry, David. We've plenty of time to figure things out. We're lucky in that way—very lucky. We, both of us, have to remember that. Otherwise we'll begin to pity ourselves and become ungrateful toward each other."

She kissed him a second time—again quickly—and said, "I have to go now. I will see you tomorrow and we will find a way to be alone."

—⁓—

At that moment, at a German airfield near Cherbourg, in northwest France, just across the Channel from southern England, the remnant of what once had been the Luftwaffe's Jagdfliegergeschwader 9 prepared to launch a bombing raid.

During the summer of 1940 the group had been among those that had relentlessly bombed southern England in preparation for what everyone then thought would be a Nazi invasion from occupied France. But the RAF had driven off the German bombers and the invasion had never come. Since then, the Luftwaffe had turned its attention to the bombing of London and then to Germany's campaigns in North Africa, Greece, Italy, and Russia.

Now Jagdfliegergeschwader 9 prepared to fly what would turn out to be its final mission of the war over England, and its target was Southampton.

TWENTY-FOUR

—⁓—

AT ABOUT TEN MINUTES AFTER ONE A.M. THE TELEPHONE RINGING
in the downstairs hall awakened Lamb. He reached for his wife, Marjorie, and found that she still was sleeping. He pushed himself out of
bed and down the steps to answer the phone.

"This is Lamb."

He recognized the voice on the other end as that of the nick's night
desk sergeant, who said that a woman had just called to report that
the pub in Marbury was on fire.

"She said specifically to tell you, sir," he said.

"Did she give her name?"

"No, she refused. She said only that the pub was on fire and 'to
tell the chief inspector.' Those were her exact words."

"Where's the nearest fire brigade with a working appliance?"

"More than ten miles away."

"All right. Please call Rivers and tell him to meet me at the nick in twenty minutes."

Lamb rang off and headed upstairs to dress. As he passed the closed door of Vera's bedroom, his first thought was to let her sleep. But he knew that she would not forgive him for excluding her and seeming to coddle her in the bargain. He knocked gently on her door, then pushed it open.

"Vera," he said. She stirred in bed. "Vera. Wake up, dear."

She sat up slowly. "What is it, dad?"

"Get dressed. We're going to Marbury."

—⁂—

They picked up Rivers at the nick and arrived in Marbury less than an hour later, only to find that the pub itself was not aflame, only a small storage shed behind it. By then, a good many people in the village had left their beds to help extinguish the fire, among them Arthur Brandt, who, as air raid warden, had sounded the fire alarm and organized the response.

Lamb, Rivers, and Vera found Brandt standing in the midst of a knot of people in front of a smoldering shed behind the Watchman. He was wearing a dark cotton cardigan sweater over his pajamas and a Home Guard helmet. The people with him—who, Lamb noticed, included Janet Lockhart wrapped in a light blue bathrobe—stood back from the shed, some still holding buckets. Its roof and three of its four walls had collapsed; the ground surrounding it was sodden. Only the western-facing wall continued to stand, though it, too, appeared ready to fall at the slightest breath. The place smelled of burned wood as smoke lazily rose from the charred remains of the shed, which appeared to have mostly held old furniture and garden implements.

"Chief Inspector," Brandt said, noticing Lamb. "How did you know to come?"

"I received a telephone call from a woman who refused to give her name. What happened here, Mr. Brandt?"

"This shed burned. I also received a call from a woman who said the pub was burning. I got up and ran down here and saw that it was not the pub, but the shed. I rang the fire bell by the church and we soon had enough people to start a bucket brigade. We kept dumping water on the thing until we got the better of it." `

"Did the woman who called you identify herself?"

"No, and I thought that curious. But I didn't think about it much in the moment, to be honest."

Lamb glanced round the scene. "Is Theresa Hitchens here?"

"You know, I hadn't noticed," Brandt said.

"And Horace Hitchens?"

"Yes, he was filling the buckets in the pub's kitchen."

"Does the shed belong to him?"

"Yes."

Lamb turned to Rivers. "See if you can find Hitchens and his daughter, please," he said.

"Right."

"What about Alan Fox?" Lamb asked Brandt.

"I've not seen him, either."

A distant sound caught Lamb's ear—a sound that, though faint, he instantly recognized. He had not heard the sound in nearly two years.

Vera heard it, too, and recognized it.

"That's an air raid siren," she said.

"It must be coming from somewhere nearer to Southampton," Lamb said.

Gradually, others began to hear the sound as well and for several seconds the crowd milling by the shed went quiet. Then someone said, "Bleeding hell. Have the Germans come back?"

"Maybe it's a drill," someone else said.

"It's no bloody drill. Why would they have a drill? The damned Germans haven't dropped a bomb here in two bloody years."

Brandt did not need to hear more. He made for the High Street as quickly as he could, running first to his cottage, where he telephoned a contact in Southampton who confirmed the raid. He then retrieved the hand-operated air raid alarm the government had issued Marbury in the summer of 1939 and a pair of ear muffs. He hurried with the alarm to the front of the church, where he found a good dozen or more people already awaiting him. He put the device down on its legs and began to crank it; gradually, it began to emit a loud high-pitched wail.

Vera had served as an air raid warden in the Hampshire village of Quimby in the summer of 1940, when the German bombers had come nearly every day. As Brandt began to crank the siren, she shouted at him, "What can I do to help?"

Brandt handed her the ear muffs and said, "Keep cranking this for another five minutes or so. I've got to unlock the shelter."

Marbury's air raid shelter was in the church cellar, a dank place that smelled of mildew. Brandt ran there to find that the vicar already had unlocked the cellar door and, with the help of Lamb and Rivers and two local Home Guard men, who had appeared in their roundish Great War–era helmets and toting first-aid kits and electric torches, already were leading people into the shelter and helping them to be seated inside. All round the little village, its residents were heading for the shelter. All the while the siren emitted its eerie sound as Vera continued to crank it.

Brandt took his place by the door, helping to shepherd residents into the damp basement, which, though it had not been used as a shelter in nearly two years, Brandt had kept stocked with benches and chairs, food, water, blankets, and other provisions. He eventually returned to Vera to tell her that she could cease the cranking and then led her to the shelter's door where they settled in with the others to wait out the raid.

"I should think we're safe enough here," Brandt said, adding that if the Germans had indeed returned after such a long absence it was probably to bomb the Supermarine factory in Southampton, which produced Spitfire fighter planes.

Lamb looked for Janet Lockhart and found her sitting with a group of young mothers who chatted as they watched over their children.

But he also noticed that at least three residents of Marbury were not present—Horace and Theresa Hitchens and Alan Fox.

"Have you any idea where they might be?" he asked Brandt.

"No. As I said, the last time I saw Horace he was filling buckets from the kitchen tap and I have no idea where Theresa has gotten to. As for Alan, I haven't seen him in more than a week."

"What are the provisions at Elton House for an air raid?"

"They shelter in the cellar. It's actually safer there than here."

Those in the shelter began to hear, from the southwest, the rumble of bombs bursting in the far distance.

The Germans were hitting Southampton.

—⁓—

Slightly less than an hour after they had first noticed the distant air raid siren, those gathered in the church cellar in Marbury heard the sirens along the coast begin to wail the "all clear" signal.

Brandt stood and announced, "Ladies and gentleman, the Germans have gone. Hopefully they won't return for at least another two years. You can now go back to your homes. Thank you for your patience and cooperation."

With that he opened the shelter door; the Home Guard men took up their positions to help the frail and the young children find their way, for it was still dark, though the people of Marbury, veterans of the summer of 1940, already knew the drill.

Meanwhile, to keep the proceedings official, Brandt briefly cranked out the all clear on the portable siren.

Lamb begged the vicar's indulgence to use his telephone. He called Marjorie and was relieved when she answered the phone on the ninth ring. She had herself just returned home from the shelter. She was fine; the bombers had come nowhere near Winchester.

"I'm sorry I wasn't there," Lamb said.

"Don't be silly. How is Vera?"

"She's fine. No damage here. We'll be home as soon as we can."

Having assured himself that Marjorie was not hurt, he took Rivers in tow and went to see if they could track down the Hitchenses and Alan Fox. Vera was to stay with Brandt and assist him in his duties.

Lamb and Rivers could find no sign of Horace Hitchens or his daughter in or near the pub. Lamb suspected that one—or both—of the Hitchenses had set fire to the shed, perhaps for the purpose of collecting on the insurance.

From the beginning he'd considered the possibility that Horace Hitchens might have killed Lee to keep Lee from harassing Theresa. But he wondered, too, whether Lee's assertion that he possessed damning evidence about something in Alan Fox's past also had frightened Hitchens. Perhaps Lee had not been so wrong to suspect that Alan Fox was linked sexually with Theresa Hitchens. And perhaps something had come of that relationship that Hitchens, as well as Fox, could not allow to become public.

Lamb and Rivers now made for Fox's cottage, where Lamb once again banged on the front door to no avail. He and Rivers went round to the rear garden and tried the French doors that opened onto the house and found these were also locked. Lamb banged on the door, hoping that Fox might merely have become drunk and slept through the air raid.

"Alan Fox!" Lamb yelled. "It's the Hampshire police. Open up!"

But the response from within was silence.

He turned to the garden-shed-cum-painting-studio and found the door open. He stepped inside with Rivers on his heels, found the light switch, flicked it on, and went to the painting lying upon the easel.

"That's bloody peculiar," Rivers said, looking at the painting.

Lamb didn't answer. He was squinting at the stern of the departing ship to see if its name was there. He could just make out, etched in faint white paint, the name of one of the Blue Star Line ships on which Joseph Lee had served as a cabin steward.

Algiers.

TWENTY-FIVE

—✴—

BECAUSE OF THE LATE HOUR IN WHICH THEY WERE FORCED TO stay in Marbury on the previous night, Lamb, Rivers, and Vera got a late start on the following day. By the time they arrived at the nick, lunchtime had come and gone.

Larkin, though, had been busy. He had been on the telephone that morning with the man from the Blue Star Line and obtained some of the information Lamb had asked for.

"Joseph Lee served on the *Algiers* from 1922 to 1927," the forensics man told Lamb. "Believe it or not, sir, he was part of three separate voyages during that time in which a passenger jumped into the sea. Apparently, it wasn't that uncommon on some of the lesser lines and during the longer voyages for those of a certain melancholy mind-set to give into despair and end it all in the briny. The voyages in question were in April 1922, June 1925, and then again in April 1926. All were on the ship's usual route from Malta to Southampton, with stops in Gibraltar and Belfast. As you probably remember from what I told you yesterday, Lady Catherine Elton went to Malta and married a man there."

"Yes," Lamb said. "Did he have the names of the passengers who committed suicide?"

"No, but he promised me he's working on that, as it will take some digging into another set of files. I told him that it was vital we get the information as soon as possible and he promised the send it up by courier."

"All right," Lamb said. "Keep at him, and let me know as soon as you have the names."

Feeling as if the pace of the inquiry had quickened very suddenly over the past twelve hours, and now threatened to outpace him, Lamb set off again for Marbury with Wallace and Rivers to see what had become of Horace and Theresa Hitchens and Alan Fox. He worried that one or more of them might have done a runner.

At the Watchman the detectives dispensed with the front door and went round the back, where they found the utility shed still smoldering and the door to the kitchen wide open. The kitchen was in a shambles, with pots and pans strewn about and the floor still slick from water that had sloshed from the buckets used to douse the fire.

Lamb called out for Horace and Theresa Hitchens, and when neither answered, the trio moved into the pub. Here, Lamb nearly stumbled over Horace, whom they found lying passed out on the floor, reeking of whiskey and lying in a pool of vomit. Lamb knelt next to Hitchens and tried to rouse him, but to no avail; still, he could see that Hitchens was breathing. Wallace fetched a glass of water from the kitchen, which Lamb threw into the publican's face. Hitchens sputtered awake and briefly opened his eyes. But he was so drunk that he was able to muster no other response save groaning, rolling over, and curling himself into a fetal position.

"Help me sit him up, please," Lamb said; Wallace and Rivers helped the chief inspector haul Hitchens into a sitting position with his back against the bar and his eyes shut.

Lamb squatted in front of him and put his hands on Hitchens's shoulders.

"Where is your daughter?" he asked Hitchens, shaking him a bit.

But Hitchens merely mumbled something incomprehensible and his head lolled onto his left shoulder.

"He's absolutely off his bloody trolley," Wallace said.

Lamb stood. "All right, David, stay with him and see if you can't sober him up. Harry and I are going to see if Alan Fox is home."

Vera was leaning against the Wolseley as Lamb and Rivers passed on their way up the hill. Lamb asked her to hike up the path toward Elton House and search the wood just below the pond for any sign of the fireplace poker they reckoned was missing from Lee's lodgings. Though Larkin had searched the area on the morning they'd found Lee's body, and found no likely murder weapon, Lamb wanted to give the area a second run-through. He believed that Vera could handle the assignment and having her do so was preferable to asking her yet again to wait by the Wolseley with nothing worthwhile to do.

"Do you have a handkerchief?" Lamb asked her.

Vera produced one from her pants pocket.

"Good," Lamb said. "Should you find anything pick it up with that and bring it immediately back here."

For Rivers's sake, Vera addressed her father as if she were a police underling and not his beloved daughter, the one person in the world whom he could not stand losing.

"Right away, sir," she said and headed in the direction of the footpath.

When Vera was out of earshot, Rivers said, "Are you worried about them, then?"

Lamb was surprised to hear Rivers speak in this way. For one, Rivers never had been one to pry. But for another, Lamb had not realized that Rivers had even caught on to what had been happening between Wallace and Vera.

"How much do you know?" Lamb answered cryptically.

"Enough. It's fairly obvious. At least at times."

This distressed Lamb. He hadn't believed it to have been obvious. "Do the others know?"

"I'm not sure about Larkin or the uniformed men, but I think Cashen knows. But he's too gentle and discreet to speak of it to anyone and far too loyal to you."

Lamb looked at Rivers. "Do you think Harding has caught on?"

"No. His head's too far up his arse."

"In that case, then yes, I am worried just a bit, but I'm trying not to be. Vera's old enough now to make up her own mind about these things."

"Prince Charming isn't a half bad lad. She might do worse."

Lamb was about to agree, when he glanced up the hill and saw Arthur Brandt moving toward them at a trot from the vicinity of Fox's cottage—a sight that brought their conversation to an abrupt halt. Brandt reached the detectives in a clear state of agitation, his breathing labored and his face flushed red.

"Chief Inspector, thank goodness you're here," Brandt said. "I was just on my way back to my cottage to call you. I've just come from Alan Fox's house."

"What is it?" Lamb asked.

Brandt looked away for an instant as he endeavored to catch his breath. Then he looked at Lamb and said, "He'd dead, Chief Inspector. Alan Fox is dead."

—⁜—

Alan Fox lay on his back on the floor of his studio by the small table that held the phonograph, his feet facing the door. His head lay upon his right shoulder in a pool of blood; inches from his left hand lay a small revolver.

Lamb saw an obvious gunshot wound in Fox's left temple—a small, red, oozing hole—that clearly had come from point-blank range. He also noticed that a single sheet of paper, folded in half, lay upon the phonograph's turntable.

The detectives squatted next to the body as Arthur Brandt waited for them out beyond the gate that led into Fox's rear courtyard.

"It could be suicide," Rivers said. He gestured toward the phonograph. "It appears he might have left a note."

"Yes."

Rivers pushed Fox's head to the left, revealing a large jagged exit wound on the right side of Brandt's head. "Was he left-handed, do you know?"

"I think so. He painted and smoked with his left hand."

Rivers sniffed the fingers of Fox's left hand. "I don't smell anything, though," he said. "If he did shoot himself then that pistol must give off almost no discharge."

The pistol appeared to be about a .32 caliber, Lamb thought.

Rivers dug through the pockets of Fox's jacket and found a half-full packet of the French cigarettes Fox favored and a box of matches but nothing else. "His body is beginning to stiffen," he said.

Lamb stood and withdrew a handkerchief from his pocket, which he used to pick up the folded paper from the phonograph. He found that it was indeed a note, written in blue ink. He read it to Rivers:

> *This note is for the world, but also for Lamb. I don't intend to hang for the sake of Joseph Lee and so have taken my own life. My departure was past due in any case, as my best years were well behind me. All I ever accomplished came a very long time ago; since, I have merely rotted, from the inside out. Now I've had enough.*
> *Alan Fox*

Rivers stood and looked at the note; he noticed, as Lamb had, the same cartoonish drawing of a fox face they'd found on one of the bills they'd retrieved from Lee's cottage and which also was on Fox's mailbox.

"Who doodles on a bloody suicide note?" the inspector wondered aloud.

Lamb was wondering the same thing. But something else caught his attention. Fox's easel was empty; the painting of the drowning woman and the departing liner was no longer perched upon it.

Lamb went to the easel and searched its surroundings for the painting, but did not find it.

"Maybe he's finished it," Rivers said, moving next to Lamb.

"Yes," Lamb said.

"I'll go back to the pub and call Winston-Sheed and get Larkin and Cashen and a squad of men out here."

Lamb and Rivers went to the French doors off the rear terrace and found them locked. "If the front door is also locked we'll have to break this one down when we get enough men out here to do a proper search," Lamb said.

He went with Rivers back round to the front of the house and saw him off down the street, then spoke with Brandt who had stood by, waiting.

Brandt told Lamb that he'd been concerned when neither Fox nor the Hitchenses had come to the shelter on the previous night and had decided that morning to check on them. "I went to Alan's first," he said. "And I found him, just as you've seen."

"Tell me exactly what you found," Lamb said. "Be as detailed as you can."

"I knocked on the front door first, then came round the back when I got no answer. The door to his studio was open and I saw Alan lying on the floor. I have to admit that my first thought was that he'd passed out drunk. That's what I'd been thinking all along—that he'd slept right through the air raid last night. I called his name, but he didn't answer, so I went inside with the intention of shaking him, to see if I could awaken him. But seeing the blood pooled round his head stopped me. Then I saw the pistol lying by his hand. I immediately decided that I should call the police and, as I said, I was coming back down the High Street to call you when we ran into each other."

"Did you notice anything else that was strange or out of place?"

"No."

"Was there a painting on the easel?"

"I didn't notice. The only thing I saw was Alan lying there. That was enough."

"Did you touch or move anything in the studio?"

"No."

"Did you see anyone else in the High Street as you walked up here?"

"No one."

"Do you know if Alan Fox was having an affair with Theresa Hitchens?"

"I don't. As I told you before, I'm not really privy to the village gossip."

"Do you know of anyone else in the village who was his lover, even in the past?"

Brandt looked away briefly.

"Mr. Brandt?" Lamb said.

"It was a long time ago," Brandt said. "Not long after her husband killed himself. Alan swooped in on Janet; he was like that. I don't think it lasted long. In fact, I'm certain it didn't."

"And how do you know this?"

"Janet told me, years ago." He briefly looked askance again, then said, "I suppose I should have told you this as well, though I truly thought it made no difference. At least until now. Janet has begun a love affair with one of the patients at the sanatorium."

"James Travers?"

"Yes, Travers."

"Did she also tell you this or did you divine it from seeing Travers come round?"

"Janet told me. She confides in me, you see; we confide in each other. Janet and I are more alike than you might think, Chief Inspector. She is also a bit of a loner in this village—she's different, you see, as I am different. She's never found an adequate replacement for her late husband, though many men have tried to replace him through the years. Despite her attractiveness to men, Janet is quite lonely—so lonely, in fact, that she's dedicated her life to proving that the living can still communicate with the dead and that therefore hope remains that she and her husband needn't be apart forever. I think her attraction to Travers is partly due to the fact that he reminds her of Cyril Lockhart."

"And how are you different, Mr. Brandt?"

"Well, look round you, Chief Inspector. I've never been married and have no children. I live alone, spending my time writing plays and stories and novels that no one wants to publish. Were it not for the money my parents left me, I might well be destitute. On top of that, my best friend in the world is a snake."

Lamb thought he understood what Brandt was saying.

Brandt sighed. "Janet is the only person who knows the truth," he said. "And now you are the second. And yet I trust you, Chief Inspector; trust in your discretion. Though I can't help what people might think or conclude about me, I've had no real trouble here in Marbury and would like to keep it that way, obviously."

"As long as it has no bearing on my inquiry, I consider your personal life none of my business, Mr. Brandt," Lamb said.

"Thank you, sir," Brandt said.

"One more thing, Mr. Brandt. Do you know if Alan Fox was left-handed?"

"Yes, he was."

TWENTY-SIX

—ɯ—

LAMB SENT BRANDT HOME, THEN STOOD BY THE SCENE FOR NEARLY an hour, during which he wondered if Alan Fox was really the type of man who would resort to suicide. Based on his lone meeting with Fox, he wouldn't have thought so. Fox had seemed to him defiant and egotistical, the kind of man who, though he might have felt despair keenly enough, had too much pride to give in to it. In the meantime, he was not surprised to discover that Travers and Lockhart had become lovers. He had sensed a bond between them that was stronger than the one they pretended to have in public.

He thought, too, of what Arthur Brandt had confessed to him and realized that Brandt must have come to trust him implicitly. He hoped that he would have no reason to betray that trust—and especially that Brandt himself would not give him reason to. Even so, he had to consider, at least for the moment, the idea that Brandt might have killed Fox.

Rivers finally returned with Winston-Sheed, followed ten minutes later by Larkin and Sergeant Cashen, who arrived with six uniformed men, two of whom stayed with Horace Hitchens—who had not yet come round enough to be interviewed—so that Wallace could join the team at Fox's cottage.

"The thing appears to be rather straightforward," the doctor told Lamb after having a look at Fox's body. "He was shot—or shot himself—at point-blank range in the left temple at a point of about an inch inward from the brow and an inch above the eye. The bullet went through his brain and exited the skull on the right side in roughly the same area as the bullet entered on the left, though the center of the exit wound is at a slightly higher spot than that of the entrance, which suggests that the bullet traveled at a slight upward trajectory. It seems to have gone straight through his brain."

"Does he have any other wounds?" Lamb asked.

"Not that I could see. Obviously, I'll know more once I get him on the table."

"Would the shot have dropped him instantly?"

"Yes."

Winston-Sheed was silent for several seconds, then said, "He had to have been left-handed. He couldn't have shot himself in this fashion with his right hand."

"He was left-handed," Lamb said.

"Well, that brings me to something else that I must tell you, Tom," the doctor said. "I finished Joseph Lee's autopsy last night. Whoever killed him was almost certainly right-handed."

"Lee was dead by the time he went into the pond," Winston-Sheed continued. "The blow to the back of the head killed him, though I'm not sure how much time elapsed between the moment he was struck and when he went into the water, though I shouldn't think it was long. The alcohol level in his blood was quite high, and I've no doubt that he was drunk at the moment he was killed. It's possible that the killer put him into the pond just to make sure that he was good and truly finished off."

"Why do you say the killer was right-handed?" Lamb asked.

"He was struck only once and from behind. The blow caved in the upper right rear portion of his skull, which means the killer could not have been left-handed, unless he swung the murder weapon backhanded, in the way a tennis player does who is returning a serve to his free-hand side, which seems to me unlikely. If the killer was left-handed then I would have expected to see more damage to the left side of the head."

"And the murder weapon?"

"I'd say that your guess of a fire poker is good one."

Larkin interrupted the pair to show them a spent slug he'd extracted from the frame of the window that was just beyond Fox's easel.

"It looks to be a .32," the forensics man said. "The doctor is right about the trajectory, by the way. The bullet was lodged in the frame with the front angled upward."

"It's possible that if someone else shot Fox, then that person was shorter than he, hence the trajectory," Winston-Sheed said, theorizing.

"Walter Brandt is shorter that Fox," Rivers said.

"So is Theresa Hitchens," Lamb said. "And she still hasn't come home yet."

—∞—

A light rain arrived as Vera had moved up the pathway toward Elton House.

When she reached the sign announcing the boundary of the sanatorium property, which was just below the pond, she entered the wood on her right and began a careful search of the forest floor. Although she thought the chances of finding a murder weapon were slim, she nonetheless appreciated her father having shown he trusted her enough to send her on such a mission. If she *did* find the murder weapon, that would be something indeed, she thought.

Off the trail, the woodland ground sprouted profusions of fern, low bramble, and yellow, white, and blue wildflowers, damp and glistening from the misty rain. Vera continued to move uphill, toward the pond and the house. She had walked only twenty yards or so when she reached a remnant of a wooden fence—a gray, splintered post, well into a state of disintegration, sticking from the ground like a sentry who refused to leave his post long after the threat against which he'd guarded had passed. It must have marked the estate's property at some long ago point in time, she thought, when the land she now trod likely had been cleared for the raising of crops and livestock.

She continued through the wood until it began to peter out into underbrush as she approached the pond. She returned to the trail and left the wood at a spot just below the pond. The tenuous rain continued to fall, coating everything, including Vera's uniform, in an airy dampness.

She picked her way out of the wood and through the brush to the pond's edge, at a point near where the old wooden dinghy lay. She walked out onto the small rickety pier and looked into the dark water, its surface vaguely rippled by the rain. She recalled David plunging into the water and her briefly comforting him afterward. She'd told him then that he needn't worry about proving himself anew to her father, or to Harry Rivers, or any of them. But he had said that no man fully trusts another whom he knows for certain to be weaker than himself. The stronger man might be patient, even compassionate, toward the weaker man, but his faith in that man is never complete and can never be.

"But you're not weak," she had said.

"I'm weaker than I was," he said. "That's a fact, and your father knows it."

She began to circle the pond, sticking close to the edge, in the hope of finding something that might prove to be worthwhile to the inquiry. She moved slowly, deliberately, and had made it about halfway round the circumference when she spied something lying in the tall grass just ahead that appeared to be covered with a blue cloth. She moved toward it and soon realized that she had found a person—a woman—curled on the ground with the cloth atop her. The woman didn't move and seemed not to have noticed her approach. Vera knelt beside the woman and touched her. She was relieved to find that the body was warm and that the woman seemed to be sleeping.

"Hello," she said tentatively. The body stirred and emitted a low groan. She could not tell if the woman was injured, though she seemed not to be.

"Hello," Vera repeated, touching the woman's shoulder. "Are you hurt?"

The woman made no sound. Vera pulled at her shoulder to turn the woman toward her. The woman put up no resistance and allowed Vera to roll her onto her back. She stared up at Vera, her eyes open but brimming with confusion; she seemed not to know where she was and did not try to speak. She was young, perhaps no more than eighteen; her long tawny-colored hair was filthy and matted and partially obscured her face.

Vera had never seen the woman before. But she reckoned that she had found Theresa Hitchens.

The young woman offered no resistance as Vera helped her to her feet.

"Theresa?" Vera said. "Are you Theresa Hitchens?"

The woman nodded.

"There now, Theresa. We're going to get you home."

Vera noticed that Theresa wore no shoes and that her feet were muddy and scratched.

"Where are you shoes?" Vera asked.

"I don't have any," Theresa said blankly. She looked away and said, "I've lost everything. I've lost it all in the pond."

"What have you lost?"

"Everything."

"You and I are going to walk down the path to the village now," Vera said. "I'm going to take you home."

Theresa wrapped the damp, woolen blanket more closely about her but did not speak. Neither did she resist as Vera began to guide her along the edge of the pond toward the footpath.

She walked, Vera thought, as if she'd been hypnotized. And yet, when they reached the footpath, she suddenly buried her face in the blanket and began to cry.

TWENTY-SEVEN

—⁊⁊—

RIVERS EASILY SHOULDERED OPEN THE FRENCH DOORS INTO FOX'S
cottage, as he, Wallace, Larkin, and the uniformed men began a search
of Fox's studio and house. Lamb especially wanted to see something
written in Fox's hand that he could compare to the apparent suicide
note, and asked the men to keep their eyes open, too, for the missing
painting of the drowning woman.

Thirty minutes later, Rivers showed Lamb numerous documents
in Fox's handwriting that appeared to match the writing in the letter
they'd found on the Victrola. On many of them Fox had drawn the
"fox" caricature next to his signature.

"Any sign of the painting?" Lamb asked.

"No, but I think we've found something better," Rivers said. He
produced a sheaf of papers that he placed on a table in Fox's sitting

room. "They're love letters from Theresa Hitchens. It appears that Fox had gotten her pregnant and was pressuring her to abort the child. In the last letter, which is dated only two days ago, she tells Fox she doesn't want to go through with the termination."

Lamb leafed through the letters and read portions of them. As he finished, Vera came into the room.

"I've found Theresa Hitchens," she said. "She was lying in the grass by the pond. I think she's in shock."

Lamb went to Vera. "Are you all right?"

"Yes, I'm fine. But I'm worried that something has happened to her. She seems to have lost her senses. I took her to Mr. Brandt's house. I thought that I couldn't take her to the pub, given the shape her father is in. And I couldn't bring her here."

"You did right," Lamb said.

He turned to Rivers. "Tell Wallace and Larkin and the others to keep searching and make sure the doctor has the assistance he needs to move Fox's body, then join me at Brandt's," he said. "It's just down the hill on your right, just before you reach the church."

"I should go with you," Vera said. "I think she trusts me. She hasn't said much of anything but neither did she fight me."

Lamb looked at Vera. He felt proud of the way in which she'd handled herself. "All right," he said.

—⁂—

A few minutes later, Lamb, Rivers, and Vera were gathered round Theresa Hitchens at Arthur Brandt's dining table. Brandt, who now stood off by the door, had fixed Theresa a cup of tea and coaxed from her the damp blanket that Vera had found her lying beneath, which he'd replaced with one of his own. She now sat huddled with the dry blanket round her shoulders as she sipped the tea. Her eyes were red-rimmed.

"How are you, Miss Hitchens?" Lamb said.

Theresa did not answer.

Lamb thought that Vera probably was right; Theresa Hitchens likely had experienced some sort of shock. But he sensed that she also might be at least partially playacting, and decided to test this.

"I know about you and Alan Fox, Theresa," he said quietly. "I've seen the letters you wrote to him. He kept them. Can you tell me about that?"

Theresa put her hand to her mouth and her eyes began to well with tears. Clearly, she understood of what he was speaking.

Theresa bit her hand in an effort to stop her tears. "How do you know about the letters?" she asked.

"We came upon them as part of our inquiry."

"Alan gave them to you?"

"Yes," Lamb lied. He was not yet prepared to tell her that Fox was dead for fear that the news might tip her over the edge. He also had to consider the possibility that she might have killed Fox over his pressuring her into an abortion and then tried to make it look like suicide. He moved his chair a bit closer to the table, so that he could speak to her in a quieter tone.

"When did you find out that you were pregnant, Theresa?" he asked. He almost whispered it.

Theresa slumped in the chair and closed her eyes. She said nothing and made no movement.

"I know that Alan was not happy about the baby," Lamb continued. "That must have been terrible to endure. You must have felt as if you had no one to turn to."

Theresa squeezed her eyes shut and tightened her lips.

"I know that you can hear me, Theresa, and that you understand," Lamb said. "And I know that although this must be almost impossible for you to speak of, I believe that you had the termination last night. Is that right? Is that why you ran away?"

Theresa burst into tears and buried her face in her crossed arms on the table. Lamb backed off and let her cry. After a couple of minutes, he looked at Vera and gestured for her to go to Theresa. Vera moved next to Theresa and gently touched her hair.

"It's me, Theresa. Vera; I found you by the pond."

Again, Theresa didn't move or make a sound, other than some low sobbing that signaled that she had, for the moment, cried herself out.

"I don't blame you for being frightened," Vera continued. "I would be too. And angry. Are you angry? Angry at what you have been forced to do?"

Theresa's head moved, almost imperceptibly, in affirmation.

Vera glanced at Lamb, to be certain that she should continue. Lamb nodded his assent.

"Who forced you, Theresa? Alan Fox?"

Again, Theresa nodded, though barely.

Lamb pulled out his notebook and hastily wrote in it a question, which he showed Vera, and which she asked Theresa Hitchens.

"Did Alan take you to Elton House? Is that where it happened?"

"Yes," Theresa murmured, though she did not raise her face.

"Is that why you stayed by the pond? You said that you'd lost everything there."

"Yes." She began to cry again, and Lamb touched Vera's arm, signaling for her to refrain for the moment. Once again, they waited several minutes for Theresa to finish crying before Lamb said, "Can I pour you some more tea, Theresa?"

She shook her head. And then she raised it and looked at Lamb and Vera, who were sitting next to each other only a couple of feet away. She dried her eyes with her fingers, whereupon Rivers pulled a handkerchief from his shirt pocket and handed it to her. She wiped her face with the cloth, then straightened in her chair and sighed deeply.

When she spoke, she looked more toward Vera than Lamb.

"That's where they did it, at Elton House," she said. "Dr. Hornby and the nurse. They did it, while Alan watched. Dr. Hornby put me to sleep and when I woke up it was done. Alan walked me home. My father was there. I didn't speak to him; I couldn't. Then Alan left."

Lamb ventured a question. "Did you set fire to the shed behind the pub because you were angry at Alan and your father?"

Theresa looked down at the table. "Yes."

"Then what did you do?"

"I ran away."

"Did you go to Alan Fox?"

"No."

"Where did you go?"

Theresa looked at Lamb for the first time. "I went to the pond. To be with my baby. Alan told me; he said it was a boy and that Dr. Hornby had thrown it in the pond."

TWENTY-EIGHT

—⚛—

LAMB BELIEVED THAT THERESA HITCHENS HAD MUCH MORE TO tell him about Alan Fox, but that she was in no fit state to undergo a heavy interrogation. He arranged for Vera and Rivers to drive her to the hospital in Winchester, where a doctor could treat her and confirm that she had undergone an abortion. In order to make sure that she did not try to leave of her own accord, Rivers was to charge her with malicious destruction in the setting of the shed fire. And before he sent Vera and Rivers to Winchester with Theresa, Lamb asked Vera to gently prod Theresa on the question of whether Alan Fox had ever sent her love letters.

If her claim that Hornby had aborted her unborn child was true, then he would also put together an arrest warrant for the doctor on a charge of violating the laws against performing abortions. The charge would give him the probable cause he needed to obtain a warrant to thoroughly search Elton House.

In the meantime, he would leave Cashen, Larkin, and the uniformed men to continue processing Fox's cottage for evidence while he and Wallace hauled Horace Hitchens to the nick and charged him with impeding a murder inquiry, giving Lamb an opportunity to sweat him properly.

Lamb believed that Horace Hitchens had failed to come to the air raid shelter on the previous night because he had gone to find his missing daughter. He was fairly certain, too, that Horace knew that Theresa had set the shed on fire. But had he known for certain that Fox had impregnated Theresa and forced her to terminate the child? If not, he might have suspected something regardless—a suspicion that Joseph Lee might have heightened when he told Hitchens that he could ruin Alan Fox. Lamb knew from what Theresa had just told him that Fox had crossed paths the previous night with herself, Horace Hitchens, Frederick Hornby, and Matilda Stevens. And before the night had ended, Fox was dead.

By the time Vera and Rivers headed off with Theresa, Horace Hitchens was beginning to come round. He had awakened from his stupor enough to sit at a table in his pub, where he complained of having a headache and asked for a drink, which Lamb allowed him.

Before Hitchens reached the point of becoming recalcitrant or combative, though, Lamb and Wallace hustled the publican, handcuffed, into the backseat of one of the motorcars Cashen and the uniformed men had come to Marbury in. Wallace sat in the back with Hitchens while Lamb drove. Lamb expected Hitchens to complain on the drive to Winchester and perhaps to even become abusive and testy. But he sat quietly next to Wallace, staring out the window.

In Winchester, Wallace completed the process of charging Hitchens, and then put him in a cell so that he could stew while he and Lamb found something to eat.

They went to the pub across the street from the nick and each ordered a pint of ale and some cheese-and-pickle sandwiches, which they ate at a table. They had nearly finished, neither of them having said much of anything, when Wallace spoke up. He decided that he was tired of waiting round for the right minute and had nothing to lose by speaking frankly to Lamb, who, he believed, valued candor.

"I don't quite know how to say this, sir, so I guess I'll just say it straight out. I want to marry Vera. I know you're aware of our relationship."

"I am," Lamb said, looking directly at Wallace.

"Well, then, I'd like to ask your permission for Vera's hand in marriage."

Lamb pushed aside the plate in front of him. He pulled out his cigarettes and offered one to Wallace, who took it. Lamb lit the sergeant's and then his own. When he had settled back into his chair, he said, "Are you sure, David? Completely sure?"

"Yes, sir. Completely."

"Have you said anything to Vera about it?"

"Yes. I haven't asked her outright but I've made my intentions clear enough."

"And how has she responded?"

"That's just it, sir. I don't know, really. She seems torn."

"But you are not torn?"

"Not in the least."

Lamb took a drag from his cigarette, and sighed as he exhaled.

"I understand your predicament, David, and I don't envy your being in it," he said. "But it's not really my permission you need—though I'm glad you think enough of me to ask for it. It's Vera's you need. But you know that already, of course."

Wallace also sighed. "Yes, I know."

"I'm sorry," Lamb said. "I'll tell you a secret; I have tried too hard to protect Vera from the vicissitudes of the world—the fact that life is unfair and that people can be ugly, stupid, ignorant, and violent. But I've learned that I can't protect her and that, in any case, I've no right to even try. She's a woman and must live her life—and I must allow her to live her life and to make her own decisions about the future. I know that probably doesn't make you feel any better, but there it is."

"I understand," Wallace said.

"Look here, David," Lamb said. "I realize that I haven't been fair to you either since you were wounded. I've sought to protect you, too, you see, and am guilty of coddling you from time to time, even though I know you must despise that. What I did out at the pond a couple of days ago was wrong. I should have just sent you in after Lee. Even with your leg the way it is you're stronger and more agile than Harry. But I misjudged you. And, at the very least, I can promise you that I won't do that again." Lamb stuck out his hand to Wallace and said, "Will you forgive me?"

Wallace was dumbfounded. He had never considered that Lamb owed him an apology and hadn't been asking for one. All the same, he appreciated what Lamb had said. "But, sir, I'm not asking for an apology" was all he could think of to say.

"Take it anyway," Lamb said. He stubbed his cigarette out on his plate and smiled. "It might be the last one you'll ever get out of me."

—⁓—

They returned to the nick, where Lamb sequestered himself in his office to smoke another cigarette and clear his head before he interrogated Horace Hitchens.

His telephone rang; it was Rivers calling from the hospital.

"The doctor says Theresa has definitely undergone a termination and very recently, probably within the last twenty-four hours," Rivers said. "And it was no butcher job. Whoever did the operation knew what they were doing medically."

"Anything else?"

"Well, he's only had a chance to examine her preliminarily but she doesn't appear to have any other physical injuries, though she appears to be suffering dehydration. The doctor said she's had a definite psychological shock, likely connected to the abortion. Also, your daughter managed to wrangle a fair amount out of Theresa on the ride to the hospital; Theresa finally seemed to come to, like, and began talking. She said that her father knew about the pregnancy and was with Fox in wanting her to abort it. She said that Fox agreed to pay for it and that Horace had a plan to send Theresa away for time afterward, to allow everything to settle. After setting the fire, she went back to the pond alone and claims that Hitchens came after her and tried to convince her to come back to the pub, but that she refused and so he left her there."

"Anything else on Alan Fox?"

"Only that she swears that the last time she saw him was when he dropped her at the pub after bringing her down the hill from Elton House."

"Did Vera ask Theresa if Alan Fox had ever sent her a love note?"

"She did and Theresa said that no, Fox had sent her nary a one."

"All right, Harry. Thank you."

"But that's not the end of it, sir, though I think we have to take this with a bit of caution, given how angry Theresa is with her father at the moment."

"What is it?"

"She claims that Horace left the pub in the wee hours on the night that Joseph Lee was murdered. She said she woke up when she heard him come in. She told Vera that she wouldn't be surprised if her father had killed Lee—not for her sake, but for Alan Fox's."

TWENTY-NINE

—⚬—

IT WAS NEARING EIGHT O'CLOCK BY THE TIME LAMB SEATED himself across from Horace Hitchens in the interrogation room.

By then, he had begun the process of obtaining a warrant to search Elton House, though he would have to wait until the following morning for a judge to approve it. Winston-Sheed had moved Alan Fox's body to the morgue, and Cashen, Larkin, and the others had returned to Winchester from Marbury.

Hitchens sat bleary-eyed and sour-faced at the bare wooden table in the windowless room. Thankfully, he had not requested a lawyer. Lamb thought that this might be because he wasn't aware he could do so, though he was more inclined to conclude that Hitchens believed he hadn't a need for a lawyer—that he could lie, bluff, and threaten his way out of any interrogation. Lamb planned to use Theresa as a kind of wedge with which to pry Hitchens open.

Lamb had with him, concealed in a cardboard folder, one of the photos of Fox that Larkin had shot at the scene; the shot showed Fox lying on the floor of his studio with the blood pooling round his head. He went right to heart of the matter.

"Alan Fox impregnated your daughter and then forced her to terminate the child—an arrangement you approved," Lamb said.

Hitchens looked fiercely at Lamb. "That's a damned lie, I'll not stand for it!"

"Are you calling your daughter a liar, then, sir?"

"What are you talking about?"

"We found her earlier today, by the pond at Elton House, and she told us everything. She even admitted to setting fire to the shed. She said that she was mad at Alan Fox and at you, Mr. Hitchens."

"What have you done with Theresa? Where is she?"

"I've sent her to the hospital."

"But you've no leave to do that."

"That simply isn't correct, Mr. Hitchens. I have all the leave I need."

Hitchens slapped his hands against the table. "You're a bloody liar, Lamb. A liar." He stood.

"Sit down, Mr. Hitchens," Lamb said.

Hitchens continued to stand. He said nothing, staring down at Lamb, his chest heaving and his eyes filled with rage.

"Sit down," Lamb repeated. "Or I'll have you handcuffed to the chair."

Still, Hitchens did not sit.

"You can take a swing at me if you want to," Lamb said, speaking calmly and remaining in his chair. "But I would advise against that."

Hitchens sneered. "You mean you'll call in your gorillas."

Lamb looked directly at Hitchens and quietly said, "Not at all. I have no doubt that I could handle you quite easily, Mr. Hitchens. You're all bluff, after all. On the other hand, I spent most of 1917 on the Somme, where for four months my main job was to crawl through the mud across no-man's-land in the middle of the night to raid the

German trenches in search of intelligence. In performing that duty I unfortunately was forced to kill exactly three men with my bare hands."

Lamb paused for just a hitch, then said, "Each time I felt the life draining from them and each time they pleaded with me to stop. But I kept on because if I didn't kill them then they would have killed me."

Hitchens, stunned, stood for a few seconds more before sitting. Lamb pulled his ever-dwindling packet of Player's Navy Cut cigarettes from his pocket, along with the matches, and slid them across the table to Hitchens, who silently took one and lit it, but otherwise did not acknowledge the gesture.

"Why did you leave your daughter by the pond after you found her there during the air raid? I know for certain that neither you nor your daughter were in the shelter, because I was there. A woman called here and reported that the pub was on fire; that same woman called Arthur Brandt and reported the same thing. I'm quite sure that the woman was Theresa. She was angry at you and Alan Fox and because of that set the fire and ran away."

"She didn't want to come home," Hitchens said sullenly. "She wanted nothing to do with me. I didn't blame her so I let her be."

"One other person also failed to show at the shelter that night and I think you know who that is," Lamb said. He was fishing again—testing a theory.

Hitchens looked surprised. "Why would I know?"

Lamb removed the photo of Alan Fox's body from the folder and slid it across the table so that Hitchens could see it.

Hitchens looked up at Lamb with alarm in his eyes. "You're saying I did that? I didn't even know Alan Fox was dead until this very minute."

"You agreed with Alan Fox that Theresa should have an abortion and even had a plan to send her away for a while, after the job was done, so that she could recover away from the gossip and the prying eyes of Marbury. But I think you had no idea, really, how losing the child would affect her. I think you believed it would be much like any

175

other medical procedure and that Alan Fox probably convinced you of that. Then, when Fox brought her back to the pub last night you saw how wrong you had been—and when Theresa set the fire you realized how truly traumatized she was. She ran away and you braved an air raid to find her, but she sent you away, told you she wanted to have nothing to do with you anymore. How am I doing so far, sir?"

Hitchens looked at the table, but didn't speak.

"Any man—any decent man who loved his daughter—would be left reeling from that," Lamb continued. "And it would be only natural, then, to turn some of that rage onto the man who had seduced his daughter and then led her astray for his own selfish pleasure."

Hitchens looked up at Lamb open-mouthed. "Are you saying you think I killed Alan Fox?"

"Did you?"

"No!" Hitchens protested.

"But you hated him for what he'd done to Theresa," Lamb said, allowing his voice to rise a bit. "You knew Alan Fox well enough. He did whatever the bloody hell he pleased and got away with it. His wealth and his position always protected him from the consequences. And you decided that had to end."

"No!" Hitchens said again. "I'll admit that I despised Fox for what he'd done; I'd even warned Theresa against him. I knew what he was like, just as you said. But once it happened I did what I did only for Theresa's sake, not for his. I couldn't afford for her to have the operation, but Fox could. And so I went along with it. I thought it would be best for Theresa, but I was wrong. But I didn't kill Fox. I swear to you, Lamb. I had no idea he was dead until just now. After I left Theresa, I came back to the pub and drank myself nearly to death, as you saw. I was hoping that I might never wake up."

Lamb remained calm. "Did you kill Joseph Lee? He came to you after he'd fought with Fox and claimed he had something on Fox that could 'ruin' him. Maybe he found out somehow that Fox had gotten Theresa pregnant. He had a love note that someone convinced him had been written by Alan Fox, but I think it was a fake. Whoever gave him the note might also have known about Theresa. You did your best to keep everything secret, but these things tend to get out regardless. And so when Lee told you what he knew, you had to silence him."

"No, I swear it."

"Your own daughter just admitted to me not an hour ago that you snuck from the pub on the night Lee was killed and returned a short time later."

Hitchens's eyes shifted quickly from right to left, like those of a trapped animal looking for escape. "No! She's lying; she's confused."

Lamb exploded. He pounded his fist so hard that it shook the table. "Stop lying to me, goddamn you!" he yelled.

He looked fiercely at Hitchens and even pointed his finger at Hitchens's face. "I swear to you, Hitchens, that if you killed Alan Fox I will see you hang for it. But if your daughter did it, then I'll see her hang. It makes no bloody difference to me. I've been patient with you, but I'm finished. You have one chance—one bloody chance—to tell me the truth, here and now. Don't squander it, for your daughter's sake if not yours."

Hitchens began to waver. "But Theresa didn't . . ."

Lamb interrupted him. "The *truth*, Hitchens. I warn you."

Hitchens slumped in his chair.

"I didn't know anything until about three weeks ago, though I suspected," he said, his voice weary. "The thing is Theresa practically threw herself at Fox, even after I had warned her about him, how he is with women. Even some of the bloody customers began to notice the way she acted toward him."

"Did Joseph Lee notice?"

"He must have, hadn't he?"

"How did you find out that Fox had gotten Theresa pregnant?"

"Fox himself. He came by the pub one afternoon while Theresa was out at the shops. He told me as if he were telling me he'd just bought himself a new motorcar or something like that. Very matter of fact. He told me what had happened and said he wanted to terminate it and that he would set it up and pay for it. He promised it wouldn't be one of these botched jobs—that he knew medical people who would handle it the proper way and Theresa wouldn't be hurt. He said the doctor would just put her to sleep for a bit and that would be the end of it."

He looked away. "Stupid bloody girl," he said quietly. "She thought Alan Fox was some sort of bloody Prince Charming. She had no idea what she was doing, and neither did I."

He looked back at Lamb.

"Fox took her to Elton House last night and Hornby did what Fox paid him to do. Then Fox told her that Hornby threw the remains in the pond. That was bloody cruel. Alan Fox was a bastard. The more I thought about it, the more ashamed I felt."

"Where did you and Theresa sit out the air raid?"

"In the trees by the pond. I wasn't worried about the bloody Germans. I knew they had no reason to come to Marbury. We waited it out together. She refused to go to the shelter because she thought Fox would be there."

"Did Theresa shoot Alan Fox?"

"No, Lamb. I told you. I swear it. She doesn't even own a gun."

Hitchens looked at the table. "All right, Lamb," he said in something close to a mumble. "I admit I lied. I did go to see Joseph Lee on the night he was killed. But I didn't kill him. I asked him what he had on Fox, but the little bastard refused to tell me. He was like that; he liked it when he had something over you. But I was worried that he might know about Theresa's pregnancy and might put it about the village to embarrass Fox. And I couldn't let that happen."

"So you went to his cottage?"

"Yes, but he wasn't there. The door was open and some candles were burning on the table but Lee was gone. That's when I took my chance; I turned the place over looking for anything he might have had on Fox. And I found something, but not what I expected."

"What did you find?"

"A newspaper clipping. It had to do with Fox being a suspect in a woman's murder years ago. He was accused of pushing someone from a ship on which Lee was a steward. I've kept the thing in a bloody drawer in the table next to my bed. I can show it to you. You see, I had no reason to kill Fox. I was trying to protect him because I thought it the best way to protect Theresa in the long run. He said he was going to see Theresa through, even after I sent her away—that he would make sure that she was provided for."

"Did the clipping say when this incident on the ship occurred?"

"There's a date written on the clipping: April 22, 1922. I remember it because it repeats the twos."

"How about the name of the ship?"

"Something with an 'A.'"

"*Algiers?*"

"Yes, that's it—*Algiers*."

"Why didn't you destroy this clipping?"

"I kept it as insurance, in case Fox went back on his promise to see to Theresa."

"Did you see Lee that night?"

"I did not; again, I'll swear to it. I got the clipping and found what I thought I needed, so I left."

"Did you see anyone else in and around Lee's cottage that night?"

"No one."

"Will you grant me permission to search your pub for this clipping?"

"Yes—yes. When you find it, you'll see that I'm not lying."

—⁂—

The pins were beginning to fall, Lamb thought, as he left Hitchens in the interrogation room and went to the incident room, where he found that Rivers and Vera had returned from the hospital. After briefly greeting them, he went to his office to call Arthur Brandt, who said he was only too happy to go to the Watchman and search for the clipping.

Brandt found the rear door of the pub unlocked; he then found the clipping in the drawer of Horace Hitchens's night table, just where

Hitchens said it would be. He called Lamb from the telephone in the pub to report that he'd found the clipping.

"Describe it to me, please," Lamb said.

"The name of the paper and the date of publication have been cut away, though someone has written what I take to be a date on it in blue ink: 22/04/1922. There's a photo with the article that shows a policeman escorting Alan Fox down the gangplank of a liner called *Algiers*; there are several people behind them who are unidentified; some in naval garb. The captions reads:

> *Belfast police escort Alan Fox, of Hampshire, from the Blue Star Line's* Algiers *yesterday. Police questioned Fox in the disappearance at sea of Mrs. Catherine Berkshire, of Malta, on the liner's journey from that country to Liverpool, via Belfast. Police later cleared Fox in the incident and ruled Mrs. Berkshire's death a suicide.*

"Hold on," Lamb said. "You said the woman's name was Catherine Berkshire?"

"Yes, that's it."

"Read me the story, please."

Brandt read:

> *Officers of the Royal Ulster Constabulary questioned a Hampshire man in the disappearance at sea of a Malta woman, but later released the man having ruled that Mrs. Catherine Berkshire had committed suicide by jumping from the Blue Star liner,* Algiers, *in the early morning hours of April 20, while the ship was en route from Malta to Southampton, via Gibraltar and Belfast. Mrs. Berkshire was traveling with a two-year-old son and a woman described as a companion, neither of whom police named.*
>
> *Officials detained Alan Fox, of Marbury, Hampshire, in Mrs. Berkshire's disappearance after several passengers told police investigators that they had seen Fox speaking and interacting with*

Mrs. Berkshire on several occasions during the voyage, including once in the first class dining room several hours before it is believed Mrs. Berkshire went missing. She was not reported as missing until eight A.M. April 20, by a female companion whom police did not name. However, investigators determined that Fox played no role in Mrs. Berkshire's disappearance. Police subsequently determined that the Malta woman took her own life by jumping from the ship and did not therefore refer the case for an inquest.

The Algiers was scheduled to depart Belfast for Southampton yesterday, but was delayed because of the inquiries. The ship is scheduled to sail for England tonight.

"That's it, Chief Inspector," Brandt said.

For the second time that night, Lamb found himself knocked back upon his heels. The story was alleging that Alan Fox might have pushed the woman formerly known as Lady Catherine Elton into the sea from the deck of a second-rate ocean liner.

He thanked Brandt and asked him to take the clipping and put it in a safe place until he was able to retrieve it. Then he went to look for Larkin. He found the forensics man staring into a microscope in his lab, studying the slug he'd pulled from the wall of Alan Fox's studio.

"Did you receive the passenger lists from the Blue Star man?" Lamb asked.

"Yes. They came in by courier while we were in Marbury tending to this mess with Alan Fox."

"Let's have a look at them."

Larkin retrieved the packet, which was addressed to him and still sealed. He pulled out the contents, and he and Lamb began to study them. Lamb immediately went to the list from the April 1922 voyage, which had carried seventy-nine passengers. He had to go to the very bottom of the two-page list to find what he was looking for.

Lost at sea, suicide, 20.04.22: Mrs. Catherine Berkshire. British subject, embarked at Malta 14.04.22.

Now he scanned the rest of the list, in which the passengers were listed alphabetically and by class, along with where they embarked and whether they were "British subjects" or "Non-British subjects."

Under the list of first class passengers he found the name *Fox, Mr. Alan.* He then scanned the list to see if he could find the name of Catherine Berkshire's two-year-old son. He found that name and another, which stunned him anew.

Berkshire, Master James
Stevens, Mrs. Matilda

"Matilda Stevens?" Larkin said, peering over Lamb's shoulder as the chief inspector underlined the name. "And she's married? That didn't turn up in the police records I checked."

"Yes," Lamb said. "And *James* Berkshire."

"Are you thinking that's Travers, then?"

"Nothing would surprise me at this point, Mr. Larkin," Lamb said. He picked up the passenger list and headed for the door. "The only way to find out for sure is to go back to Elton House."

Lamb met with the team in the incident room and told Rivers and Wallace that they were returning to Elton House immediately.

"You'll need a driver," Vera said, concerned that her father apparently wasn't including her in his plan.

Lamb looked at Vera. He would have preferred that she go home to eat a decent meal and get a proper night's sleep. But she had found Theresa Hitchens at the pond and deserved to see the thing through with the rest of them.

"We will indeed," he said.

THIRTY

—w—

DR. FREDERICK HORNBY ANSWERED LAMB'S KNOCK UPON THE DOOR
of the Elton House Sanatorium at a little past ten P.M.

"Chief Inspector," he said, clearly surprised by the fact that Lamb, Rivers, and Wallace were standing upon his doorstep. "It's rather late, isn't it?"

"I'd like to speak to you for a moment, sir."

"About what, if I may ask?"

"I'd rather discuss it in your office."

"Well, it is rather late, as I said, Chief Inspector. We're past lights-out. Can't this wait until tomorrow?"

"No."

The bluntness of Lamb's answer startled Hornby. He stepped back from the door.

"All right, then. Come in."

The doctor ushered the detectives through the foyer and into his office. A single tumbler full of whiskey sat on his desk. "I was just having a drink before retiring," Hornby said. "May I fix you gentlemen something?"

"No, thank you," Lamb said. He, Rivers, and Wallace remained standing. Hornby stood by his desk facing them.

"I do hope this has nothing to do with your suspicions about us hiding stolen goods and the rest of it, Chief Inspector," Hornby said. "I feel as if I've cooperated with you to my utmost on that point and can assure you yet again that we have nothing to hide here."

"I asked you during our first interview if you knew a man named Alan Fox and you said that you did not," Lamb began.

"And now you want to ask me about him because he's dead," Hornby said. "Word has filtered up here from Marbury about his suicide."

"Did you know Alan Fox?" Lamb repeated.

"I might have met him once, but I didn't know him. I don't think I'd even recognize him on the street if I saw him."

"Have you seen Alan Fox since the morning Joseph Lee's body was discovered?"

"No."

"Do you know Horace Hitchens, the man who owns the pub in Marbury?"

"No. I'm afraid I haven't had much time to explore Marbury. My work here has kept me too busy."

"How about his daughter, Theresa Hitchens?"

"No."

"Theresa Hitchens claims to have been here just last night, with Alan Fox. She said that Fox paid you to abort the child that he had fathered with her. She also claims that you took the child's remains and threw them in the pond. Now Alan Fox is dead."

Hornby's face flushed red and his composure finally began to crack. "But that's a lie," he said. "I did nothing of the kind."

Someone entered the anteroom. "Dr. Hornby!" It was a female voice.

A second later Janet Lockhart burst into the room, breathing heavily, as if she had been running.

"But Mrs. Lockhart, what are you doing here at this hour?" Hornby said.

"Please, Dr. Hornby," she said. "It's James. I can't wake him. You must come quickly."

Janet Lockhart looked at Lamb. "Please, Chief Inspector," she said.

"Calm down, please, madam," Lamb said. "What are you talking about?"

"It's James. He seems to have taken an overdose of sedatives. I fear he might be dead."

The four men followed Janet Lockhart to James Travers's room, where they found Travers lying still and silent in his bed, his body straight, his head on the pillow facing up, and the blanket tucked beneath his chin.

Lamb moved to the bed and shook Travers and yelled his name. But Travers did not move. He put his ear to Travers's chest and heard his heart beating, though faintly.

"He's alive," he said.

"Let me see," Hornby said. He took Travers's wrist in his hand and held it, measuring the lieutenant's pulse. "His pulse is weak."

Wallace stood by the small table in the middle of the room at which Lamb had earlier interviewed Travers. Upon the table sat a partially full bottle of sherry and a single glass.

"It looks as if he was drinking," Wallace said.

Hornby went to the table and picked up the glass. "There's residue in the bottom," he said. "He must have put something in the sherry."

"Does he take sedatives?" Lamb asked.

"Yes," Hornby said. "And he took an overdose of sleeping pills before he came here in a botched suicide attempt. So he has tried this before."

"We've got to get him to hospital immediately," Lamb said. He turned to Rivers and Wallace and said, "Let's get him to the car. We've no time to waste."

They loaded Travers into the rear seat of Frederick Hornby's large saloon. Vera, who had been waiting by Lamb's Wolseley, came to assist. Janet Lockhart stood by, silent and obviously still frantically worried.

Lamb instructed Hornby to stay in the back seat with Travers. "The constable will drive and I'll go with you," he said.

Matilda Stevens appeared, still in her nurse's uniform. "What is wrong?" she asked Hornby. "I heard noises."

"Travers has tried to take his life again," the doctor said. "We're taking him to hospital."

"Is he dead?" the nurse asked.

"No, thank God," Hornby said.

Janet Lockhart wheeled to face the nurse. "You did this," she said to Stevens. "You're not going to get his money. He knows now that he's made a mistake."

The nurse reached out a hand toward Mrs. Lockhart. "You're delirious," she said. "Let me help you."

But Mrs. Lockhart recoiled and said, "Don't *touch* me."

Lamb heard this exchange but had no time to follow up on it. He pulled Rivers aside and told him to stay with Wallace and take statements from Lockhart and Stevens and anyone else whom they deemed appropriate.

"Lockhart and Travers are lovers, according to Brandt," he said to Rivers. "Hornby did not know that Lockhart was here, but Stevens might have known. She and Stevens dislike each other."

"What about the abortion and this business with the *Algiers*?" Rivers asked.

Lamb glanced back at Hornby's car, anxious to leave. "That will have to wait until tomorrow," he said.

—⁂—

James Travers awakened on the following morning, lying in a hospital bed. Lamb and Dr. Hornby had passed the night with him, each taking turns dozing, after a doctor had worked to flush from Travers

the poisons that had threatened to slowly shut down his body's func-
tioning. The doctor reported that Travers had ingested a combination
of barbiturates and sherry, which would have killed him within the
hour of their discovering him had they not brought him to the hospital.

Lamb had much still to do, including serving Hornby with a
warrant to search Elton House, which he expected to receive that
morning. Lamb believed that the doctor had aborted Theresa Hitchens's unborn child and continued to suspect Hornby of harboring
stolen lend-lease goods. But Lamb also did not doubt that Hornby's
efforts to save Travers's life had been sincere.

After managing to locate a cup of coffee with the help of the nurse on
duty, Lamb called the nick and instructed the desk sergeant to tell Rivers
that he should obtain the warrant to search Elton House as soon as possible
and to bring it to the hospital. Lamb also wanted to know from Rivers
what Nurse Stevens and Janet Lockhart had said in their interrogations on
the previous evening. He had an inkling of the relationship each shared
with Travers, but wanted to be certain he was correct. He hoped that
Travers could—and would—tell him that morning. He also asked that a
uniformed man be sent to the hospital to stay with Hornby; although the
doubted the doctor would bolt, he wanted to make certain of it.

An hour later, as Hornby cooled his heels in a spare room guarded
by the uniformed man, Lamb stood by Travers's bed with the doctor
who had treated the lieutenant. Travers, his eyes still showing weari-
ness, looked up at Lamb.

"Hello, Lieutenant Travers," Lamb said.

"Chief Inspector," Travers said, sounding bewildered. He glanced
round the room. "What is this?"

"You're in hospital. You had a rather rough night of it, I'm afraid."

Lamb introduced the doctor and briefly explained to Travers what
had occurred. "You took too many sedatives and drank them down
with sherry," he said.

Travers put a hand to his head. "Sedatives? But I took no sedatives,
Chief Inspector—or I took only the one I normally take. But I took
nothing else."

"I'm afraid you did. Did you also drink a glass of sherry before going to bed last night?"

"Yes."

"Were you alone when you did?"

"No, Aunt Matilda—Nurse Stevens—was with me. She brought the sherry to my room. She wanted us to toast the . . ."

Travers stopped in mid-sentence as he suddenly realized what had occurred.

"My God," he said. He looked at Lamb with the expression of a man who had just jumped out of the way of a speeding train. "But where is Janet?" he said. "Is she all right?"

"Yes," Lamb said. "Was she in your room last night?"

"No. It was . . ." He paused, then added, "Irregular. We planned to meet later, in my room."

"Nurse Stevens—your aunt Matilda—gave you the sherry, then?"

"Yes, but it can't but true." He looked at Lamb again with the same look of amazement.

"I'm afraid it is," Lamb said, pushing ahead and not wanting to lose the opportunity to pry the rest of Travers's story from him. He recalled the testy exchange between Janet Lockhart and Matilda Stevens the night before and Lockhart's mention of how Stevens would not get an of Travers's "money."

"You said she brought the sherry to your room so that you could toast something? What had the two of you to toast? Had you decided to give your aunt some money?"

"Yes. My late mother left me quite a lot of money. But it has been in trust until I turn twenty-three, which I will do in October. I had agreed to give Aunt Matilda a sum of money for herself and another sum on top of that, which she would donate to the Elton House Sanatorium, to the fund that Dr. Hornby has set up for men who can't afford the treatment."

"What is the sum?"

"Five thousand. Half would go to her and she would give the rest to the sanatorium."

"Why would you not just give the money to the sanatorium yourself?"

"I did it for Aunt Matilda—so that she could make the donation in her name. She wanted it that way, and I agreed." He looked away from Lamb. "I trusted her, you see. I never thought . . ." He shook his head in disbelief.

"You said that your late mother left you this money."

"Yes."

"Her name was Catherine Berkshire," Lamb said quietly. "She died on a sea voyage in 1922, when you were only three years old."

Astonished, Travers sat up. "But how could you possibly know that, Chief Inspector? No one knows that."

"Certain facts have come to light," Lamb answered cryptically. "I also have reason to believe that Mrs. Lockhart knows of your mother and what happened to her."

"Yes. Janet has been helping me—with my grief, you see, and all the rest of it. I'm beginning to see now how it's all connected. How what happened to me when I was young—losing both my parents so soon together—and then my experiences in France are all part of the same problem." He looked at Lamb. "Janet has used her gift to help me to commune with my mother, Chief Inspector, and the experience has been eye-opening."

"And your aunt Matilda—she also was on the voyage on which your mother died, traveling as your mother's companion."

"Yes. She is my mother's sister."

"Did you come to Elton House Sanatorium in part because of your aunt?"

"Yes, she contacted me and asked me to come; she believed I would benefit from the program Dr. Hornby has set up. I had tried to commit suicide only two months earlier, by swallowing a handful of sleeping pills. But they weren't enough in the end. I suppose I didn't really want to die."

"Are you aware of your mother's past, Lieutenant—of who she was before she came to Malta and married your father?"

"All I know is that she and my aunt grew up in Warwickshire and that their parents died when they were young women, and that later, after they left the orphanage, they went to Malta, where my mother met my father and Aunt Matilda became a kind of companion to my mother and helped to raise me. After the incident on the *Algiers*, I was adopted by an older couple from Liverpool, Morris and Diana Travers. Hence my surname. They knew little to nothing about my mother, except what Aunt Matilda told them. They welcomed her into our lives and, though she never lived with us, she did visit often during my boyhood and I became close to her."

Lamb was uncertain if Travers was lying. But he decided that if Travers in fact did not know the full truth of his mother's past and her connection to Elton House that informing him of this could wait. Travers's ignorance would not hinder his inquires for the moment and the matter could be sorted out in due time.

"Tell me about Alan Fox," Lamb said, purposely phrasing the question in a way that made it sound as if he believed that Travers knew Fox.

"Alan Fox? I know no one of that name. Should I?"

"So neither your aunt, nor Mrs. Lockhart, nor anyone at the sanatorium has ever spoken to you of Alan Fox?"

"No. Who is he?"

"He also was a passenger on the *Algiers* and for a brief time was suspected of having pushed your mother into the sea. He is also a resident of Marbury—or he was until last night, when he was shot to death."

"My God," Travers said. "Marbury? But I'm sorry, Chief Inspector, I don't know the man at all. And if you say that he was on the *Algiers* then I have no choice but to believe you. But other than my mother and my aunt, I don't know who was on that ship; indeed, I have no memory of the incident at all, though Janet has been helping me to pull bits and pieces of it to the surface."

The surface, Lamb thought. *All of the bits and pieces—the secrets and lies—now were coming to the surface, like so much detritus breaking free from a sinking ship.*

THIRTY-ONE

—◦◦◦—

RIVERS ARRIVED AT THE HOSPITAL BEARING THE SIGNED WARRANT to search Elton House and ready to debrief Lamb on his and Wallace's interrogations of Matilda Stevens and Janet Lockhart on the previous night.

"Lockhart admitted that she and Travers have become lovers," Rivers said. "She claimed to be surprised that Travers would have tried to kill himself and said outright that she believes Stevens spiked his sherry. According to her, Travers has agreed to give Stevens some of his money—apparently he's worth a bundle—and Lockhart believes that Stevens has in effect 'hypnotized' him—that was her word—into doing her bidding. For her part, Stevens flatly denied all of this and turned it on Lockhart. She said Lockhart had been filling Travers's head with a lot of nonsense about communing with the dead and that that is why Travers tried to kill himself."

Lamb told Rivers what he had discovered from his conversation with Travers.

"Bloody hell," the detective inspector said, stunned. "Do you believe him?"

"About the sedatives, yes. I don't see him as having a reason to kill himself. I'm not sure about the rest of it. He claimed to have no knowledge of Fox."

"We'll have to go after Stevens as soon as possible, then."

"Yes. I'm going to have Hornby call her and tell her that Travers never regained consciousness and has died. Hopefully that will keep her in place at least for a while. As soon as I'm done with him, we'll discuss the best way to approach her and the search of Elton House."

Lamb now turned his attention to Hornby. The two sat facing each other in a pair of chairs in the room in which Lamb had left Hornby under guard.

Although he was grateful for Hornby's efforts on behalf of Travers, he nonetheless wasted no time in pressing the doctor. He informed Hornby that he had obtained a warrant to search Elton House on suspicion of Hornby having violated the law prohibiting abortion and that he intended to charge Hornby under the act, never mind the additional charges that would follow if he found stolen lend-lease goods hidden in the house.

"I *will* find what I am looking for, Doctor," Lamb said. "Despite your denials. But if you cooperate with me now, I will cite that in arguing for a mitigation of your punishment. As it is now, you face a possible charge of treason. I also might be able to help you with the trouble you will face with whoever put you up to this. From my experience, they hate those they consider snitches and like to take their revenge. They have long tentacles that reach even into prison."

"But this would mean the end of my practice—my mission," Hornby said in a pleading tone.

Lamb thought that Hornby seemed not to have understood what he had just told him. He seemed unconcerned with the fact that he faced a long prison sentence and the possible retribution of the gang with which he'd conspired to hide the stolen lend–lease goods.

The doctor covered his face with his hand for a second and sighed deeply. He looked at Lamb. "But don't you see, Chief Inspector?" he said. "You must. You were on the Somme. You must see that what I am doing is important."

"But I'm afraid you are the one who is failing to see the truth. If I find what I believe I will find at Elton House, your practice is finished. I'm offering to help you possibly receive some mercy from the court and to protect you in prison."

"But everything I've done is to make the sanatorium work for the benefit of the men I treat," Hornby said. "And I've succeeded in that. Ask Travers himself; he will tell you."

"Nevertheless, I've given you a choice, Doctor," Lamb said flatly. "I strongly advise you to cooperate, or you will have much more than the end of your practice to worry about."

Hornby slumped in his chair. He seemed nearly about to cry, Lamb thought. He looked at the floor and said, in almost a whisper, "I don't know where it's hidden."

He looked up. "I swear to you, Chief Inspector. I agreed to it only for the money. A man came to me not long after I bought the house. He offered me a very large sum of money, up front, in cash. He said he wanted to use the cellars of the house to store goods. I told him I wasn't aware of the cellars; but he assured me they existed. All I needed to do was to give them access to the rear doors of the house and they would handle the rest. The only proviso was that I ask no questions. I was to forget about the cellars. I was not to look for them or speak of them. And I was to take on a man of his choosing as gardener, who would 'keep an eye on things,' as the man put it."

"Joseph Lee."

"Yes."

"So Lee had a key to the house?"

"Yes."

"And he knew where the goods were stored?"

"I can only assume. I kept up my end of the bargain. The man gave seven hundred and fifty pounds in cash on the very day on which we spoke and promised that, if all went as he hoped, I would receive another seven-fifty a year hence, which I have received. Had it not been for that money I would not have been able to keep the sanatorium open."

"Did they make use of the lorry in the carriage house?"

"Again, I can only suppose. I was as surprised to see that lorry there as you must have been. I had no idea that it had been stored there. When I showed you the stables I was certain they were empty."

"Who was the man who offered you the deal?"

"He said his name was William Smith. I knew it was an alias. I don't know his real name. He made it clear that if I compromised the operation I would pay what he called a 'severe' penalty. Then Lee was murdered. I knew I couldn't hush that up because it was simply too public, and that it would only look worse if I did. When I went to Southampton on the night Lee's body was found, I spoke to my contact. I explained to him what had happened and why I had acted as I did. He advised me merely to lay low and wait out the inquiry. In the meantime, if you or anyone on the police began to suspect anything regarding the goods I was to deny knowledge of it, and continue to deny it. He admitted that they had become worried about Lee; that they were getting word that he was acting strangely in public, saying too much. They were in the process of removing him, though I'm certain they didn't kill him—at least not in the way he was killed. They would have taken him elsewhere and made it appear as if he'd quit his job or just gone missing."

"Did you abort Theresa Hitchens's unborn child?" Lamb asked.

"Yes," the doctor muttered, so quietly that Lamb almost didn't hear him. "Again, I needed the money."

"Alan Fox paid you for the operation. Was he in attendance?"

"Yes."

"Did he leave with Theresa afterward?"

Hornby nodded.

"Did Nurse Stevens assist you?"

"Yes."

"When the air raid came, where did you and the patients and your staff take shelter?"

"In the cellar, the kitchen mostly; there's also a pantry."

"Was anyone among the staff or patients absent during the raid?"

"No. I took the count myself."

"Did anyone leave the house later that night, or in the early morning hours?"

"Not that I know of, though Nurse Stevens has a penchant for wandering about at night. She has trouble sleeping."

"Did you know or suspect that James Travers had developed a closer-than-normal relationship with Janet Lockhart?"

"I suspected it, yes."

"But you never confirmed your suspicions?"

Hornby looked at the floor again and shook his head. "I was too busy. I told myself I had nothing to fear from Janet Lockhart, in any case. I actually thought that she probably was doing Travers some good."

"Did you know that Janet Lockhart had a key to one of the rear doors of the house, through which she let herself in last night and used on other occasions to come and go after hours?"

"No."

"Were you aware that Alan Fox, Joseph Lee, Matilda Stevens, and James Travers shared a common event in their past and that this event also connected them to the death of Lady Catherine Elton, who had once been mistress of Elton House?"

Hornby looked up, clearly startled. "No. I had no idea. What incident?"

Lamb did not answer the doctor's question, but pressed ahead with his own. "But you did know that Matilda Stevens recommended to Travers that he come to the sanatorium for treatment."

"Yes, she knew his family and so knew of the problems he'd encountered since his breakdown in France."

"Do you know of any other connections Nurse Stevens has to James Travers?"

"No."

"Did she mention to you that Travers was prepared to give her a large sum of money, part of which she promised to donate to the sanatorium?"

Hornby again appeared shocked. "No, she said nothing to me of any donation. This is the first I'm hearing of it."

"How often does James Travers take a sedative?"

"Once a day, at lights-out, to help him to sleep. He suffers from nightmares. The kind of which you are aware, Chief Inspector."

"And is Nurse Stevens responsible for providing Travers with his sedative?"

"Yes."

"Now, sir, I want you to call Nurse Stevens and tell her that James Travers never recovered consciousness and has died and that you are taking care of matters here in Winchester. I also want you to make clear that she is in charge of the sanatorium until you return."

"But I thought we'd gotten to Travers in time," Hornby said.

"We did," Lamb said, and left it that.

THIRTY-TWO

—✺—

LAMB ARMED HIMSELF WITH A .45 CALIBER WEBLEY MARK IV, which he put into a holster beneath his jacket, and issued identical pistols to Wallace and Rivers. He intended to send uniformed men to guard the front and rear entrances of Elton House, to prevent anyone escaping, and then issue Nurse Stevens the warrant. His plan was to arrest her on a charge of violating the law and interrogate her while Rivers, Wallace, Larkin, Sergeant Cashen, and some uniformed constables, including Vera, searched the house, beginning with the cellar, including the kitchen and the strange corridor that contained the staircase that led nowhere.

The team quickly swarmed upon Elton House. Lamb rang the front door bell and announced the presence of police with a search warrant. A full minute passed, but no one answered. Lamb rang the bell again and rapped loudly on the door. He was on the verge of breaking down the door, when it opened and the young nurse to whom he'd spoken on the first day stood before him. The sight of so many policemen standing before the door surprised her.

Lamb showed her the warrant and announced that they had come to search the premises. The nurse stepped aside to let them in and watched the team file into the foyer in the same way a child might watch a group of exotic animals parade down a city street. Lamb asked the young nurse to fetch Stevens.

"She's gone into Winchester, to the hospital, to help Dr. Hornby with Lieutenant Travers," she said. "She left a note in the nurses' room explaining what happened last night."

"So you have not seen her at all this morning?" Lamb said, realizing that the nurse had not bought his ruse about Travers never regaining consciousness and dying.

"No, sir. I haven't seen her since last night. With her and Dr. Hornby both gone, the place has gone a bit awry, I'm afraid. There was no one here this morning to give the men their medicines."

"And Janet Lockhart? Has she been in today?"

"No, sir."

"Where is Nurse Stevens's room?" Lamb asked.

The nurse explained how to reach it. Lamb then sent Larkin and Cashen to search it, discreetly telling Cashen before they left: "Turn it upside down if need be."

He turned back to the young nurse. "Are you in charge, then?"

"Yes, sir. I suppose I am."

"All right then, miss. No one is to leave the house, either staff or patients, until I say it is permitted. Is that understood?"

"Yes, sir."

With that, Lamb went with the others to begin the search of the cellars, though he gathered them in the kitchen for a brief meeting first.

"It appears that Nurse Stevens is on the run," he said. "Either that, or she's holed up somewhere here on the property. She won't have known that we'd be searching the house today, so, if she is hiding in the house or on the grounds, and waiting for an opportunity to make an escape, that gives us an advantage. She's possibly armed, so we must proceed with that in mind."

Lamb then left the search of the kitchen in the hands of Wallace and the others, while he and Rivers went down the hall to search the alcove that contained the mysterious staircase. They found the door locked, but, taking turns, kicked it down with relative ease. They stepped into the narrow alcove and began to examine it with electric torches.

Rivers peered up the stairs to where they abruptly ended at the wall. "It must have been used as a direct way out of the cellar to the stables and was sealed off once the stables became redundant," he said.

"Yes," Lamb said. "I think there might be something beneath the stairs, a space of some kind. The nurse who answered the door said that Joseph Lee had tried to lure her here with the promise of showing her proof that the ghost of Lord Elton haunted the place. He had a key to the house and he might have rigged something up in here that he thought he could use to impress the young nurses."

"There had to have been a door up there at the top," Rivers said. "But if you're going to close off the place and wall up the door to the outside, why keep the bloody steps? Why not seal it off at the hallway and be done with it?"

"Unless you had a use for the steps," Lamb said. He began to ascend them, stomping hard on each one as he reached it.

"They don't sound solid," Rivers said.

Lamb carefully descended the steps back to their base, where he squatted and began moving the beam of his torch over each board, looking for a finger hole or some other way in which one of the boards could be removed. He saw what appeared to be a narrow opening at the place where the second step met its supporting board. He asked Rivers to shine his light upon the space as he tried to work his fingers into it. He felt the board give as he managed to get his fingers partly beneath it.

"This has been pried up before," Lamb said. He withdrew his fingers from the opening and said, "I need something else; something with more leverage."

"Wait here," Rivers said. He left the alcove and returned a few minutes later with a large metal soup spoon.

"This is all I could find," he said.

"It might do."

Lamb wedged the end of the spoon into the opening and began to work it like a lever. Gradually, the board began to come loose. After a few seconds the step popped free of the supporting board and Lamb found himself staring into a dark, open space beneath it. He shined his torch into this space and saw that it was deep enough to accommodate a standing man, though it was only as wide as the steps. He noticed the stubs of several candles lying on the stone floor.

Lamb began to work on the step above the one he removed and soon lifted it free. He tugged at the supporting board between the two, but could not move it. Then he realized that he might be trying to free it the wrong way and instead tried yanking it upward, which did the trick.

Lamb played his torch into the space again, expecting to see some sort of ladder or other method of climbing down into the pit but saw nothing.

"Let's get one of the chairs from the kitchen," he said to Rivers, who returned a minute later with one of the stout wooden chairs. Lamb began to undo his necktie and asked Rivers to do the same. Lamb knotted the ties together and then knotted one end of the make-shift rope to one of the chair's rear slats. He then carefully lowered the chair into the hole so that it came to rest upright on the stone floor, with its seat about four feet below the rim.

"We should be able to lower ourselves onto the chair without breaking our necks," Lamb said. He went first, turning so that he faced the rear wall of the hole, after which he easily lowered himself to the chair. He stepped off the chair onto the stone floor and waited for Rivers, who also made the descent without incident.

They shined their torches into the chill, dark space that lay before them—seemingly a tunnel that went on for some distance. Lamb led the way forward, away from the chair. Neither spoke, as they listened for some telltale sound that might give them a clue as to what lay ahead.

They moved forward roughly the length of the staircase, which ran above their heads, before they found themselves facing another wall—though this one, unlike the one above, was not made of stone, but of brick that appeared to be very new indeed. Lamb reckoned that they had come to a point that put them at a place just beneath the rear wall of the house. He shined his light on the wall and ran his hand over it.

"Still smooth," he said. "It can't be more than a few years old."

"So the tunnel goes on—or it did?" Rivers said.

"It must."

The two became silent again as they tried to picture in their minds where the tunnel led—beneath the rear courtyard and then under the carriage house . . .

"Bloody hell," Lamb said aloud.

"What is it?"

"The lorry."

"Which lorry?"

Lamb turned and began to move back to the chair.

"We're in the wrong damned place," he said.

THIRTY-THREE

—∞—

AS LAMB AND RIVERS WERE EXITING THE HOLE, LARKIN APPEARED
at the door to the alcove, holding several items that he and Sergeant
Cashen had found in Matilda Stevens's room. The two detectives
followed Larkin into the hall, where the forensics man showed them
three .38 caliber bullets.

"These were in the top drawer of her dresser," he said. "Just lying
there, scattered about. It's possible she had a box of them and these
three fell out as she removed it. We've found no pistol, though."

He then produced a half-dozen nine-inch-long white candles
he'd found stored in a box beneath the nurse's bed. "They look to be
identical to the stubs we found by the lake and in Lee's cottage and
those you found at Lord Elton's gravesite," he said.

Finally, the forensics man handed Lamb a paper lily.

"We found several of these as well," he said. "They were in the
same box as the candles, under the bed, along with a box of matches.

She also has a small typewriter in her room, along with several sheaves of writing paper."

"Excellent work, Mr. Larkin," Lamb said.

But he hadn't the time to stop for more. "Let's go, Harry," he said to Rivers, and the two hustled down the hall to the kitchen, where Lamb grabbed Wallace and searched for a heavier tool than the soup spoon. He found a meat cleaver he thought would suffice. The three detectives then left the kitchen and moved across the courtyard to the door of the carriage house.

Lamb brought the meat cleaver down on the old padlock and chain that ensnared the doors—once, then twice, then a third time, before the lock cracked open. Lamb removed it and opened the double doors, moving right to the small delivery van.

"Hornby claimed he hadn't known this lorry was in the carriage house," Lamb said. "And yet it had fresh mud on its tires when I checked it yesterday, meaning that it has to have been moved recently. The problem is, though, that the mud is only on the front tires. The rear tires are clean. But at the time I couldn't see why that was."

He pointed at the house.

"The tunnel would have come out of the house over there and led here if you follow a straight line." He looked at Rivers and Wallace. "What if Lord Elton's ancestors made their fortune two centuries ago by smuggling—cotton, rum, whatever it might have been, and all of it to avoid paying the steep tariffs the government levied to pay for its wars with the French? Smuggling was common round here then. Even the clergy took their cut from time to time. They built these tunnels to hide the contraband until they could sell it, and I think whoever employed Hornby is using the cellars for the same purpose now, only the contraband is lend-lease goods stolen off the American ships coming into South-ampton and Portsmouth. But they first had to disconnect the tunnels from the house, in case someone working in the sanatorium stumbled upon one of the entrances. So they walled them and up and created other entrances, apart from the house. They've kept the stables and carriage house locked, just as they've been for twenty-five years or more."

He turned toward the small lorry. "That's why the front tires are muddy, but the rear ones aren't," he said. "They have to push its nose into the courtyard to uncover the access hole. I should have seen it before but was too bloody dense."

Lamb climbed into the vehicle and made certain it was out of gear. Then he went to the back and began to push the vehicle forward; Wallace and Rivers moved to assist him. A few seconds later they had pushed the van's nose through the door and into the courtyard. "Stop here," Lamb said.

He looked at the floor that had been hidden beneath the lorry and saw what he expected to see—a wooden trap door. It was about two feet square with a pair of black iron hinges at one end and a U-shaped iron handle at the other. Next to the handle was a metal flap and eye fastened with a new padlock.

"This one is going to take more muscle to get loose," Lamb said. He looked at Wallace and said, "Have at it, please, David."

Wallace went at the lock with the meat cleaver as if he were Jack the Ripper, and a minute later had cracked it open and removed it.

Lamb pulled up the door to reveal another darkened pit like the one beneath the stairwell in the cellar, though this one had a newly built wooden stair leading into it.

"It's here," Lamb said. "This is the rest of the tunnel."

"Shall I go first, sir?" Wallace asked.

Lamb nodded. "Look for a light switch. They won't have been working in the dark."

Wallace eased himself through the opening and down the steps and had a look round with his torch. "It leads both ways," he said. "Back toward the house and in the opposite direction as well."

He scanned the wall for a light switch and found one less than a foot from the opening. A line of bare lightbulbs strung along the tunnel's ceiling flashed on, illuminating the tunnel in both directions.

Lamb moved down the stairs next, followed by Rivers. The tunnel was just wide enough for the three of them to stand shoulder to shoulder within it, while the ceiling was high enough that they could move without stooping. Lamb pointed his torch down the corridor that led in the opposite direction, toward the unknown. He withdrew the pistol from the holster beneath his jacket; Rivers and Wallace followed suit.

"If she's down here, we have to assume she's armed," Lamb said, repeating his earlier warning. He looked at Wallace. "Don't fire unless I give the command."

Wallace nodded.

"All right, then. Let's see what's down the other end of this bloody hole."

—⁂—

Lamb led the way, with Rivers behind him and Wallace following. The dim, close-in walls reminded Lamb of those of the trenches on the Somme and he wondered if the tunnel was dredging up similar memories for Rivers. Lamb slowed, looked back over his shoulder, and whispered, "Are you all right, Harry?"

"I'll let you know if the bullets start flying," Rivers said drily.

They moved forward another fifteen or so yards when Lamb's beam suddenly fell upon several wooden crates stacked upon each other in what looked to be a place where the tunnel widened, forming a kind of small room. They moved into this space, which was about six feet or so wider than the tunnel and went on for about twenty feet before narrowing again. Here, they found the walls on either side of them stacked with the wooden crates, each of which was about four feet long by perhaps three feet high and three wide, and marked in black lettering that read: PROPERTY OF THE UNITED STATES ARMY.

"I'd say we hit the jackpot," Wallace whispered.

"This has to let out at a place somewhere down the hill from the house," Lamb said. "They can't have left it with only one way in and one out."

"Lee's cottage, maybe?" Rivers said. "It would be down the slope as the crow flies and if the gang employed him to watch over this lot then it would make sense that he had access. Though when I searched I saw nothing that looked like a trap door."

"Or that decrepit little bloody ice house," Lamb said.

He spoke to Wallace. "Go back and tell Cashen what we've found. Suspend the rest of the search and get three or four men down here to secure this place. Then I want you to take no less than two men with you to Lee's cottage and the old ice house to see if you can find the other end of this hole. Harry and I will go forward from here."

Wallace nodded, turned, and disappeared down the tunnel.

Lamb and Rivers readied to move again—but Rivers halted suddenly when he thought he heard a sound coming from the unexplored end of the tunnel.

"Did you hear that?" he whispered.

"No."

Rivers peered forward, and moved a bit ahead of Lamb. "It sounded like a muffled voice, a kind of muttering."

From just up the tunnel, they heard a woman yell, "Help!"

Lamb recognized Janet Lockhart's voice.

In the next instant the lights strung along the ceiling went out. Lamb heard a shot and saw a muzzle flash ahead; he heard Rivers grunt, "Jesus," and saw Rivers's torch fall to the ground and rattle against the stone floor. Instinctively, Lamb pressed his back against the boxes. Rivers seemed to have fallen, though he could not tell for certain in the darkness, which was blindingly complete. Another muzzle flash lit up the blackness as a second shot fired. Lamb heard the bullet whiz past him, inches from his chest. He went to his belly. His immediate instinct was to return fire, but he did not want to risk shooting Rivers in the confusion. Neither did he want to give away their position by calling to Rivers. He briefly played the beam of his torch along the stone floor up the corridor and caught sight of Rivers crawling toward him. He doused his torch and crawled forward until he collided with Rivers.

He grabbed the rear collar of Rivers's jacket and dragged him back along the floor to a place about two yards distant, where they sheltered against the wall behind some of the stacked crates. Lamb expected another shot, though none came.

Lamb whispered. "Where are you hit?"

"Right shoulder. Just a nick; hurts like bleeding hell, though."

Lamb briefly shone his light on Rivers. He removed a folding knife from his pocket and cut open the sleeve of Rivers's jacket and shirt, exposing the wound.

"Okay," he whispered. "You're not going to bloody die at any rate."

"Stevens, then?" Rivers said. "And she has Lockhart?"

"Yes."

Wallace had just reached the steps when the shot that hit Rivers was fired. He was about to head back into the tunnel when the second shot struck the stone wall just to his left. He went immediately to his stomach and scrunched himself as closely as possible against the right tunnel wall, by the steps.

Sergeant Cashen was in the carriage house now, with Larkin. He heard the shot and looked down the hole, but could see nothing.

Lamb guessed that Stevens was heading for the other exit to avoid being trapped. He wanted to follow, but had to get Rivers help as soon as possible. He helped Rivers to his feet and wrapped his arm around the inspector.

"Can you walk?" Lamb asked.

"Yes."

"Off we go, then."

Lamb hustled Rivers back the way they had come, shielding his friend with his body and praying to God that a third bullet didn't strike him in the back.

As they reached the stairs, Wallace rose from the ground and helped Lamb hoist Rivers up to the waiting Cashen, who eased Rivers onto the floor of the carriage house, where he sat holding his wounded shoulder.

Lamb drew in a deep breath and steadied himself. "I think she's gone out the other way," he said. "We must get someone down the hill and find out where the tunnel lets out. I'm going to go back in from this way. We might be able to trap her. But we have to move now."

"I'll see to Rivers," Cashen said.

"I'll be all right," Rivers said crankily. "I just need a bandage."

Lamb asked Wallace, "Have you still got your pistol?"

Wallace patted the holster beneath his jacket. "Right here."

"All right," Lamb said, then he turned and descended the steps into the tunnel.

THIRTY-FOUR

—◊—

NURSE STEVENS KNEW WHAT LAMB HAD GUESSED: THE TUNNEL'S other secret entrance lay concealed within the old ice house. The escape hatch consisted of nothing more than a small square opening covered by a pair of floorboards that were hammered into stringers that contained small finger holes that could be used to lift them free.

A drunken Joseph Lee had shown Nurse Stevens the hole late one night as she ascended the path from Marbury after having lit a candle at Lord Elton's grave. Lee understood the nurse's importance to Dr. Hornby and had wanted to impress upon her the importance of his own station. And so he had stopped her—startling her at first—by the pond, in the dark of the wee hours, with the promise of revealing to her a secret of Elton house "that even Dr. Hornby himself does not know." He had then shown her the exit and demonstrated for her how to lift the floorboards. And he had told her where the tunnel led and what its purpose once had been, and what its purpose had become. He'd added that his "employers" had renovated and improved the tunnel so that it even boasted electric light.

"I've been down and had a look round myself a few times," Lee had boasted. "A person could hide down there for weeks and no one would know."

On the previous night, as she had retreated to her room to think after Lamb and Dr. Hornby had hustled James Travers to the hospital, Nurse Stevens remembered the tunnel and decided she would use it if necessary. She had shown the patience of a saint in bringing her plan to fruition and now it seemed that all was falling apart. Her only hope of not being found out was that James should never regain consciousness; if he did then the truth would be obvious to him.

When Hornby had called that morning to say that James had never awakened and had died in the night, she had first felt relieved. But almost immediately something—a suspicion—took hold of her and would not relent: What if Hornby were lying and Lamb had put him up to it? The eagerness with which the doctor had cooperated with Lamb on the previous night in transporting James to the hospital had given her pause. In the end, she had decided that she could not risk waiting to find out if Lamb had concocted a ruse designed to put her off her guard and that she must act to ensure her escape. On the other hand, she could not yet immediately run, as she had no motorcar. Then, too, she couldn't have predicted that Lamb would show up just as James was falling off to sleep and threaten everything. Neither had she counted on Janet Lockhart's interference and Lockhart's efforts to influence James and turn him against her.

It was then that she'd glanced out her window—which looked down upon the pond, where all of her trouble had begun so many years before—and seen the beam of a torch bouncing along the path and realized that Janet Lockhart was heading home. One of the detectives had interrogated her after they'd taken James away and she realized now that the police must also have spoken to Lockhart. She was certain the meddling bitch had blamed her for what had happened to James and would continue to do so if she allowed things to continue as they were. And so she had decided on a plan of action, hoping—believing—that she could once again escape fate and reinvent herself.

—◈—

Now, she reached the place in the tunnel that was just below the decrepit ice house, her .38 caliber revolver pointed at Janet Lockhart's head. A wooden ladder led from the floor of the tunnel to the hatch. She saw that she would have to unbind Lockhart's hands to get her up the ladder and through the hole.

"Turn round," she demanded.

She placed the torch on a step of the ladder so that its beam illuminated Mrs. Lockhart's back, and gently placed the pistol in the pocket of her smock. She then loosened the green cotton scarf she had used to bind Mrs. Lockhart's hands. This done, she retrieved the pistol and ordered Lockhart to turn back round.

"Get up the ladder and push the boards away," she said. "There are two of them. When that's done come back. If you try to run I'll kill you."

Terrified, Janet Lockhart did as Stevens commanded; the floorboards came loose easily and she descended the ladder.

Stevens ascended the ladder and lifted herself through the hole and into the old ice house. She pointed her torch and pistol down the hole at Mrs. Lockhart and ordered her to climb. A minute later, Stevens stepped out of the shed into the darkness, behind Janet Lockhart, at whose back she pointed her pistol.

The pond lay directly ahead of them, just beyond the trees, its surface glistening in the moonlight. Stevens intended to head down the path into Marbury. She hoped to find a car there, but if not, she would make her escape on foot. The situation was far from what she had planned, but she had found herself betrayed and left alone three times before in her life and survived each time. She intended to do so again now.

She pushed Lockhart forward and commanded her to move. As they emerged from the wood and onto the path, Wallace, Larkin, and the uniformed constables, including Vera, arrived at the pond. Wallace saw them first and yelled for them to halt.

Stevens pointed the gun at Mrs. Lockhart's head. "No closer!" she called out. "I'll shoot her and any one of you who moves."

Stevens aimed the pistol at the sky and fired a single warning shot that echoed over the pond and up and down the path.

Wallace raised his hand; his group halted about thirty yards from where Stevens held Mrs. Lockhart. They froze there in a standoff.

Lamb was just struggling out of the hole in the garden shed when he heard the shot. He saw, illuminated by the moonlight, the figures on the pathway—one woman clutching another, who he knew must be Matilda Stevens and Janet Lockhart. Neither seemed to be wounded and Lamb guessed that Stevens had fired a warning shot—or so he hoped. From where he stood, he could not see Wallace and the others but knew that they must be close.

Rivers, his shoulder now wrapped in a makeshift bandage Cashen had applied, also heard the shot. He stood with the sergeant in the kitchen of Elton House.

"Holy Jesus," he said and ran out the door and toward the pond with Cashen at his heels. As they reached the path, they saw Wallace and the others stopped cold about fifty yards distant, and beyond them the dark figures of Stevens and Lockhart.

"Stay here and make sure no one from the house comes down here," Rivers ordered Cashen. Then he moved off the path to the left and began to make his way slowly toward the pond under the cover of the bushes and young trees that grew along the pathway and along the pond's edge. Some of the patients and nurses had become aware that something was happening at the pond and begun peering out the windows toward it.

Lamb had to think quickly. He did not intend to let Stevens pass unmolested as long as she held Janet Lockhart hostage. His conversation with Travers had left him convinced that the nurse probably was desperate and might kill Lockhart and even, perhaps, attempt to kill herself if she concluded she had no other way out. The plan she seemed to have set in motion a long time ago—perhaps as far back as the incident on the *Algiers*—was coming unraveled before her eyes, and just at the moment that she must have believed that all of her efforts and scheming finally had come to fruition.

Stevens began to back down the path, her arm still wrapped tightly round Mrs. Lockhart, who was visibly quaking, and the gun pointed at her head. Lamb saw that her only route of escape lay down the hill and so began to move through the wood in that direction. He made it to the path and stepped onto it just below the place where Stevens and Lockhart were, cutting off Stevens's route to Marbury.

"That's far enough, Nurse Stevens," he said.

Stevens turned quickly round and saw Lamb. She moved toward the left side of the path, jerking Lockhart with her. She looked back up the path at Wallace and the others, then down at Lamb, frankly surprised that he stood unprotected in the middle of the path with his hands raised. By now, Rivers had reached Wallace and stood with him and the others.

"You haven't any place to go," Lamb said. "Let Mrs. Lockhart go and we will talk."

"Back away," Stevens said to Lamb. She pressed the pistol against Mrs. Lockhart's temple. "I'll do whatever I have to do."

"I believe you," Lamb said. "That's why I'm willing to offer you a deal. I spoke with Travers this morning and I know everything. I have a car parked just up the hill. Exchange me for Mrs. Lockhart and I give you my word that I will make sure you get what was promised to you, along with a ten-hour head start. It's not much of a deal, I agree, but it's better than what you're facing now. Look round you; you're surrounded and have no place to go. Killing Mrs. Lockhart will only ensure that you hang. But I'm offering you a chance, at least."

"You're lying."

"I'm willing to use myself as collateral. Let Mrs. Lockhart go and you can take me as your hostage. It's your only chance."

"What about your men?"

"They'll do as I command them. I promise you that they will stand down for ten hours."

Nurse Stevens looked nervously up and down the path a second time. Rivers, Wallace, Vera, and the others stood their ground.

"I'm armed," Lamb said. "I'm going to open my coat now and remove my pistol from its holster and throw it into the wood. I want to prove to you that I mean what I say. Here I go now. Don't be alarmed."

"What is he doing?" Wallace whispered to Rivers.

"I don't know."

As Vera watched her father, a feeling of dread flooded her, and she had to stop herself from running to him.

Lamb slowly unbuttoned his coat, withdrew the pistol from its holster, and tossed it into the wood's edge.

"You see?" he said. "I'm willing to take the risk. Are you?"

Stevens already had decided to say yes to Lamb's offer, though she had no intention of going with him to his car. Instead, she had her own plan about what she wanted to do next and she needed Lamb to ensure that she could carry it out to its rightful end, unlike the old plan that he and Lockhart and the rest of them had ruined. She could see it clearly now; even Hornby had betrayed her, as had Lee, who had stumbled back into her midst at exactly the wrong time and place, forcing her to remove him for good and all.

"All right," she said to Lamb. "Come here and stand between myself and your men."

Lamb did as she asked. Once he was in position, Nurse Stevens let Janet Lockhart go—she'd grown exhausted of clinging to Lockhart and was glad to be rid of her—and stuck the barrel of her gun into the small of Lamb's back, as Janet Lockhart ran into the wood near the spot where Lamb had exited it a minute earlier.

"Go find her," Rivers said to Wallace as the pair of them watched Lockhart disappear into the wood. "And keep quiet. Stevens mustn't know."

Wallace slowly moved to the rear of the clutch of policemen standing on the path so that Stevens could not see him enter the wood. Vera was there, at the back. She touched Wallace's arm and said, "Be careful, David, please."

"I will," Wallace promised, then moved into the wood.

Stevens shoved the gun firmly into the small of Lamb's back. "Tell them to leave," she said. "I want the lot of them gone. If I see even a hair of any one of them I will shoot you dead."

Lamb looked again at the group gathered up the path and was surprised—but heartened—to see Rivers's familiar figure among them. He reckoned that Rivers must have sent someone through the wood to fetch Mrs. Lockhart.

"Stand down and go back to the house," he said to the group. "No one is to follow or Nurse Stevens will shoot me."

"I understand," Rivers said, more for Stevens's sake than Lamb's.

Rivers herded Larkin, Vera, and the others up the path toward the house.

Stevens, who had no intention of following Lamb to his car—or of going to the gallows—now put her alternative plan into action. A part of her had always known that she would end her life in this way and indeed she had longed to do so since the day her sister had stolen from her the only man she had ever loved.

She had tried to grab for herself what she wanted and deserved in life—to boldly take it, as her sister had done time and again. Now she would have the one prize in the next life that had so cruelly eluded her in this, the man whose spirit she was certain dwelled in its true final resting place, the pond of Elton House.

THIRTY-FIVE

—◦◦◦—

AS STEVENS BEGAN TO MARCH LAMB ALONG THE PATH BACK TOWARD Elton House, Rivers sent Cashen to lock down the building, then moved the rest of the team into the rear courtyard, where he sequestered them behind the carriage house. He wondered what the nurse was on about and if she actually believed Lamb's promise that he would give her his car and ten hours' lead. He worried that she had something else entirely different in mind.

Rivers moved alone to the stone wall built into the slope opposite the house and stole a peek over the rampart in an effort to follow what was unfolding by the pond.

Lamb also wondered what Matilda Stevens actually had in mind. He did not believe that she had really bought into his offer and had agreed to it only to buy herself time to think and a chance at escape.

He kept himself poised to jump at any opportunity to disarm her or, failing that, to act in accordance with whatever Rivers was planning.

Even so, he was surprised when Stevens told him to leave the path and begin to move along the edge of the pond toward the rickety pier and dinghy that lay in the grass near it. He began to get an idea of what she might be planning.

"I know what you want," he said. "It was you, wasn't it, who put the candles and flowers on his grave, you who tossed the lily onto the pond. You knew him once; he was your sister's husband. And this is where he died."

Stevens said nothing.

The sight of Stevens marching Lamb toward the pier alarmed Rivers, who had also gotten an inkling of what the nurse might be intending. Holding his aching shoulder, he hurried back to the carriage house, where he addressed the uniformed men, Larkin, and Vera.

"I need the strongest swimmer among the lot of you."

Vera spoke up first. "I was swimming champion of my secondary school."

"Can anyone else swim?" Rivers asked.

"I can give it a try," Larkin said.

Rivers looked at the forensics man and his thick glasses; he was well aware that Larkin could barely see without his glasses. "Thank you, Mr. Larkin, but there can be no shortcuts. Anyone else?"

No one raised a hand.

Rivers looked hard at Vera. He would have preferred someone who was better trained. But neither did he want to be left with a man floundering about in the pond when every move they made from here out would be crucial.

"There can be no room for error—and no holding back," he said to Vera, fixing her with his eyes. "No hesitation or second thoughts when the moment comes. Do you understand?"

The words terrified Vera. Even so, she knew she should not—could not—back away from doing whatever Rivers thought was necessary to save her father.

217

"I understand," she said.

Rivers nodded. "Come with me, then," he said.

By this time, Wallace had located Janet Lockhart as she had been moving through the wood toward the house. He had expected her to be hysterical but instead found that she had remained remarkably steady. He guided her up the hill through the wood, where they passed the old ice house. From there, they saw what was unfolding at the pond.

Nurse Stevens stood by the dinghy, pointing her pistol at Lamb.

"My God," Mrs. Lockhart said. "She's going to kill herself; I know it. And she probably intends to shoot the chief inspector too."

"Can you make it up the hill the rest of the way on your own?" Wallace asked.

"Yes, of course."

"All right, then. Go quickly. Someone up there will find you."

As Mrs. Lockhart moved away, Wallace sat on the ground and quickly removed his shoes and socks and jacket. He pulled the pistol from its holster and moved toward the pond. The last time he had found himself in a similar situation he had nearly bollixed everything by moving too hastily. He resolved not to allow that to happen this time.

At the same moment, Rivers and Vera were moving down the hill—Vera barefoot—through the cover of the young trees to the edge of the pond that was opposite the one on which Lamb and Nurse Stevens stood. They stopped about five feet from the pond and sheltered in the high grasses on their stomachs.

Rivers's plan was to first attempt to get off a clean shot to fell Matilda Stevens—a feat he knew would be close to impossible to achieve as long as the nurse kept Lamb close to her. Failing that, he would wait for the right moment to fire a shot into the air, hoping to startle the nurse and knock her off balance for at least an instant, during which Lamb could act to disarm Stevens and Vera could rush to assist him. Rivers reckoned that the nurse intended to use the dinghy in some way and he had instructed Vera to go into the water and do whatever she could capsize the little boat as he covered her.

Sure enough, they saw Lamb step into the dinghy and sit in its bow, as Stevens, who still held the gun on him, seated herself in the stern.

Vera's heart throbbed and she realized that she had begun to perspire heavily.

Rivers laid his hand upon her shoulder and said, "I know that you are frightened and so am I. But it will all go very quickly."

Stevens ordered Lamb to take up the oars and begin rowing toward the center of the pond.

"I know about the *Algiers*," Lamb said as the little boat began to nose away from the pier. "I know that Lady Elton was your sister and that James is her son, and that Alan Fox pushed her into the sea and got away with it."

"Alan Fox was a coward," Stevens said. "*She*, on the other hand, had true courage, real strength. But she stole Henry from me and, no matter how much I loved and admired her, I could never forgive her for that. She always acted in her interests firsts, but I was too weak to follow her lead in that and she knew it. I'm changing that now. She took his body, but his spirit remains here, in this pond where she discarded him. She threw him away. But I never let him go; I always kept him close. Now I shall join him."

They reached the center of the pond.

Wallace watched from just inside the wood, also hoping to get off a shot at Stevens. But she was too close to Lamb and the boat was moving too steadily to risk it. Even so, he raised his pistol and readied to squeeze off a shot the instant he believed that Stevens intended to shoot Lamb.

Stevens commanded Lamb to stop rowing and the little boat began to drift. For perhaps twenty seconds no one spoke or made even a sound. Dead silence pervaded the pond. In the next instant, Stevens stood and raised the pistol and whispered to herself, "I'm coming, Henry."

"Go," Rivers said to Vera, who ran toward the pond and dove into it headfirst.

Rivers stood and fired his pistol into the air, startling everyone, including Wallace, who at first thought that the shot had come from Stevens's gun and that he had been too late. And yet he saw Lamb standing. In the same instant he saw someone dive into the pond just beyond the boat and so he limped to the pond as fast as his bad leg would carry him, leapt in, and began to swim furiously toward the boat.

When Rivers fired the gun, Stevens froze and instinctively turned in the direction from where the shot had come, giving Lamb the opening he had sought. He stood and flung himself at Stevens, rocking the little boat. They both lost their balance and tumbled into the pond, Stevens falling backward and losing her grip on the pistol, which fell into the water.

Lamb hit the water face-first, his body atop Stevens's. A second later the pair were struggling beneath the opaque green surface of the pond, their feet becoming tangled in the long aquatic grasses that sprouted from the muddy bottom. Lamb pushed himself free of Stevens and surfaced, gasping. In the next instant, Stevens also raised her head above the water. Their eyes met; Stevens moved her arms beneath the water in an attempt to escape Lamb. But he dove toward her and caught her by the collar.

"Let me go!" she said.

Lamb got his arm around her neck and began to pull her toward the bank closest to the house, where Rivers was now wading in to help.

Vera reached them and helped her father to subdue the kicking, struggling Matilda Stevens. Then Wallace arrived and the three of them pulled the nurse to the bank, where Rivers, who had gone into the pond up to his knees, helped to pull her ashore with his good arm.

All of them were soaked to the skin and partly entangled in long blades of the pond grasses, which clung to their shoulders and arms. Wallace and Lamb turned Stevens over and Wallace secured her hands behind her back with cuffs that Rivers handed to him.

"Let me go, damn you!" the writhing Nurse Stevens gasped. "I want to go to Henry."

THIRTY-SIX

TWO DAYS LATER, LAMB STOOD YET AGAIN ON THE EDGE OF THE pond at Elton House, this time with Superintendent Harding, as they watched two three-man teams probe the pond from row boats, searching for Matilda Stevens's pistol and, Lamb hoped, Alan Fox's painting of what he believed depicted Lady Elton drowning as the *Algiers* steamed away over the horizon.

In the wake of the standoff two days earlier, Lamb had found himself in the hospital in Winchester, where doctors examined Janet Lockhart, Matilda Stevens, himself, Vera, and Wallace, and released each with a clean bill of health. They had also properly treated and bandaged Harry Rivers's shoulder.

Lamb worried about the shock he knew Vera must have endured, though she had endeavored to keep up a brave front, telling him as he led her, soaking wet, back to Elton House that she needn't go to the hospital. Indeed, she was more concerned for him, asking repeatedly if he was all right. He had nonetheless insisted that she take a couple of days off, during which they would have the promised talk with her mother over her future. As they ascended the path to Elton House in their dripping clothes, Lamb had pulled Vera close to him and kissed her on the head.

"Thank you," he'd said. "I'm very proud of you."

To which she answered, shivering, "Thanks, dad. I'm proud of you too."

On the following day, Lamb had interrogated Matilda Stevens. She seemed to Lamb defeated and exhausted, the opposite of the frenzied woman he'd faced down on the previous day. She answered most of his questions in a subdued, flat voice that sounded noticeably older than the one he'd grown used to hearing.

He had gathered a trove of evidence against her, which included the items they had found in her room at Elton House, and which he laid out as they spoke—the candles, which proved identical to those they'd found in Lee's cottage, by the pond near Lee's body, and that Lamb had taken from Lord Elton's grave; the bullets, which matched one that Larkin dug from the stone wall in the tunnel beneath the carriage house; and the typewriter and a sheaf of writing paper that they successfully matched to the machine and the paper used to compose the love note Alan Fox supposedly had written to Theresa Hitchens and that had so upset Joseph Lee.

The team's search of the tunnels also had turned up, hidden among the boxes of stolen lend-lease goods, a fireplace poker wrapped in a towel that was stained with blood that matched Joseph Lee's type, along with Lee's fingerprints and those of Matilda Stevens. Larkin also recovered two sets of fingerprints on the pistol found lying next to Alan Fox's body—Fox's and Stevens's. Finally, Lamb had the newspaper clipping detailing the incident on the *Algiers*, the ship's passenger list, and the testimony of James Travers, portions of which Lamb had confirmed with Travers's solicitors, including the fact that Travers was set to give a large sum of money to Stevens, part of which she would then donate to the sanatorium in her name.

From this evidence and his interrogations of Stevens, Travers, and Janet Lockhart, Lamb had pieced together a narrative of the murders of Joseph Lee and Alan Fox.

The story began nearly forty years earlier in Southampton, when two sisters, ages thirteen and twelve, were orphaned after their parents died in a fire that had started in the grate of the hearth in their bedroom.

The girls—Catherine and Matilda Ambrose—had come of age in a children's home in Portsmouth. When Matilda was seventeen, she attended a charity event meant to raise money for the home, where she met one of its benefactors, a well-to-do young man named Henry Elton. She and Henry talked and, to Matilda's surprise, Henry told her that he found her to be very pretty and asked if he might visit her on the following day at the house. Everyone involved agreed the visit was a good idea, and so Henry Elton kept his promise and came to the home.

Catherine, who was a year older, had not wanted to go to the charity event and had feigned a fever to beg off. However, by the time Henry Elton appeared she had made a miraculous recovery and awaited his arrival in her best dress. Everyone, even Matilda, had to admit that Catherine was very beautiful in her dress, with her long auburn hair tied up in a neat bun and her large, expressive hazel eyes—and, indeed, once Henry Elton saw her, he was smitten and very soon politely cast Matilda aside in favor of her sister.

Although Matilda had fallen in love with Henry Elton, she swallowed this rejection, as she had other defeats that she had suffered at the hands of her older sister, who had always ruthlessly pursued what she wanted and—at least as far as Matilda was concerned—gotten it. Indeed, Catherine had so loathed their strict father that she had murdered her parents by purposely setting the fire that had killed them. Matilda had kept this secret all of her life.

Henry had married Catherine in 1912 and they spent two years traveling in Italy because the country's sunny landscape inspired

Henry, who fancied himself a painter. When the war began in 1914, they returned to Elton House. By then, Matilda had married a maritime man named Stevens. But the marriage had not lasted long and the two separated but never divorced—though Matilda kept her married surname because she reckoned that doing so might prove useful some day. She was, even then, bent on taking revenge on her sister for stealing Henry Elton from her, though she worried that she lacked her sister's cunning and ruthlessness and therefore might be no match for Catherine.

Then Catherine had done something that even Matilda had not expected. She killed Henry Elton, not in self-defense as she had claimed, but to inherit his money. Matilda knew that Catherine had seduced a sallow man from Marbury, Alan Fox, who, like Henry, fancied himself an artist, and convinced him to dump Henry's poisoned body in the pond with the promise that, once the deed was done, the two of them could be together. Although the scheme had nearly come undone, Catherine had seen it through and convinced a judge and jury that she, rather than her husband, had been the victim. She had never implicated Alan Fox in the scheme because she knew he could contradict her story. Her acquittal meant that she could inherit Henry Elton's fortune; once she secured it, she abandoned Fox and fled to Malta. Then, unknown both by name and reputation, she quickly ensnared an elderly, rich, dim, and lonely man named Charles Berkshire and bore him a son named James.

Matilda, who hated and loved her sister all at once, and had always been in thrall to Catherine—even to the point of helping Catherine set the fire that had killed their parents—had traveled with Catherine to Malta and acted as her female companion and nanny to James. Charles Berkshire had never known that she was Catherine's sister because both of the sisters had come to Malta under their married surnames.

Catherine eventually convinced Berkshire to make her the sole beneficiary of his will. Once she reckoned that enough time had elapsed that she could safely return to England and freshly green pastures under her new surname, she also killed Berkshire, just as she had killed Henry

Elton. She had learned her lesson, though, and before performing the deed this time she read extensively on the properties of poisons. In the end she had given Berkshire a dose of something—Matilda had never known what exactly, because Catherine had refused to tell her—that caused the old man to suffer a heart attack, which a coroner ruled as the cause of his death. Catherine also had written to Alan Fox, beckoning him to come to Malta and sail home with her and to help her establish herself anew in England, once again dangling before him the promise of their being together. She told him that she had left England not because she no longer cared for him but because she had to escape the country after the trial. Now she was ready to return—and return to him, she wrote. And Alan Fox had believed her.

Matilda also acquiesced—as she always had—though this time Catherine had promised to share her fortune with her, which now included both what was left of Henry Elton's estate and Charles Berkshire's as well. She meant to share her wealth with her younger sister, she had claimed, as a way of repaying Matilda for her long-suffering loyalty. But during the voyage on the *Algiers* Catherine admitted to Matilda that she intended to leave her fortune solely to her son. Matilda suspected her sister did so out of sheer cruelty—to humiliate Matilda and thereby keep her under her thumb.

But in fact even before this revelation Matilda had guessed that her sister was only lying to her anew about sharing the money and never intended to share it with her. And it was then that Matilda began to see the initial glimmerings of a way in which she could finally break free of her sister's grip and still take possession of some of Catherine's wealth. She didn't want it all, but neither did she intend to live through her sister's controlling charity. Indeed, she decided that she must become more like Catherine, strong and ruthless, in order to live in the way Catherine did. And she hoped that, in the end, when her life had run its course, she would be with Henry Elton once more as Catherine burned.

They sailed from Malta in April 1922—Catherine, Matilda, James, and Alan Fox, who had come to be with Catherine, just as she had instructed him to do. Matilda knew that Catherine had no intention of passing her life with the weak and errant Alan Fox, and that once Fox had outlived his usefulness to her she would reject him anew. And yet, at the same time, Matilda understood that Catherine had to tread lightly with Fox because he knew the truth behind Lord Elton's death. She reckoned that Catherine meant to push Fox into the sea at some point during the voyage, to be rid of him for good. Another man from her life gone as the result of an unfortunate accident.

And so it was on the *Algiers* that Matilda began the transition to the new person she hoped to become.

THIRTY-SEVEN

—◊—

LAMB RELATED THE STORY TO HARDING AS THEY WATCHED THE TEAM search the pond, adding that he remained unconvinced that Alan Fox had committed suicide.

"But I haven't been able to prove that yet," he told Harding, adding that, although Matilda Stevens had admitted to killing Joseph Lee she had steadfastly denied killing Fox and instead had accused James Travers, who also flatly denied killing Fox.

"Who is more creditable?" Harding asked.

"Travers, obviously, though I have to say that Stevens's denial bothers me," Lamb said. "She freely admitted to killing both her sister and Lee; she also admits to helping Travers plot to kill Fox but claims that Travers acted alone in the end. Travers claims that his aunt planted into his mind long ago, when he was just a boy, the idea that Fox had pushed his mother into the sea because Catherine had rejected him. After the old couple adopted James, he saw his aunt regularly at holidays and on other visits. But he claims he had no idea that Fox lived in Marbury. Indeed, to him Fox had always been a name only; his aunt had never shown him a picture of Fox, or told him anything of Fox's life, including where he lived or that he was a painter."

Harding stared out over the pond. "And yet she admits to having known Fox and that Lee was blackmailing him and that she eventually killed Lee to get him out of the way?" the superintendent asked, making sure he was following the twisted path of the story Lamb was unraveling for him.

"Yes, she killed Lee because she believed he was becoming too volatile and cocky, and worried that he might become a problem for her. You see, when she discovered that Hornby had opened a sanatorium for shell-shocked men at Elton House, she came to believe that Providence finally was moving in concert with her and saw the chance to bring her 'plan,' as she calls it, to its full fruition. She had been working as a private nurse off and on for nearly twenty years and so had the necessary experience. And once she was on the staff of the sanatorium she made herself indispensable to Hornby. Indeed, in some ways she essentially ran the place.

"From the beginning, her intention was to get Travers here for treatment and convince him to transfer a sum of his mother's fortune to her, part of which she promised to give to the sanatorium—to a fund for men who couldn't otherwise afford to be treated here. At the same time she began plotting a way to get rid of Alan Fox. She had kept a close eye on both Fox's and her sister's movements during the sea voyage from Malta and on the night her sister was killed she had brought Fox with her to the dining room and invited him to sit with her and Catherine, although she knew that Catherine had been seeking to limit her public interactions on the ship with Fox, so as not to come under suspicion of his death once she rid herself of him. But Matilda turned the tables on him and her sister later that same night. She knew that Catherine had a habit of spending a bit of time late each evening by the rail watching the sea, and told Fox that Catherine had asked her, Matilda, to tell him that Catherine wanted to meet him there to discuss their future together. But when Fox showed up, Catherine was surprised to see him and she tried to send Fox away, which Fox resisted. And that is when Matilda struck, darting from the shadows of the promenade deck and pushing Catherine into the sea, shocking Alan Fox. Matilda now was the only living soul, other than Fox himself, who knew that Alan Fox had helped Catherine Elton dispose of Lord Elton's body and so she made a sort of devil's pact with Fox then and there—her silence on his crime for his on hers. When they reached Belfast, several of the nosier first class passengers identified Fox as someone who had been seen trying to gain Catherine Berkshire's attention from time to time, and so police questioned him. But Stevens provided him an alibi by telling them that Fox had been with her in her cabin all that night and had never left."

Harding shook his head and emitted a heavy sigh. "Something always comes along to shock you anew, some new low in human depravity," he said. He stared at the men poking along the bank. "And so she then bludgeoned Lee to death in this very spot?"

"Yes. Hornby once told me that she had trouble sleeping and often went for walks late at night. But in fact she was visiting Lord Elton's grave, which is in the church cemetery, where she would light candles in his memory and occasionally leave paper lilies that she made herself. When I first interviewed her on the morning we found Lee's body, she denied having much interaction with Lee, though she saw him regularly and even befriended him. He understood her importance and tried his best to get her to notice him, even going so far as to showing her the tunnels. Lee was a stupid man and Stevens used that and Lee's eagerness for notoriety to her advantage. When she first came to the sanatorium she was surprised to find that Lee was the gardener; she remembered him as the man who had served as Alan Fox's steward on the *Algiers*, although he had no recollection of her, as he'd had no reason to encounter her aboard the ship. She reasoned that Lee might have come to Marbury because of some connection he maintained with Fox, and vowed to discover what that connection might be, believing that she might use it to her advantage. She flattered Lee's pretensions, pretending interest in the trivial subjects in which he considered himself an expert. She won his trust and he eventually told her that he was blackmailing Fox, and showed her the news clipping from Belfast, which he'd kept since the incident. It was one of many clippings Lee had collected, but the only one that he could use in a scheme to enrich himself. Once again, I think that he admitted all of this to Stevens because he believed that it would impress her."

Harding shook his head again. "Pathetic," he said.

"In the end, she did use Lee's connection to Fox to her advantage. Lee told her about his interest in Theresa Hitchens and she likely understood from the beginning that it was all a fantasy, as was so much of the rest of his life. She began to whisper in his ear that she had heard that Fox was a notorious Lothario who had his eye on Theresa—which, it turns out, was true. She wrote a bogus love letter that Fox was supposed to have written to Theresa in which he insulted Lee, hoping that this would spur Lee into a confrontation with Fox, which is exactly what happened. She told Lee that she had seen Fox drop the letter by the door of the pub and that she had swept in and nicked it on his behalf."

"She read Lee like a bloody book," the superintendent said.

"She had a knack for that," Lamb said. "She is a very intelligent woman who nonetheless has always felt vastly inferior to her sister. At any rate, Travers witnessed the set-to between Lee and Fox in front of the church as he was leaving Janet Lockhart's house after one of the sessions in which she put him in touch with his dead mother."

"Ridiculous," Harding said. "All this mumbo-jumbo about ghosts."

"But Travers believed in it. In fact, he believed in it so thoroughly that Stevens began to worry that Janet Lockhart was beginning to exercise undue influence over Travers's mind and emotions, and that he in turn was falling in love with Mrs. Lockhart. Stevens worried that Travers would see Lockhart as an older woman who could play the role of the mother figure he'd lost so many years ago. Because

Lockhart had convinced Travers that she could facilitate his communication with his late mother, she might become psychologically indispensable to him.

"Travers mentioned to Stevens on the following morning that he had seen Lee fighting with someone she recognized as Fox, confirming that the scheme had worked and she could now kill Lee and point the finger at Fox, which she did brilliantly. As she came up the hill from visiting Lord Elton's grave in the late hours, she found Lee drunk and sitting alone by the pond. She went to his cottage, retrieved the poker from the stove and killed him with it, after which she kicked his body into the pond. In doing so, she dropped one of the burnt-out candles she'd retrieved from Lord Elton's grave; it likely fell from her smock without her realizing it. Larkin found it and we found more of the same candles in Lee's cottage, all of which matched those we found in her room.

"A few hours later, Horace Hitchens came to the cottage to confront Lee about what he supposedly knew that could compromise or 'ruin' Alan Fox, as Lee had claimed in the pub after he'd fought with Fox. But Hitchens found Lee gone and so ransacked the place until he dug up what he was looking for—which turned out to be the newspaper clipping about Fox having been a suspect in Catherine Elton's death. The entire time in which Hitchens was tossing Lee's cottage, Lee was floating dead in the pond, but Hitchens never went to the pond. Stevens's plan in killing Lee was to point us at Fox, then to shoot Fox and make it appear that he had committed suicide because he'd buckled under the pressure of being a prime suspect in a murder and feared the gallows.

"But this is where her story diverges from Travers's. She claims that she and Travers planned Fox's murder together; that the two of them would kill Fox and together avenge Catherine Elton's murder. Stevens had spent a lifetime convincing Travers that Fox had pushed his mother into the sea and even that Travers himself had witnessed the killing but repressed that memory. What Travers didn't know is that Stevens then planned to do the same to him—to give him the sleeping pills and make it appear as if he had succeeded in doing what he had tried to do once before but failed in. She wanted them both out of the way so that she could enjoy living off the money Travers had agreed to give her—which, in the end, had been the money her sister had promised her and then cruelly withdrawn. Despite all this, she still steadfastly denies that she had any hand in Fox's death and that Travers killed Fox with a gun he brought solely for that purpose."

"But her fingerprints were on the gun and Travers's weren't," Harding pointed out.

"That's true," Lamb said. "Stevens claims that Travers tricked her into touching the gun—that he showed it to her one day as it lay in the drawer of the dresser in his room at the sanatorium and that she made the mistake of picking it up, though she only realized that this was a mistake later, after Travers shot Fox and then tried to frame her for the crime. She believes that, after that moment when she touched the gun, Travers handled it only with gloves. When I asked her the caliber of the pistol she claims Travers showed her, she said it was a .32, which is the caliber of the gun that fired the bullet that killed Fox. She says that, despite his outward appearance to the contrary, Travers has inherited his mother's ruthlessness. As she said to me, 'It's in his blood.'"

"Nonsense," Harding said. "We've got her to rights and she knows it, and so is making a last desperate attempt to implicate her nephew. She obviously cares nothing for him. She tried to bloody kill him after all, not to mention the fact that she took advantage of his having suffered shell shock to lure him here in the first place."

Lamb had to agree. All of what Harding said was true.

And yet, a small flame of doubt, like that of a candle burning down to its nub in a dark room, continued to flicker in the nether regions of his mind, illuminating a thought that he could not entirely dismiss.

What if Matilda Stevens was telling the truth?

THIRTY-EIGHT

—ᴍ—

SERGEANT CASHEN HAILED LAMB AND HARDING FROM THE BOAT in which he was searching. "We've got something, sir."

A minute later, Lamb was helping Cashen from the dinghy onto the dock, where a uniformed sergeant handed Lamb a small ceramic statue of what appeared to be a woman emerging from a deep green pool of water.

"No sign of the pistol or the painting yet, but we found this," Cashen said.

Lamb immediately recalled Lady Elton's so-called Ondine defense and the way in which Brandt had depicted her in his story for the *Times*—as a far cry from the victim she had convinced the judge and jury she was. And he remembered how Brandt had said that he'd spoken to a maid who had worked for the Eltons who had told him that she believed that Lady Elton, rather than her husband, had the interest in the tale of the water nymph and even that Lady Elton had kept a small, cheap statue depicting Ondine emerging from the water. Lamb was certain that the statue he now held in his hand—obviously cheaply made, its colors faded and detail less than fine—was the same one Lady Elton had kept and that she must have thrown it into the pond to ensure that no one outside the house would ever see or identify it. A sliver of pond grass clung to the figure's upraised right arm—the grass was exactly like that which had clung to him, Wallace, Vera, and Stevens as they had emerged from the pond two days earlier—and seeing this brought to the surface a memory from the depths of Lamb's mind.

"Ondine rising," he muttered to himself.

"What's that?" Harding asked.

"Ondine bloody *rising*," he said. "I had Fox's painting wrong; the drowning woman wasn't sinking, she was rising. She had sea grasses clinging to her hand as this one does and as I did, and Wallace and Vera and Stevens did, when Rivers pulled us from the pond."

"You're not making any sense, Tom," Harding said.

"Arthur Brandt said that Alan Fox painted his life—that he tended to depict the events of his life, which, at least to Brandt's mind, limited his range and ability as an artist. But there it was; Fox even doodled a little figure of a fox next to his bloody signature. He was a thoroughgoing narcissist in that way. It makes perfect bloody sense but I didn't see it—something that is sinking would not be entangled with underwater grasses, only something rising from the bottom would. Travers claimed he never met Fox, but I now think that is a lie. Fox painted Ondine rising because that's how it must have seemed to him—that Lady Catherine Elton was rising again into his life in the form of her son. James Travers must have seemed like a spirit come back from the dead to Alan Fox."

Lamb turned to look up the slope once again at the looming gray edifice of Elton House. "I must find Travers."

"But you released him," Harding said. "You had no cause to hold him."

"I might have made a mistake."

Lamb handed the statue back to Cashen. "Keep at it until you find the gun and the painting, if it's there," he said, then left the pier and headed up the path to Elton House.

—॰॰—

The sanatorium was in a mild state of disarray. The staff were preparing to send the patients home or move them to other facilities. In addition, Harding had informed the Home Office of the discovery of the stolen lend-lease goods, and in response the army had posted a sentry at the tunnel entrances until the material could be catalogued and moved.

Lamb went to Travers's room but found it empty and cleared of the lieutenant's possessions. After a brief search of the house, he found Nurse Anderson, whom Joseph Lee had tried to coax into the blind staircase in the cellar with the promise of seeing a ghost, who told Lamb that Travers had been to the house that morning but had not stayed long and had left about thirty minutes earlier with Janet Lockhart.

Lamb descended the hill and rapped on the front door of Janet Lockhart's cottage. When no one answered, he tried the door and found it open and went inside, where he found Mrs. Lockhart sitting silently in her living room before a single candle and a photograph of her late husband. She looked up at Lamb but said nothing.

"Where is James?"

"I don't know," she said without looking up.

"You just left Elton House with him not thirty minutes ago."

"I don't know what you mean."

"You can't protect him Mrs. Lockhart, and if you attempt to you will suffer the consequences."

She looked up at Lamb but did not speak.

"I see now that he lied to me about Alan Fox and that he did so not only to protect himself, but you," Lamb continued. "He didn't want you to become entangled in all of this because he'd fallen in love with you. After he shot Alan Fox, he took the painting from Fox's easel because he knew what it depicted."

Tears welled in Janet Lockhart's eyes.

"I fear that I am responsible," she said. "I thought I was helping him, but *she* had buried deep in his psyche the idea that Alan had killed his mother. She poisoned his mind for her own greedy ends."

"You must tell me where he is," Lamb said. "Otherwise he might hurt someone else. Surely you see that. Don't compound Matilda Stevens's sins. It's past time for the lying and the killing to end."

"He is at Arthur Brandt's," she said. "When he returned from Alan's cottage that morning, he had the painting, as you say. But I told him that we must hide it. The sun was only then rising and we had no time, so I suggested he hide it among the clutter in Arthur's study, to lean it against the wall and to pile some of the boxes and papers in front of it. And that is what he did, while Arthur slept."

"You knew, then, that he had shot Fox," Lamb said.

Mrs. Lockhart looked at Lamb, he eyes seeming to plead for his forgiveness.

"I was dazed and shocked," she said. "I couldn't believe that James had killed Alan; I refused to believe it. And now I've put Arthur's life in danger."

—ɯ—

Lamb rushed into Brandt's study to find James Travers standing with his back to the door, Fox's painting beneath his arm, and holding a small pistol aimed at Arthur Brandt, who stood very still by his desk, about three yards away, with his pet snake hanging from his shoulders and his hands in the air. Papers and other objects littered the floor.

Travers turned toward the door. He held the pistol high and told Lamb to put his hands up and not to move.

"I don't want to hurt anybody, Chief Inspector," Travers said. "But I will if you force me to."

"No one is going to force you to do anything, Mr. Travers," Lamb said.

"Now move out of the way," Travers said to Lamb.

Lamb did not move. "But where will you go, James? You haven't a car."

"Janet has a car."

"And how far do you think you'll get?"

Travers gestured with the gun. "Move aside, Chief Inspector," he said angrily. "Don't make me shoot you."

"I was on the Somme," Lamb said. "For an entire bloody year. I know what it was like—what you went through in France, how all of what you'd kept down since the time you were a boy must have come rushing back at you, forcing you to break down. Some of them must have called you a coward then. But you weren't a coward. I know; I saw it in the trenches, brave men breaking down. It got to all of us in the end, one way or another. You've nothing to be ashamed of in surviving. But why kill again? You had your reasons for killing Fox, but now the killing must stop. Think of those men you knew who died in France and how you grieved their loss and still grieve it, and how you grieved the loss of your mother. Your aunt took advantage of your youth and innocence to implant an idea in your mind, James. That's a mitigating circumstance."

"But Fox was guilty," Travers said. "Janet helped me to see that. I remembered what I had long ago repressed; I remembered seeing Alan Fox push my mother into the sea. I went to see Fox for the first time a week ago, but not to harm him, only to see if he was real. He seemed a disheveled, sad man, and after leaving him I even began to doubt what Aunt Matilda had told me. But then I made contact with my mother with Janet's help and she showed me what I had forgotten. And so I had to act."

"Think of Janet—of what it would do to her if you killed again."

Travers looked hard at Lamb. "Stand aside, Chief Inspector," he said.

Lamb took a small step backward. As Travers began to move toward him, Lamb glanced at Brandt and saw him nod, as if saying to Lamb that he understood what he must do.

"Lieutenant, you forgot your painting," Brandt shouted.

Stunned, Travers checked to see that he still had the painting; he then looked at Brandt, who, in that instant, took Terry from his shoulders and tossed the snake at Travers.

As Travers instinctively raised his hands to cover his face, Lamb tackled him; the pistol and the painting both fell from Travers's grip. A second later Brandt was also atop Travers and he and Lamb together subdued the lieutenant. Lamb retrieved Travers's pistol from the ground and pointed it at Travers.

"Stand up," he said to Travers.

As Travers stood, Brandt searched for Terry and found him curled in a ball upon the floor, terrified but unhurt.

"Terry, old friend," Brandt said to the snake. "I'm so very bloody sorry. Will you ever forgive me?"

Alan Fox's painting lay at Lamb's feet, torn in two.

THIRTY-NINE

—〰—

FOR THE SECOND TIME THAT DAY, LAMB STOOD BY THE POND, watching Sergeant Cashen and his squad of men continue their search. Harding, Rivers, and Wallace had returned to Winchester with James Travers in custody, charged with the murder of Alan Fox. They had also arrested Janet Lockhart, whom Lamb intended to charge with abetting Travers.

As Lamb waited in the sun, smoking and trying his best to feel at ease, Arthur Brandt appeared up the footpath with Terry round his neck.

"I thought I might find you here, Chief Inspector," Brandt said, joining Lamb by the edge of the pond. "Still searching I see."

"Yes," Lamb said. He had thanked Brandt for his assistance earlier, but felt compelled to do so again. "I want to thank you again for your help, Mr. Brandt."

"Oh, please, Chief Inspector. I was glad for the chance to be part of it." He smiled at Lamb and added: "Who knows, perhaps I'll write about it. It mightn't make a half-bad novel in the end."

"But I thought you wrote plays?"

"I do. But I haven't had much luck with that, I'm afraid. It might be time to try my hand at something else."

The pair looked over the water for a couple of seconds, as Terry moved slowly round Brandt's shoulders, flicking its tongue and testing the fragrant summer air.

"You know, I must say I was quite smitten with Constable Lamb," Brandt said. "Not smitten in the usual sense of the word, obviously, but very taken with her spirit and optimism and the easy way she has with people. You have quite a gem there, Chief Inspector. I daresay she wouldn't make a fine detective herself some day."

"I also am very impressed with her," Lamb said. He turned to Brandt. "I suppose I should tell you that she's my daughter. She didn't want you to know because she feels embarrassed by the obvious nepotism."

"Well, she shouldn't be; she seems to have earned her place well enough. But in any case, I figured out the connection on my own."

"How so?"

"Well, you know what they say about the apple never falling far from the tree, Chief Inspector. Besides, I wondered why you or she never mentioned your surname. I wonder if she has a beau, by the way? I certainly hope so."

"She does."

"And does she love him?"

"I believe so."

"Well, that's something."

"Yes."

They watched as two of the boats drew together at the center of the pond, one of which contained the familiar figure of Sergeant Cashen, who began to wave at them.

"We've found the pistol, sir," Cashen said.

Brandt put his hands together. "Bravo," he said. He touched Terry's snout, and said to the snake, "What do you think of that, old boy? Success!"

He followed Lamb to the pier. As they made their way through the reeds and grasses, Brandt glanced back at Elton House.

"I wonder what will become of it," he said. "I suppose someone else shall buy it. I imagine it shall come rather cheap under the circumstances."

Cashen's dinghy drew alongside the pier. He laid the wet pistol, which was partially ensnarled in pond grass, as the statue had been, on the pier.

"We also found this," Cashen said to Lamb, gesturing for the constable in the boat to hand him the other item.

Lamb felt his anxiety spike as he realized what the other item Cashen had found must be—the remains of Theresa Hitchens's aborted child.

But the only thing Cashen laid next to the pistol was a small, sodden and tattered paper lily.